# MIDNIGHT VOW

# MIDNIGHT VOW

WOLVES OF MIDNIGHT

BECKY MOYNIHAN

Published by Broken Books
www.beckymoynihan.com



ISBN-13: 979-8-9883737-0-4

Cover design by Becky Moynihan
Cover model by Ravven
www.depositphotos.com

*Be wild. Be free.*

# CHAPTER 1

Sneaking out the back door in the dead of night wasn't the best idea I'd ever had.

Then again, I wasn't exactly known for my brilliant ideas.

But tonight, of all nights, should have kept me indoors. Tonight, I was the most vulnerable. Most *weak*.

With a soft click, I secured the door's lock. Not that it mattered. Not when I was on the *wrong* side of the door.

*Lock yourself in the cellar, Nora.*

*Don't come out until dawn, Nora.*

*It's for your own protection, Nora.*

*Nora.*

*Nora, are you listening?*

*NORA!*

Yeah, yeah, yeah. I was breaking the number one rule. The rule that had kept me *alive* for twenty-two years. Even during my time away at college, I'd obeyed the single most important rule: Don't go out at night on a full moon.

I knew what would happen if I did. Knew firsthand the consequences should I be caught.

But I'd finally found someone to help me with my little problem. A *legit* someone. I wasn't chasing after a wild dream this time. This was *real*.

My family—my *pack*—would understand. Would support my brave venture. Right?

Wrong.

They'd lock me in the cellar for the rest of my life if they knew what I was attempting to do.

Best to keep my plans to myself. That way, no one would feel compelled to rat me out to Alpha Hendrix. He'd just about had enough of me and my hairbrained schemes.

*Nora, are you trying to put me in an early grave?* he'd say, then delegate me to some menial job as punishment.

If I had to dispose of deer guts one more time, I'd pull my hair out. The pack should be cleaning up their *own* messes, thank you very much.

I was tiptoeing around the side of my parent's old white farmhouse, yards away from my yellow rustbucket pickup in the driveaway, when a shrill alarm went off—the one I'd accidentally set out of habit.

Cursing, I reached into the front pocket of my duffel bag and ripped out my screeching phone. With a swift tap, silence descended once again. Except for my heart. It pounded out of control, louder than the crickets singing in the long grass.

I stood stock-still. Waiting. Hoping against hope that no one had heard.

Several seconds passed and I started to breathe easier. Until my ears picked up a sound.

A howl.

All the hair raised on my body.

The eerie noise shivered through the pine and maple trees backing the thirty-acre property. Followed by another. And another.

"*Crap*," I hissed, and bolted for my truck. My bag slapped against my thigh as I ran the short distance. Frantically unlocking the door,

I wrenched it open and dove inside. Once the door was firmly shut behind me, I scrambled to start the ignition.

A pathetic wheeze filled the interior.

"Please, baby, *please*," I begged the old Ford pickup and tried again. "I promise I'll change your oil this week." Another wheeze. "New brake pads? I know you've been wanting those." Wheeze. "Come *on!*" I shouted, banging the wheel.

She started with a sputtering cough.

"Yes, yes, *yes!*" I crowed and flicked on the headlights. When the beams caught on a pair of glowing yellow eyes near the treeline, I bit back a scream.

Time stood still as the eyes simply stared at me. Unmoving. Unblinking.

Slowly, ever so slowly, I put the car in reverse.

The eyes winked out.

My heart jumped into my throat and I stomped on the gas, gunning backward down the dirt driveway. My poor truck clanked and groaned over the rough path, the headlights fishtailing every which way. I frantically searched for the eyes again, but they could be anywhere. *Anywhere.*

I was nearly to the road when something *huge* rammed into the truck. I screamed for real this time as metal creaked and shuddered under the impact. Yanking the wheel, I plowed right into the mailbox before switching gears and stomping on the gas. The truck lurched forward and I cleared the drive, shooting down the road at breakneck speed.

Only then did I dare to glance in the rearview mirror. To watch as the pair of yellow eyes gradually faded from view.

I spent the next several minutes calming my racing heart and fighting off the need to laugh. Not that anything was funny. Not even a little bit. Laughter was just my natural response to stressful situations.

*There's something wrong with you, Nora, but there's nothing we can do to help.*

Laugh.

*Stay away from the other pack members, Nora, or they might lose control of their instincts and kill you.*

Laugh.

*When you graduate college, you must come back home. It's for your own protection.*

Laugh.

Laugh.

LAUGH.

I should be crying. Bawling my eyes out right now. *Screaming.* A member of my pack had just tried to kill me. After all these years, I was still a target. I hadn't seen the wolf clearly enough to know who it was, but it didn't really matter. My own *mother* would have attacked me if I'd been caught outside unprotected.

It was a fact I'd known for years. Ever since I'd been old enough to shift . . . and hadn't.

Something was wrong with me, all right.

I was a natural-born werewolf who couldn't shift.

In all honesty, I should be dead right now. The instinctual need to shift into animal form should have driven me wild with insanity. Should have torn me apart from the inside. But here I was, stuck in my human form on the night of a full moon. *Full moon.* And my wolf was still dormant inside me as if she didn't exist.

The other members of my pack couldn't understand it. Something like this had never happened before. A child born of two werewolf parents was fated to become one too. No ifs or buts about it.

The *disease*, as some called it, was highly contagious. Even a scratch could trigger the change. No one knew exactly when or how werewolves had been created, only that our toxin was linked to the moon's cycle. Every full moon, we had no choice but to wolf out. Over time, it was possible to control the shift, but not fully. A wild animal could never truly be tamed, after all.

And then there was me. A purebred werewolf, descended from several generations of wolves. Powerful werewolf toxin pumped through my veins.

And yet, I was wolfless. Weak. Practically human.

*Prey.*

My very presence threatened pack dynamics. But, for better or worse, I was their responsibility. It was dangerous for me to go off into the world alone. I was still a wolf, even if half my pack had tried to convince me otherwise.

But tonight, I was going to prove them wrong. Tonight, I was going to finally—*finally*—unleash my wolf.

No matter the cost.

The drive to Burlington only took me half an hour. I'd driven this route countless times during my college years, returning to my childhood home every weekend. *It's not safe for a wolf to be alone for too long,* Alpha Hendrix had repeatedly told me. *Especially a weak and unpredictable one like you, Nora.* Not that my pack had missed me while I was away. My absence had probably been a relief for them, even for my parents—despite them never saying so to my face.

No matter. All those years of them barely tolerating my presence were about to be a thing of the past. After tonight, they'd welcome me back with open arms. The risks would be worth it when I saw their surprised—and happy—faces. I'd no longer be Underhill Pack's shameful little secret. I'd be a *true* member. One they could be proud of.

Arriving at my destination, I claimed the farthest available space in the parking lot near the docks. Even though I was risking everything by coming here, I still had an inane instinct to be cautious. I didn't know these people. I'd found them through a chatroom on the *dark web*, for heaven's sake. Still, I believed they were legit. I'd spent weeks tracking down sources and confirming that Blackstone Coven was a bonafide witch community.

They specialized in hexes, which meant that they could *break* them. With that kind of power, they should be able to unleash my wolf.

Hopefully.

"Leave your doubts at the door, Nora Elizabeth Finch," I scolded myself and killed the engine. My poor beat-up truck pitifully sighed and fell silent. Pulling the tie off my wrist, I quickly corralled my wild ginger mane into a messy bun. One look in the visor mirror told me what I already knew: I was nervous. *More* than nervous. My lightly tanned skin looked pallid, the dusting of freckles on my cheeks standing out in stark relief. And my pupils were so dilated that the aqua blue of my eyes was barely visible.

Squeezing them shut, I took several calming breaths before reopening them. I could *do* this. What's the worst that could happen? The urge to laugh bubbled up again. I viciously bit into my lips and reached for my phone.

*I'm here*, I texted my contact and hit send.

Less than a minute later, I received the reply: *Last boat slip on the east side. The Black Maid. Come alone and unarmed. No phones or wires.*

My heart rate soared once again. I almost chickened out this time. If I wasn't so desperate, I would have. But I couldn't live like this anymore. Couldn't bear one more second. I'd rather die trying than barely exist. Than remain this . . . this *thing*. Not a human. Not a wolf. Not *normal*.

So I unbuckled my seatbelt and reached for the door handle. At the last second, I turned my phone back on and hurriedly sent another message.

*Love you*, was all the text said. Anything more would alert my best friend that I was up to no good. As my college roommate for the last four years, there was little Brielle Lacroix didn't know about me. I'd even caved and told her about the supernatural world. But she was human, and I couldn't let her get caught up in this. Witches weren't the friendliest bunch.

On an impulse, I sent the same message to my parents, just in case. In case I never came home again.

Before doubt could badger me once more, I tossed the phone onto the passenger's seat and grabbed my duffel. Slamming the door shut, I swung the bag over my shoulder and headed for the marina. At least it was well lit. Having a dormant wolf meant no night vision. No *nothing*. Not a single supernatural ability.

Which meant that I was powerless against these witches if they decided to pull anything.

"Great pep talk, Nora," I grumbled with an eye roll. "Way to see the glass half full." I wasn't usually this pessimistic, but I was really going out on a limb here. More than usual.

I shivered, tugging my oversized plaid shirt closed over my white tank top. Vermont nights could get a little chilly, even during the summer months. I'd worn ripped shorts and white Converse shoes, which I was second-guessing now. Maybe I should have dressed up a little. My casual outfit didn't exactly scream "I know what I'm doing so don't mess with me."

Before I could turn around, my feet hit the dock. The sound of creaking wood beneath my soles gave me a fresh boost of determination, and I strode forward with purpose.

*Almost there. This will all be over soon. Just put on a brave face and show them that signature Nora Finch swagger.*

I didn't know what I expected witches to look like—it's not like I'd ever seen one in person before—but the wildly eclectic group that greeted me wasn't it. For one, they weren't all female. I knew that warlocks existed, but I didn't expect to find one here—especially one who looked like a young *Jackie Chan* with a top knot.

"Hey," I said and stuck out my hand. "I'm Nora. Nora Finch."

His dark eyes narrowed on my hand, then went to my duffel. "I thought my instructions were clear."

"Oh, you're my contact?"

His eyes narrowed further. Okay, wrong thing to say.

I switched tactics. "Your instructions were perfectly clear. I just brought a change of clothing with me. You know, in case I wolf out and shift back afterward. Then I would be naked, and that could be kind of—Hey!"

I lunged for my duffel as a dark brown hand appeared out of nowhere and snatched it from me. The warlock stopped me with a firm head shake.

I raised my hands complacently. "Okay, fine. That's fair. We're understandably a little distrustful. Witches and werewolves don't typically do business with each other."

We all watched in silence as a curvy little witch with boho braids rummaged through my bag. Finding only clothes, she beckoned at me with a pointy bejeweled nail. "Come."

I blinked. "Oh, okay. Thanks. Should I just . . . ?" The hot asian dude stepped aside, allowing me entrance into the boat's covered interior. "Cool."

Biting my lips so I wouldn't ramble—or laugh—I boarded the expensive boat and followed Boho Braids through the open door. Another brown-haired witch with pale skin watched me pass, her expression more curious than unfriendly. When I offered her a small smile, she quickly looked away. She and the warlock brought up the rear as we descended a few short steps into a rather spacious cabin.

"Nice boat," I couldn't help but say, scanning the pristine interior. It smelled of herbs and what I could only guess was magic. "Are you sure you want to do this here? I'd hate to ruin anything, especially that leather seating area. We could—"

"Stop talking," Boho Braids demanded, whirling around to face me. My mouth snapped shut. She dropped my duffel before reaching out to grab my arm. "Payment first. Then we discuss."

It took everything in me to hold still as she yanked up the sleeve of my plaid shirt. But when she positioned a dagger-sharp nail at the crook of my elbow, I shied away with a grimace. "Wait, hold up. You said a vial of my blood as payment. Don't you have a syringe?" Or something *sanitary?*

"Do you want our help or not?" the witch said in clipped tones, her accent heavy.

"Yes, but—"

"Then stop delaying. We only have a short window before the moon reaches its zenith."

Okay, that made sense. Still, I—

I emitted a short cry of pain as she jabbed her nail into my skin. Deep. Deeper. The other witch placed a shallow bowl beneath my elbow just as blood trickled from the wound.

"*Manifesto*," Boho Braids crooned, waving her other hand over the wound. My mouth fell open as cerulean blue lit up her hand.

*Magic*. "Reveal to me all that is hidden. The past, the present, and the forbidden. Unlock thine secrets, they are now mine. I command the passage of time."

With morbid fascination, I watched as the blood in the bowl started to bubble. She repeated the words, yanking her nail from my flesh to grab the bowl. The bite of pain barely registered; I was too focused on the magical ritual. Pressing on my wound, I waited for something to happen. Maybe the blood would form words. Or start talking. I didn't know how these things worked. Maybe—

Boho Braids stuck a finger into the blood and brought it to her lips.

*Ew*.

When she sucked the digit into her mouth, her eyes fluttered shut and she moaned.

*Double ew*. I thought they were witches, not *vampires*.

"Such *power*," she breathed, drawing her finger back out. "It speaks to me. *Calls* to me. Come out and play, little wolf. I want to see you with my own two eyes."

Okay, this was getting a tad creepy.

I slowly began to pull away, but she snatched up my arm again.

Surprised, I met her eyes, only to find them blank. Glazed. She started to tremble, digging all five of her pointy nails into my skin.

"Hey, let go," I warned, and attempted to tug my arm free.

"Keisha, what is it?" the brown-haired witch whispered, excitement flashing in her hazel green eyes. "What do you see?"

I tugged again, but her grip only tightened.

"Stars and moon above, help us," Keisha moaned, shaking so hard that the bowl in her hand slipped. With a flick of her wrist, the other witch stopped the bowl midair. Not a single drop of blood spilled. "A wolf she is, that is true. But something else lies hidden within, making her two."

"What does that mean?" The warlock this time. "Can we free her wolf or not?"

Instead of answering, Keisha latched onto both my arms and wailed, "*Reveal* yourself, little wolf. I must see you. I must *know*."

Her eyes had regained their clarity, and I cringed away from the manic look she was giving me.

"Look," I started, unable to hide the tremor in my voice. "Maybe this wasn't such a good idea. I don't feel any different, and this is kinda freaking me out. Plus, your nails are wicked sharp and I don't want to lose any more blood."

My words only amplified the crazy in her eyes.

"You must not leave. She must not leave. Fang, don't let them leave."

Aaaand that was my cue.

With a swift yank, I broke her hold on me and whirled around. Only to come face-to-face with the warlock.

"Oh," I loudly groaned, doubling over. "I think the change is happening. My wolf is coming out. AH!"

I fell and grabbed onto his arm. As he bent forward under my weight, I snapped back up. My forehead smacked him square in the nose. With a curse, he stumbled back. I helped him along with an added push, and he crashed into a table.

I raced for the door as if my tail was on fire.

"*No!*" Keisha screeched. "Stop her, Raelyn!"

I'd almost made it up the stairs when the boat suddenly heaved. The violent motion knocked me sideways into the wall. My shoulder took the brunt of the impact, further adding to my injuries. The boat bucked again, sending me to my knees.

Jeez. Were they controlling the *water*?

When the rocking motion continued, I resorted to crawling on all fours to escape the crazies. I should have known this deal was too good to be true. The *blood* payment should have tipped me off. When would I ever learn?

"Stupid, Nora, *stupid!*" I hissed, scrambling to get my bearings. I'd just made it topside when something came whistling at me. Glancing over my shoulder, I shrieked and hit the deck. Not a moment too soon. A glowing ball of what looked like *fire* shot past.

Hell, no. I was *so* out of here.

Deciding to take my chances in the water, I swan-dived overboard. Good thing I was an excellent swimmer, because the water continued to buck and writhe. I dove down deep, desperate to escape the chaos. To escape *them*. I didn't know what Keisha had discovered, but I wasn't going to be held prisoner while they *experimented* on me.

I stayed underwater for as long as I could, only coming up when my lungs screamed for air. Then, in a flash, I vanished beneath the waves again, slowly inching farther and farther away. I didn't know how long it took, but by the time I made it to shore, I shook with exhaustion.

The deal might have gone bad, but at least I'd escaped in one piece.

I doubted this was over though. Sure enough, the sound of hurrying footsteps and urgent whispers reached my ears only moments later.

Ah, hell. I was being *hunted*.

# CHAPTER 2

They knew my name.

My *name.*

Why hadn't I used an alias?

I'd seriously messed up this time.

Even if I made it safely back home, they could track me to my front doorstep. Which meant . . .

I couldn't go back home.

I'd spent the past three hours trying to wrap my head around that fact. My emotions kept ping-ponging from dread to excitement. Back and forth. Back and forth. I was on my own now. My *own.* A lone wolf.

Correction: a *wolfless* lone wolf.

So what did that make me exactly?

"Pathetic," I muttered, flicking a glance in the rearview mirror for the gazillionth time. Good thing I excelled at running from dangerous beings bent on causing me harm. I'd managed to give the witches the slip and hightailed it out of dodge before they could catch me.

But I didn't know where to go.

I'd simply peeled out of the parking lot and headed south, eventually sliding into New York. Probably because Brielle lived there, and running to her with my problems came naturally to me. Not that I was *actually* going to visit her. I'd missed her terribly since graduating a month ago and moving back home, but I wouldn't bring my problems to her doorstep.

Maybe I would just do a quick drive-by and torture myself by sneaking a peek at the future I'd almost had. The apartment I'd planned to share with my best friend. The *life* that had been within my grasp, then snatched away, all because of my screwed-up DNA.

Even though I'd been allowed to attend and graduate college, I still hadn't left the nest. Maybe never would. Not if my parents and Alpha Hendrix had anything to say about it.

*We need to keep an eye on you, Nora,* Alpha Hendrix had said on the day of my graduation. *Who knows when your wolf will decide to emerge. You wouldn't want to accidentally hurt someone, would you? Plus, any wolf outside of our territory will see you as fair game. Do you want your death to be on my conscience? Or on your parents'?*

With a guilt trip like *that*, how could I argue?

I'd wanted to though. I'd wanted to so badly.

I wasn't exactly the submissive, do-as-your-told type. A flaw that had gotten me into trouble countless times over the years.

But returning home could hurt my family. My *pack*. I didn't know how far these witches would go to get to me. Didn't know if they'd *kill* if someone stood in their way. This was my chance to finally cut the umbilical cord and create a whole new life for myself.

If only I'd been able to free my wolf first.

"And win the lottery," I sarcastically muttered, turning on my blinker for the next exit. Despite the dire circumstances, seeing the sign for Albany sent a shiver of excitement through me. I'd never been allowed to visit a city bigger than Burlington before. I understood why—that an unpredictable werewolf in a big city was a recipe for disaster—but that only made me want to go more.

As the city rose up before me, my guilt for disobeying pack rules gradually faded. I wasn't truly trying to run away. I simply had a better chance of escaping those witches in a city. In a *crowd.*

Another wave of giddiness stole over me.

*Nightlife.*

This city was sure to have some fun late-night adventures. I might be broke—thanks to college expenses and being jobless—but I could afford a few drinks. And maybe a little dancing, if I was lucky.

Sure enough, I had no trouble finding clubs and bars open this time of night. I chose one that looked a little nicer than the rest, a nightclub called Hexagon. It was smack in the middle of downtown, a few blocks from the New York State Capitol. When I finally found a parking spot, adrenaline was coursing through me.

Just one night.

One night of being anonymous for once. Of being *normal.*

I wasn't the pack's black sheep. The girl who went into hiding every full moon. The broken wolf. The disappointment. The idiot currently being hunted by diabolical *witches.*

I was just me. Nora Finch.

"The girl who smells like fish guts," I bemoaned, remembering how awful I must look after my little late-night swim. Would they even let me in looking like this? I no longer had a spare change of clothing. Not even a hairbrush, which I needed most.

Sighing, I grappled with the hair tie for a few minutes before it finally let go of my fiery mane. Parts of it were still damp, but the majority was now a tangled mess of frizzy curls. Shaking out the heavy mass, I scrutinized my apparel next. Removing the plaid shirt would help, but my white tank top was stained in a few spots.

Oh well. What's the worst that could happen? They'd turn me away?

No big deal. I was pretty used to rejection.

With one last glance in the visor mirror to make sure I didn't have *algae* in my hair, I hopped from the truck. When another car pulled into the packed lot, I froze, suddenly aware of how exposed I was. What if the witches had tracked me here?

Firmly shaking my head, I dismissed the notion and began to walk. I'd checked countless times. No one had followed me here. I was *safe*. For now.

The only thing I should be focused on was getting inside that club and having some fun for once. Because after this night was over, I had no idea what would happen next. I'd need a place to stay, that much I knew. And a job. I desperately needed cash. Other than that, I wasn't going to think about the challenge before me.

I was more of a "do first, think later" kind of gal.

Thankfully, the nightclub's bouncer seemed more interested in my hair than what I was wearing. I smiled at him brightly, tugging on a curl to keep his attention squarely above my chin. He barely glanced at my ID, enraptured by the lock of hair as it sprung back into place. Not an abnormal response to my wild tresses.

My spine tingled with awareness again as I heard a feminine exclamation directly behind me. "Wow, is your hair color natural?"

I glanced over my shoulder, relaxing when all that greeted me was a gaggle of curious college girls. "Yeah," I replied, slowly easing into their circle as if I belonged there. "This Bobo the Clown look is completely *au naturale*."

"Hell, nah," she said, presenting her ID to the bouncer. "Natural curls are so in. And that *color*. So hot."

I completely forgot then what I was wearing or how I smelled. Forgot everything but the boisterous girls surrounding me. Their easy acceptance of me into their group was an experience I'd never had before. Besides Brielle, I'd always been carefully held at arm's length.

The next two hours passed in a colorful blur. I drank. I danced. I laughed. And, for the first time in what felt like forever, I let loose.

For once, I wasn't my problems. For once, I was just me.

Carefree. Independent. Normal.

And then, just like that, I wasn't.

One of the girls I was dancing with cried out in surprise and stumbled against me. I caught her before she could go down. In that same moment, I looked up into a pair of familiar dark eyes. All the blood drained from my face.

Ah hell, the witches had found me.

Reacting on instinct, I pointed at Fang and screamed as loud as I could, "*GUN!*"

Oh, wow. That worked a little *too* well. Nearly every head in the loud room swiveled my way. Then to my pointing finger. Then to the warlock.

"He threatened to shoot me if I didn't leave with him," I continued to shout, letting my voice rise hysterically. "Call the cops. Don't let him get away!"

Just like that, the room erupted into chaos.

People pushed and shoved me every which way, their fight or flight instincts kicking in. I welcomed the crush of bodies, using their panic to my advantage. In no time, I lost sight of Fang. The second I did, I slipped from the crowd. Keisha and Raelyn were no doubt waiting out front for me, but I was used to finding other routes of escape.

While the crowd caused a distraction, I hurried toward the long hall leading to the bathrooms. When I rounded the corner, I smacked face first into something *hard*. My hair tumbled forward, obscuring my vision. But not before I saw an expensive dark suit and crisp white shirt stretched across a broad chest.

"Move it or lose it, buddy," I blurted, trying to shove past. *Try* being the word. The guy was like an immovable brick wall. Whipping the hair from my face, I paused to shoot a glare up at him, wasting precious seconds. "Look here, mister. You're going to be in a world of pain soon if you don't—"

At that exact moment, our gazes locked.

Eyes of dark amber pierced mine, and—wow, those thick black lashes should be illegal.

Not one to get distracted by a pretty face—okay, fine, his face was *gorgeous*—I opened my mouth to finish telling him off. Before I could, something strange happened. So unexpected that I lost the ability to speak.

A sensation stirred in my gut. A startling, breath-stealing one. So deep and foreign and *hot* that I simply gaped up at him, utterly stupefied.

What the hell?

Completely caught off guard, I nearly forgot about my need to escape the witches. But only for a moment. Struggling to orientate myself, I blinked and shook my head. The action threw me off balance and I listed sideways. Before I could right myself, strong hands gripped my bare biceps.

Whoa. The startling sensation *ripped* through me this time.

Gasping, I wrenched my arms away and stumbled back. "Don't . . . don't touch me." Nausea rolled through my stomach and I pressed a hand to it before shoving past again.

This time, he let me.

Without a backward glance, I lurched down the hall and burst into the women's bathroom. A few girls were inside, but I ignored them, already plotting my escape. When I knocked the trash can over and began rolling it across the room, they gaped at me like I'd lost my mind. Now *that* reaction I was used to.

Tipping the trash can upside down, I scrambled on top and reached for the window. "Come on, you rusted piece of junk," I grumbled, straining to open it. With a *bang*, it slid all the way open. "*Yes*."

In a flash, I shimmied through the narrow opening. Just in time too. Sudden squeals from down below announced what I already knew. Fang had found me.

I pulled myself through before he could reach me and dropped to the alley below. Stumbling slightly, I straightened and shot down the alley at breakneck speed, knowing I had to reach my truck before either of the witches spotted me.

My hair streaked behind me like a fiery comet, my Converses pounding the asphalt. I paused briefly at the alley's mouth before scurrying to catch up with a couple crossing the street. They eyed me warily, but didn't comment as I used their bodies to shield myself. Safely making it to the other side, I was almost to the parking lot when all the hair raised on my arms. I glanced over my shoulder, frantically searching for the witches.

No sign of them.

Hurrying my pace, I jogged the rest of the way to my truck. I'd just yanked the door open when my spine started tingling, demanding I turn around. When I did, all the air fled my lungs. Ah, hell. The gorgeous guy I'd bumped into was stalking right toward me like a serial killer. Why was it always the hot ones?

Cursing, I dove into the truck and slammed the door shut. The keys in my hand rattled loudly as I desperately tried to start the engine, swearing when it rolled over. Once. Twice.

I almost sobbed when she roared to life on the third try.

Putting her in reverse, I stomped on the gas.

*BANG.*

My head thwacked the headrest as the truck jerked to a dead halt. My eyes flew to the rearview mirror and I bit back a scream. It was the guy. The guy with the dark amber eyes. Except that his eyes were now glowing a bright *yellow*. And he was gripping the back of my *truck*.

Freaking out, I stomped on the gas again. The tires spun and squealed, but the truck wouldn't budge an inch. I lit up the cab with a string of curses. This was no ordinary guy. *Definitely* not human. What he wanted with me, I had no idea.

Switching tactics, I shoved the truck into park and killed the engine. "Okay, dude, come at me. I'm ready for you," I murmured, reaching into the middle console. At the same time, I pocketed my keys and prepared myself.

I didn't have to wait long.

As soon as the engine died, he let go of the back and came around the side. When he rapped a knuckle against the driver window, my heart leapt into my throat. Inhaling a calming breath, I slowly cracked open the door.

"Yes?" was all I said, keeping my gaze straight ahead.

The deliberate move forced him to lean in closer to speak to me. Before he could utter a single word, I whipped my right arm around and shot him in the face. Not with a bullet, but with *bear* spray.

He jerked back with a muffled curse, covering his eyes.

*Bull's eye.*

Not wasting any time, I shoved the door open all the way and jumped out. My feet were already running before they could touch the ground, carrying me as fast as they could from the mystery man. I ran without direction, my only thought on finding someplace to hide. I tried slipping into a pub, but it was closed for the night. I kept running. Kept searching. But I didn't know the city, and I hit a dead end.

Wheezing and trembling with fatigue, I searched for a way out. A door. A ladder to a roof. A manhole. *Anything.*

I found nothing.

Before I could backtrack, I caught the unmistakable sound of footsteps. They were loud, almost as if the owner *wanted* me to hear them. Pressing up against the brick wall behind me, I struggled to collect myself. I still had the bear spray. Still had my own two hands. I wasn't completely defenseless. I'd survived this long in life unscathed.

Mostly.

Moments later, he appeared out of the gloom, his white shirt a stark contrast to the deep olive skin of his neck and face. His eyes were no longer glowing a bright yellow, but I knew what I'd seen. He was supernatural. A swift-healing one, which made this fight extremely unfair. The bear spray might as well be water. No matter. I'd been raised by wolves. I *was* a wolf. I wouldn't make this easy for him.

Unlike me, he wasn't even a little out of breath. He slowly approached as if I were a cornered animal. Technically, I *was* a cornered animal. When he was halfway down the alley, close enough that I could just make out his facial features, I settled onto the balls of my feet and raised the bear spray once more. "Don't come any closer."

He stopped. Stopped and took me in from head to toe. I allowed the inspection, because there was nothing I could do about it. At the same time, I observed him. He was well over six feet and powerfully built. Even though he was covered from the neck down, there was no hiding the strong outline of his shoulders and chest. His hair was dark, just shy of black, meticulously swept back off his forehead. His full broad mouth was surrounded by dark stubble. Not too much, not too little. His jaw was square and probably rock hard.

He couldn't be much older than me, yet he carried himself with an ease men twice his age hadn't yet mastered. Didn't matter. I wasn't the type of girl to swoon over the bad guy just because he was confident and *hot*.

When his feet shifted, I nearly jumped out of my skin.

"Not one more step," I said, a little too shrilly. "I know karate."

Really? Did I *really* just say that?

I could have sworn his lips twitched with amusement.

"Look, mister," I kept going, unable to stop. "I really don't have time for this dark and silent mysterious guy crap. I'm kind of in a hurry, so let's just cut to the chase. Why are you following me?"

He let the silence between us stretch for another unbearable moment.

And then he finally—*finally*—spoke.

"I want to know why a strange wolf trespassing on my territory hasn't shifted with the full moon."

# CHAPTER 3

The words knocked all the air from my lungs.

Not because his voice rumbled wickedly through my insides, tempting me to lower my guard. No, I didn't care *how* deep or sinfully sexy it sounded.

This guy knew who I *was.*

Well. Sort of.

"Excuse me? Do I *look* like a wolf?" Yup. I totally went there. I wasn't going to give up my werewolf-card *that* easily.

He shifted a step closer, making me tense even more.

"Maybe not," he replied. "But you smell like one."

Ah crap. He was either a vampire or a werewolf. Didn't matter which. Both could easily make me their late-night snack.

Switching tactics, I said, "Look, I didn't know this was your territory. If you'll just let me pass, I'll leave the city."

"It's not just this city."

I blinked. "Huh?"

"My territory," he explained, enunciating as if I were slow. "It's not just this city."

"Fine," I snapped, annoyance overpowering my fear. "How far away do I need to go to leave your *territory?*"

Males and their stupid territorial nature.

"New York."

My eyes bugged out. "What, like the entire *state*?"

He tipped his head to the side. "You don't know who I am?"

I threw my hands in the air. "Give it up for Captain Obvious."

He did smile this time. I could clearly see it, slightly crooked and completely disarming. "You're a difficult one."

"So I've been told." When his only response was to take a step closer, I gritted out, "If you're trying to intimidate me, it's not working."

"If I were trying to intimidate you, you'd be cowering on the ground before me."

"Oh wow. *Wow*. You did not just say that," I said, my annoyance flipping to anger. "I don't know who you *think* you are, but—"

He abruptly jerked up his hand as if to silence me.

My vision bled red. Hell no, he did *not* just give me the hand.

I opened my mouth to tell him off, but he was suddenly moving toward me. *Fast.*

Panicking, I deployed the bear spray again. He dodged it this time, easily prying the can from my fingers. With only my body left to defend me, I lunged at him. My arms and legs did their worst, punching and kicking and kneeing and elbowing. It was like fighting a *tree*. He barely moved under the assault. Suddenly, I was pressed up against the brick wall, both my wrists pinned to my sides.

"Stop attacking me," he hissed in my ear, gripping my wrists tightly, but not enough to hurt.

I opened my mouth to scream bloody murder.

"Don't," he said. "They'll hear."

Despite myself, I paused, knowing he wasn't the only one following me.

"Who?" I gasped as a wave of heat flushed through me. What was *happening*? Every time he touched me, my body went crazy. I didn't think it was lust though. At least, not completely. This was more acute than hormones. Almost unpleasant in its intensity.

"You tell me," he replied. "Are you in some sort of trouble?"

I froze, my eyes widening. "How did you—?"

"Three of them. Two witches and a warlock. I always keep an eye on unfamiliar guests in my nightclubs. Especially pretty little wolves with fiery red hair who haven't shifted."

*He thinks I'm pretty*?

*Not* what I should be focused on right now.

"Let me go," I said, starting to struggle again. "I can't let them find me."

He easily stilled my movements. "What will they do if they catch you?"

My breathing grew erratic as the heat became painful. "I don't know. Something bad. I just need to . . . need to . . ." Clenching my teeth as *fire* licked at my veins, I burst out, "Ah hell, please let me go. I can't stand it anymore!"

He immediately jerked back, dropping my wrists.

I curled forward and clutched at my aching stomach. "I think I'm going to be sick," I groaned, wincing when another heatwave blasted through me.

"What's wrong?" he pressed.

"You tell *me*," I shot back, breathing through the lingering pain. "I was fine until you touched me."

He was silent for a beat. Then, "Pick me up at the south end of Northern Boulevard."

I whipped my head up just in time to see him pocket his phone. "What are you—?"

"You're coming with me," he interrupted, reaching for my arm.

"No way," I hissed and jerked away from his fingers.

The slightest bit of impatience darkened his eyes. "Then the witches are going to find you. We have maybe two minutes before they arrive."

Cursing, I pushed off the wall and stumbled forward. "I can escape them on my own."

I only made it three steps before I heard, "I doubt that."

Okay, this guy was getting on my *last* nerve. "And why's that?" I threw over my shoulder, tensing when I heard him start to follow. "Because you think I'm weak and pathetic?"

"I didn't say that."

"You didn't have to—Hey!" I tried to jerk away again as he grabbed my arm, but his fingers only tightened.

"This wound is deep. And fresh," he said, stepping around me to point at the nail gouge Keisha had inflicted. "So are the marks here." His finger feathered down my forearm, stirring awake the heat again. "You also have a bruised shoulder and reek of lake water."

With a snort, I wiggled my arm free of his grasp. "Okay, you're freakishly observant, but so what? I—"

"Did you give them your blood?"

I gaped at him. My shocked silence was answer enough.

Shaking his head, as if he was *disappointed* in me, he placed a hand on the small of my back and ushered me forward. This time, I didn't resist. "Blood is a powerful tool. One that can be used against you if you're not careful."

"So, what are you saying?" I let him guide me from the alley, if only to hear his explanation. Apparently, he knew something important that I didn't.

"Witches can't track scent like we can, but if an Oracle ingested your blood . . ."

Ah hell. So they were tracking me through my blood. No wonder they'd been able to find me so easily.

"How long?" I asked, stepping onto the sidewalk at a fast clip. "How long can they track me?"

He easily kept pace, no doubt slowing his long-legged strides to match mine. "Hours. Days. Depends on the witch and how much blood you gave them."

Too much. I'd given them *too much*, like a naive idiot.

"They're here," he abruptly said, making my stomach bottom out. Just as I glanced over my shoulder and spotted three figures racing toward us from down the street, a car rolled to a stop before us. He whipped the back door open. "Get in."

I froze with indecision, trying to pick the lesser of two evils.

"I can protect you," he continued.

Yeah, I'd heard *that* one before.

A whistling sound distracted me and I glanced back again to see a fireball zipping toward my head.

*Hell* no.

I dove into the backseat. My mysterious rescuer—or kidnapper—slid in beside me, slamming the door shut just as the fireball smashed against it. The car peeled away in a squeal of rubber, leaving the witches behind.

After the initial danger was over, I started to breathe easier. Only to hyperventilate when Mr. Mystery said to the driver, "Take us to the penthouse, Max."

"Scratch that, Max," I hurriedly said, testing the door handle. *Locked*. "You can drop me off first. Right outside Hexagon, if you please."

I watched as the middle-aged driver shared a look in the rearview mirror with my backseat companion.

"Mr. Rivers?"

For a second, my brain blipped. Like a broken record, it replayed the name Rivers over and over while I tried to recall why it sounded so familiar. With a shake of my head, I forced myself to focus on the problem at hand. "Mr. *Rivers* was kind enough to give me a ride, but I've got it from here. Really. Thanks anyway."

I directed the words at Max, but they were meant for the guy next to me who was silently studying the side of my face. My fingers left the door handle and slowly inched toward my back pocket where my phone was. I didn't know who to call, but maybe an empty threat would be enough to make him let me go.

After a lengthy moment, he quietly said, "I can help you with your wolf."

I couldn't have been more shocked if he'd shoved me out of the moving vehicle.

Even though I knew he could hear my thundering heartbeats, I worked to mask my surprise before replying, "Who says I need help with my wolf?"

Another beat of silence. Then, "Your wolf."

Shock pierced me again.

"You can . . . you can sense her?"

"Yes."

Wow. I mean, I knew she was there. Even the witch Keisha had confirmed it. But, unlike me, he could *sense* her.

"You're a werewolf then," I needlessly said, clearing my suddenly dry throat.

"Yes. What did you think I was?"

I shrugged, flicking a glance at the driver. He looked human, but I couldn't know for sure. Our conversation didn't seem to shock him though. "You aren't shifted."

"No," was all he said. Then, "Will you accept my offer?"

"I can't pay you."

"I don't want your money."

I whipped my head around to face him. "Then *what?* I doubt someone as obviously wealthy as you," I said, gesturing at the expensive car, "would help someone like me out of the kindness of his heart."

The smallest of smiles curved his lips. One that could only be described as *wicked.*

"Very observant of you, Miss . . ."

"Anonymous."

The grin slowly widened. "Max," he abruptly said to the driver. "Drop the lady off, please."

Alarm trickled through me, but I didn't argue.

The next few blocks were driven in silence. Mr. *Rivers* was no longer studying me, but he didn't have to.

He'd already figured me out.

When the car pulled up to the curb right outside Hexagon, just like I'd requested, the only sound was a *click* as my door unlocked.

I opened the door, still too shell-shocked to speak. Before I could step out, a business card materialized in front of me. One of those fancy plastic ones that looked like a credit card.

"When you're ready to accept my offer, give me a call," Mr. Rivers said, patiently holding the card out. I only hesitated a moment. Then snatched the card from his fingers and jumped from the vehicle.

Without even a goodbye, I slammed the door shut in his rather smug face.

Just like that, he left. But not before I could have *sworn* I heard him chuckle.

# CHAPTER 4

He had me. He had me *good.* And he knew it.

I couldn't believe the guy I'd shot with bear spray was Kolton Rivers. *The* Kolton Rivers.

The wealthiest, most powerful alpha in America. Leader of the Midnight Pack. *King* of New York.

He was practically a god in the werewolf world.

I'd never met him before. Never even seen a picture. I didn't much follow celebrity gossip—human or supernatural—which was why I hadn't put two-and-two together. Until he'd given me his business card. He must think I was a complete *idiot.* I sure felt like one.

Of course he wouldn't want my money. But what *did* he want? What could I possibly offer him that he didn't already have? The world was literally at his fingertips.

Once again, a deal was being dangled in front of me. One too good to be true.

Giving some crazy witches a little of my blood was one thing, but what would a werewolf like Kolton Rivers want in return for his services?

Although I didn't know much about him, I'd heard a few disturbing rumors over the years. That he was a blatant womanizer. That he was a cold and ruthless leader who punished disobedience with violence. That anyone who challenged him was torn to bloody shreds.

"Nah," I said, taking the right turn out of Albany a little too sharply. I wasn't about to indebt myself to a power-hungry alpha. It would be like selling my soul to the devil. I would find some other way to set my wolf free. There *had* to be another way. Once this blood-tracking thing wore off, I could stop running and start searching in earnest for a solution.

As I drove, I couldn't help but remember my body's reaction to Kolton's touch though. It wasn't normal. The nausea. The heat. The deep shift within me. It was almost as if . . .

I suddenly swerved onto the shoulder and slammed on the brakes.

"Ah, hell!" I yelled, throwing my head back. "No. No. NO."

Not possible. Not *possible.*

His touch had *not* stirred my wolf awake.

No. Freaking. WAY.

But, no matter how much I denied it, I knew that it was a possibility. He was an alpha. An extremely powerful one. Alphas had abilities that the rest of us lowly wolves would never have.

After a few head-bangs and curses, I took off again, mindful of the witches still tracking me. Every few seconds, I'd glance at my phone charging on the passenger's seat. Then at the business card I'd tossed beside it.

It would be easy. *So* easy to dial that number.

But at what cost?

"I thought you were willing to pay any price, Nora Finch," I chastised myself, shaking my head. I really needed some food, a shower, and rest, in that order. Maybe the decision would be more clear then.

But how? The witches were obviously still tracking me, and there were three of them. They could switch off driving while the others slept. I didn't have that option. I cursed again, feeling hysteria bubble up.

Half an hour later, the sun slowly peeked over the horizon. Chancing a quick stop, I pulled into a gas station to fill the tank and grab some snacks. I was somewhere around Hudson now, traveling straight south toward New York City. If there was one place I could keep blood-tracking witches off my tail, it would be there, among the millions of other people.

I was halfway there when the texts and phone calls started rolling in.

Brielle: *Love you too, Nora Bora. Everything okay?*

Mom: *Nora, pick up. Where are you? We're worried.*

Dad: *Your mom's about to contact Alpha Hendrix. Call us back, Nora.*

Not long after, Alpha Hendrix texted: *We've been over this dozens of times, young lady. Come back home before I'm forced to discipline you.*

I ignored them all, not knowing what I'd say anyway. *No, I'm not okay. I'm in the middle of nowhere running for my life. Oh, I'd love to obey your order, Alpha Hendrix, but I can't.* Yeah, I couldn't say any of those things. They would just lead to more questions. Questions I couldn't answer.

I'd nearly made it to my destination when the truck's engine started to sound strange. Well, stranger than usual. "Come on, baby," I crooned to my truck, gently stroking the wheel. "I need you. Please don't give up on me."

But no amount of sweet talk could stop her slow demise. Five miles later, smoke billowed from the hood. Another couple miles and she trembled so violently that I was forced onto the shoulder. She coughed a few times before sputtering out with a weak sigh.

If I wasn't so busy frantically gathering my belongings, I would have cried. Stuffing everything I could carry into a plastic grocery bag, I jumped from the truck and took off on foot. If I got out of this alive, I'd come back for her. But, for now, I pushed aside my nostalgic feelings for the vehicle and searched for a place to hide.

Not knowing a thing about the city that never slept—except for what I'd seen in movies—I decided to wander aimlessly for a while. The longer I walked, the more crowded it became. Early rush hour traffic was in full swing. I'd never seen this many people in my entire life, and they were all so *busy*. My tiny hometown felt a million miles away.

There was honking horns and blaring music and loud chatter. Garbage lined the curbs and sidewalks, and the smells had nothing to do with nature—unless you counted the occasional stench of urine. Buildings rose sky-high, blocking out the morning sun. Street vendors were everywhere, their shops already open and ready for business.

I quickly stopped and bought an NYC baseball cap and t-shirt at a little tourist shop, hoping a disguise would help me further blend in. Then paused to order a footlong hotdog at a vendor cart. I wolfed it down in one minute flat, but the people around me were too busy to notice. The anonymity felt nice.

Until I tried to ask for directions.

"Rude," I muttered, as the third person in a row brushed past me without comment. Maybe some of the rumors about this city were true. People here had no time for pesky little tourists who'd lost their way. Or maybe they thought I was homeless. I *desperately* needed a shower and hairbrush.

Eventually, I learned how to follow the signs. By the time I figured out where the subway was, it was almost noon. I hadn't slept in thirty hours, and the Red Bull I'd just chugged could barely keep my eyes open. Still, I pushed through, knowing what would happen if I stopped.

I ended up purchasing a MetroCard with the little bit of cash I had left. It would allow me to ride the subway for free the next several days, and maybe—just maybe—I'd catch some shuteye. If I was constantly on the move, no one could catch me. Or so I told myself as I slipped through the crush of bodies filling the train. Searching for a seat and coming up empty, I settled for a spot on the floor. With my back propped against the train's side, I allowed my guard to slip. Only a little. Just enough to close my burning eyelids and shut out the world for a moment.

Just one moment. One little . . .

Something knocked against my shoe and I violently jerked awake. The abrupt action made the world spin, and I blinked rapidly to clear my vision. By the time I did—and realized what was happening—it was too late.

"Hey!" I yelled, scrambling to my feet. I shot after the thief, but he was young and clearly an expert at stealing from idiots who fell asleep on the subway. Especially one who carried all her stuff in a bag containing her *wallet*. Even my MetroCard was in there. The only thing he hadn't taken was my phone, which I thankfully still had in my pocket. Oh, and Kolton Rivers' fancy business card.

Belatedly realizing that the train had stopped and the doors were open, I watched as the thief slipped onto the platform with ease, zigzagging through the crowd. Still struggling to wake up, I lost him less than a minute later. After another minute spent catching my breath, I threw my head back and shouted, "Are you freaking *kidding* me?"

Okay, I received a few looks with that one. How nice that they *finally* noticed me.

The following hours passed in a blur. I aimlessly wandered the massive city, getting lost in the swell of people. I could fall down a manhole and no one would even know. Or care. I was invisible, and it didn't feel so great anymore. As the day slowly slid into night, my stomach rumbled with hunger and my feet ached from all the walking. There was nothing I could do about it though.

Well, *almost* nothing.

Hitting rock bottom wasn't what made me pull the business card from my back pocket. I was a survivor. I could handle tough situations. But what I couldn't handle was knowing that a *normal* werewolf wouldn't be in this mess. They wouldn't have snuck away from home, witches wouldn't be hunting them, they wouldn't have been robbed, and they wouldn't be lost in a big city with nowhere left to run.

If *I* was a normal wolf, I would no longer be pathetic.

I'd be strong. *Formidable.* No one would mess with me.

And *that* was why I did it. That was why I whipped out my phone and punched in the number. That was why I let the phone ring and ring instead of hanging up.

And when he answered. When he said his name and waited for a response. I replied, "Nora."

Silence. Then, "Pardon?"

"My name is Nora. Nora Finch. I'm ready to accept your help. Name your price."

He was silent for another beat. Long enough that panic tightened my chest. What if he'd changed his mind? What if he'd realized what a loser I was, one not worth his time?

Then, "Where are you?"

A lump formed in my throat. I tried to swallow and failed. "I don't know," I admitted, my voice small. Lost. Clenching my teeth, I said more loudly, "Somewhere in New York City."

Another pause.

"A landmark would help."

I looked around, not seeing anything notable other than . . . "Near that really big park they always show in movies."

"Central Park."

"Yeah, sure. I just passed this circle with a statue of a dude in the center."

"Stay there."

"You're kidding, right? I'm still being tracked by those witches."

"I'm aware. Just stay put. I'll be there in twenty."

The line went dead.

What the hell?

In *twenty?* That was impossible. Unless . . . unless he was *here.* Unless he had somehow *followed* me.

Again . . .

What. The. Hell?

Why was everyone *following* me?

It only took five minutes of frantic pacing and hair-pulling for me to call the whole thing off. Waiting for a stalker to pick me up felt like a bad idea. A *really* bad idea. Maybe I wasn't quite desperate enough to risk everything after all.

Not yet anyway.

I started walking again, ignoring my aching calves. Ignoring my burning eyes and gurgling stomach. I walked and walked, my only mission on losing myself to the city once again. With my focus on maintaining a steady pace, I almost didn't hear it in time.

When a car came to a screeching stop directly behind me, every hair on my body stood on end. Without turning around, I walked even faster.

A car door opened.

"NORA!"

I bolted.

Instead of sticking to the well-lit areas like a smart person, my instincts took me into the park. I ran for all I was worth, veering away from the paths and blindly crashing through the underbrush and trees. But no matter how hard, how *fast* I ran, my stalker quickly gained on me. Just as I jumped over a bush, a pair of strong arms tackled me from behind. My hat flew off and the ground rushed at me. Squeezing my eyes shut, I braced for the impact.

At the last second, my attacker rolled us, taking the brunt of the fall. I still felt it in every bone of my body, my teeth clacking together as we tumbled across the grass. The moment we stopped, I scrambled to get away. He rewarded my efforts by bodily pinning me down. *Face first* into the ground.

"Get off," I wheezed, spitting grass out of my mouth. "You're freaking *heavy*."

"Not until you tell me why you didn't stay put," Kolton said, his voice lined with annoyance.

"I changed my *mind*, that's why," I snapped, wiggling harder.

He suddenly flipped me over, so fast that I didn't have time to react. His weight settled on top of me again, but less heavy this time. When I tried to push him off, he pressed my wrists into the grass on either side of my head. At the skin contact, that foreign heat immediately rushed through my body again.

"You agreed," he said, a slight bite to the words. "You agreed to accept my help."

"I did not," I shot back, writhing as the heat became uncomfortable.

"And even if I did, I decided that making a deal with a rich, self-entitled *stalker* wasn't worth it."

His lips thinned. "I wasn't stalking you. I knew you were in trouble, so I made sure to remain nearby. You're the one who accepted my business card."

I stopped struggling. "Huh?"

"My business cards contain GPS tracking."

What the . . . ?

"Is that even *legal?*"

He silently raised an eyebrow. Answer enough.

"You know what? I don't even care. I'm tired, hungry, smelly, and *hot*. So just get off me, okay? I'm done being pushed around. *Done*."

At the slight catch in my raised voice, he studied my face as if seeing me for the first time. Whatever he saw made him slowly release my wrists and lift off me. The absence of his touch immediately brought welcome relief from the heat. Ignoring his offered hand, I staggered to my feet, brushing clumps of grass from my shirt.

As I turned to leave without even a goodbye, something flashed in his eyes. Something primal. Something dark. I ignored that too, making sure my phone was still in my pocket before taking off.

I made it three steps. Then . . .

"Accept my help, Nora. Make a deal with me."

The dangerous edge, the *warning* in his voice, gave me pause. But only for a moment.

"No," I said, and began walking again.

As I did, I could have sworn I heard him growl, "Stubborn, insufferable woman."

I ignored that too, continuing to march away from him.

Which lasted all of two seconds.

One moment, I was surrounded by a darkly-lit park.

And the next . . .

Nothing.

# CHAPTER 5

It had finally happened.

A wolf had killed me and I'd joined the afterlife.

It was the only thing that made sense. Nothing else could explain this blissful feeling of floating on a cloud.

I must be in Heaven then. I doubted Hell felt like this.

"I don't care *who* she is," a sharp feminine voice said, piercing my little bubble of bliss. "You don't *kidnap* people, Kolton Anthony Rivers."

My eyes flew open.

Oh no. Oh noooo. If *he* was here, then I was definitely in Hell.

The rumble of his voice as he responded to the woman should have filled me with dread. Instead, warmth shivered through my insides. *The* warmth. The startling sensation of my wolf stirring awake.

What the . . . ? Why? *Why* did she respond to him like that?

Suddenly angry at my wolf for her reaction to him, I struggled to extract my limbs from their heavenly cocoon. The white silken sheets were a *trap*, meant to lull me into a false sense of safety. It was all coming back to me now. The fight in the park. Me storming away. And then . . . nothing.

My anger boiled over and I lurched from the cloud-like bed, only to crash to the wooden floorboards. With a groan, I clutched at my spinning head.

What did he do? *Drug* me? Hit me over the head?

I was going to *murder* him.

A door to my right burst open, revealing the devil himself.

When Kolton saw me sprawled across the floor, he stepped forward as if to help me. I threw a hand up, stopping him in his tracks.

"You freaking *kidnapped* me?" I spat—or, at least, tried to. My voice rattled, rusty with disuse. How long had I been out? "Haven't you ever heard of 'no means no'? Or are you *that* much of an entitled dickhead?"

Someone burst out laughing from behind Kolton. A *male* someone.

"She called you *dickhead*, bro. What are you gonna do about it?"

I caught the briefest flash of white teeth and spiky blond hair before a brunette close to my age shoved him aside.

"He isn't going to do *anything*, Griff, other than apologize," the girl sternly said, shouldering her way into the room. One look at me on the floor and her expression flipped to pity. "Oh, you poor thing. I don't know what got into my *dickhead* brother."

She threw the last part over her shoulder with a disapproving frown.

Wait. *Brother?*

"Vi," Kolton started.

"Don't *Vi* me," she interjected, whirling to shoo him from the room. "Make yourself useful and go get her something to eat. The poor girl is starved."

Uhhh . . .

Then the most shocking thing happened. The big bad werewolf backed up and allowed her to shut the door in his face.

With a harumph, she turned back to me as if ordering around the most powerful alpha in America was no big deal. "Now," she said, "let's start over. I'm Violet, but everyone calls me Vi. The *dickhead* who brought you here is my big brother, but I swear I had nothing to do with it. Kidnapping is so not my style."

Despite myself, I actually cracked a small smile. How could I not? This girl was hardcore.

"I'm Nora," I replied back, immediately starting to like her. Which, I realized, was a flaw of mine. She was Kolton's *sister*. I needed to keep my guard up.

As if her goal was to prove me wrong, Vi casually sat on the edge of the bed and tilted her head to study me. Her hair was almost black like her brother's, swept up in a high ponytail. It was perfectly straight, not a hair out of place, which I secretly envied. She even had cute bangs, something I could never have without looking crazy. Her olive skin tone was the same as Kolton's, but her eyes were purple. Violet, like her namesake. Probably contact lenses.

"I can see why my brother is obsessed with you," she said after a beat. "You're wicked hot."

When all I did was gape at her, she threw her head back and laughed.

Moments later, she stood up again as quickly as she'd sat. "Okay, enough chit-chat. I'm sure you want to get out of here, but first, how about a shower and change of clothing?"

Okay, I was smitten with her. Just a little.

"Yes, please," I immediately replied, deciding to throw caution to the wind and play nice with this girl. She could be my ticket out of here. "I'd seriously hug you right now if you weren't Kolton's sister."

She laughed again. "Touché. But, who knows, maybe I'll convince you to change your mind."

"Who knows," I responded with a noncommittal shrug.

In no time, she showed me to the adjoining bathroom—which

was bigger than my bedroom back home—and even helped me start the shower when I couldn't figure it out. Who had *touch pads* in their bathroom? Rich people, apparently.

When I went to undress, she hopped up onto the counter instead of leaving. Okay, I knew werewolves were used to nudity, but I'd never been a part of that experience. I still had a human tolerance level to nakedness.

It dawned on me that her job might be to keep an eye on me. To make sure I didn't try to escape. But I was so tired of running. What would the harm be in staying here long enough to recharge my batteries a little? At least with me here—wherever here was—I was safe from the witches.

Or was I?

I still didn't know what Kolton's plans were for me. All I knew was that he *really* wanted me to accept his help. Enough to *kidnap* me.

Mad at him all over again for bringing me here against my will, I shucked off my clothing, unmindful of my audience. Then froze when I heard, "*Whoa*, girl, those are some sick scars. Where did you get them?"

Suddenly self-conscious, I hurried into the shower to hide them from view. "Um, car crash when I was ten."

The lie easily slipped from my tongue. *Too* easily.

She didn't buy it.

"They look like claw marks, Nora."

At the quiet use of my name, my throat closed. Instead of responding to her observation, I stepped under the hot spray. As the water washed over me, I nearly lost it. Nearly caved to the emotions I'd been holding in for way too long. Biting my lips, I shoved them back down. No way was I going to cry in front of a perfect stranger.

In front of my kidnapper's *sister*.

I already looked weak and pathetic enough.

Vi lapsed into silence after that, probably realizing she'd stepped where she wasn't welcome. I was nearly finished when she left and quickly returned with a change of clothing. We were roughly the same size, so they were probably hers.

Instead of hopping back onto the counter, she left once more, giving me the privacy I desperately needed. Ringing out my hair—which was going to be hell to untangle—I stepped from the shower to inspect the clothing. Just like I suspected, both the shirt and ripped jean shorts were expensive name brands. So were the bra and panty set, which still had tags on them.

I'd never worn these brands. Could never afford them. Goodwill and thrift stores had always been my go-to. I doubted these people had ever stepped foot inside a Goodwill, unless it was to donate all of their unused clothing.

Not that I really cared how or where they shopped. I didn't hate rich people. Only rich people who *kidnapped* me.

Ripping the tags off a bit too forcefully, I donned the clothing, trying not to notice how good they felt against my skin. Okay, maybe there was something to be said about quality. The bra and top were a little snug, but the bottoms fit perfectly. Vi had even left me sandals, which I slipped on.

As I finally looked at myself in the mirror, I had to admit that she had good taste. The plum scoop-neck top was simple, yet tastefully showed a hint of my cleavage. The white-washed shorts hugged my curves and were just high enough to cover my midsection, which I was grateful for.

Ignoring the dark circles under my eyes, I focused on the beast perched atop my head. With a quick test of my fingers, I groaned when they immediately got stuck in the thick mass. It was literally going to take me all day to untangle this mess. I was tempted to do just that. Take my time. Keep them waiting. But, in the end, I forced the wild curls into a messy braid and called it a day.

I didn't have the patience for petty revenge.

Expecting the bedroom to be empty, I left the bathroom and immediately froze solid. Because there, leaning against the closed bedroom door, was Kolton.

At the sight of me, he straightened, arms slowly falling to his sides. I didn't miss the way his gaze traveled the length of my body, pausing more than once. He'd showered and changed as well. His damp hair was slicked back, but a strand had fallen onto his forehead. He was wearing another white shirt, but without a suit coat this time. The collared shirt was open at the neck, revealing a hint of chest hair and well-defined pecs.

Not hot at all. Nope. I hated it.

What snagged my attention next was the patchwork of dark tattoos he'd unveiled by rolling up his shirtsleeves. Was that a . . . *snake?* Not that I cared. Seeing his pristine appearance stained with ink did *not* intrigue me. Not in the slightest.

When he abruptly pushed off the door, I backpedaled into the bathroom. Before I could close and lock the door, he hurriedly said, "Nora, wait."

I paused to shoot back, "What will you do if I say no? Drag me out and tie me to the bed?"

Silence. Then, "Guess I deserved that."

"You deserve a *whole* lot more than that."

With a quiet sigh, he slumped back against the door. "I brought you breakfast," he said, gesturing at the bed.

At the mention of food, my stomach betrayed me with a loud

rumble. I peeked around the corner and, sure enough, there was a fancy gold tray on the bed with one of those domed covers over the plate. I forced myself to stay where I was, muttering, "It's probably poisoned."

Kolton sighed again, with a note of exasperation this time. "I promise it's not poisoned. Do you want me to taste test it for you?"

"Maybe."

Pushing off the door, this time slower, he approached the bed. I watched him, ready to slam the door if he so much as looked at me wrong. When all he did was lift the cover and make a show of sampling the food, my deathgrip on the door handle gradually eased. Now that the lid was off, tantalizing aromas filled the air. Eggs, toast and butter—

"Is that sausage?"

I snapped my mouth shut, but the damage had already been done.

Kolton looked up at me, just as he grabbed one of the sausages and bit into it—*slowly*. I pursed my lips to keep the drool from escaping.

"It is," he confirmed, holding it out before him. An invitation.

When I stubbornly stayed where I was, he raised it to his lips again.

"*Fine*," I snapped, and marched into the room. Before he could take another bite, I snatched it from him. Backing away again, I tore into the sausage like a rabid dog. He silently watched me eat, his dark amber eyes glittering with something . . . unsettling. Squirming under his intent gaze, I said, "Where am I?"

"Upstate in the Adirondacks. At my family estate near Lake Placid."

I nearly choked on the sausage, swallowing too fast. "What did you do, stuff me in the trunk of your car?"

His lips twitched. "We took a private jet up here, actually."

I froze. Of *course* I was unconscious for my first ever flying experience. Just my luck. I stared at him a moment before demanding, "And how, pray tell, did you knock me out?"

He abruptly looked away. Ah hell. This wasn't good.

When I started backing toward the bathroom again, he shoved a hand through his hair and replied, "You weren't hurt, I promise."

I gawked at him for a second, watching as more hair fell onto his forehead. Then yelled, "Not hurt? You *kidnapped* me! I clearly said no and then you—"

"Okay," he loudly interrupted, raising his hands as if in surrender. "I handled the situation poorly. I'm *sorry*. I was desperate and that was the only thing I could think of."

"Gah!" I shouted, throwing my head back. "*Kidnapping* was the only thing you could think of? That is the most pathetic thing I've ever heard. And what now? Are you going to keep me here against my will? Because, guess what, genius? *I don't want to be here!*"

I was screaming now. Screaming at the top of my lungs. I'd finally snapped, and I didn't even care how unhinged I sounded.

Trapped. *Trapped*. Why was I always *trapped?*

"Nora, please. Let me explain," I heard him say, but I was too far gone.

Lunging at the bed, I grabbed the plateful of food and threw it at him. "Get out!" I screamed, reaching for the cover. I threw that too. "Get out, get out, *get out!*"

When he simply stared at me, I gripped the heavy tray and swung it at him. Inches from his head, he caught it. I tried wrestling it from him, but his grip was ironclad. Breathing heavily, I shot him a death glare, ready to spew hateful words. But, as our eyes locked, the words lodged in my throat.

Yellow. His eyes were burning a bright yellow.

Which should be impossible. The full moon had lost its pull. Werewolves couldn't shift—even partially—without the full moon.

I let go of the tray and staggered back, landing heavily on the bed. As my back hit the mattress, he was suddenly above me. Towering and imposing. For the first time since running into him at the nightclub, true fear spiked through me. He was an *alpha*. One of the strongest on the planet. And I'd forgotten. I'd completely forgotten how small, how *helpless* I was compared to him. How violent they said he was when provoked.

And I'd yelled at him. I'd thrown food and disrespected him in his home.

He had every right to tear me down to size. To put me in my place. I was nothing. *Nothing*. And he was going to remind me of that, probably in the most painful way possible.

But my body was weak. Frail, like a human's. I wouldn't survive. I wouldn't—

When his leg brushed against mine, I flinched as if he'd kicked me. My breaths came in short spurts as I tried to brace myself for the punishment to come. He slowly leaned down, placing both hands on the mattress either side of me. I squeezed my eyes shut.

"I will leave you now, Nora," he quietly said after a torturous moment, his breath warming the side of my face. "Take this time to calm yourself and rest, but I will be back. And when I do, I expect you to hear me out. Understood?"

Clenching my teeth as hard as I could, I nodded.

"Good," he whispered, bending even lower to inhale. To breathe in my *scent*. Then he straightened and was gone.

# CHAPTER 6

Escaping through the window wasn't an option.

I was three stories up with nothing to aid in my descent. There weren't enough bedsheets and jumping would certainly break a few bones. A *normal* werewolf would survive the fall just fine, a fact that was grating on my nerves something fierce.

After my altercation with Kolton, I decided that escape was the only viable option. He had complete control over this situation and I had none. He'd made that perfectly clear with his parting words. It didn't matter that they'd been softly spoken. He could demand my submission with barely a whisper and I'd be forced to obey.

Well, if I wanted to keep my *head.*

Running was the only guarantee that I could keep my independence—and my life. I didn't care that witches were still out there looking for me. I didn't care that I was now phoneless, truckless, penniless, and homeless. I would survive somehow. I would survive and find a way to free my wolf on my *own* terms. Not make a shady deal with a dickhead alpha.

Freshly rested, washed, and fed—sort of—I focused on the only other escape route available: the bedroom door. I hadn't tested it yet. Hadn't checked to see if it was locked. But of course it would be. I was a prisoner here, after all.

Inhaling a breath to steady my nerves, I tiptoed to the door and silently grasped the handle. Slower than molasses, I turned it. When it easily gave way, shock zipped through me. Then excitement. Maybe he'd been so upset with me that he'd forgotten to lock the door. Thanking my lucky stars, I finished turning the handle and carefully inched the door open.

All was quiet on the other side.

I peeked into the hallway and saw a banister straight ahead instead of a wall. A gigantic chandelier dripping with crystal dropped down the middle open space, while another hallway of rooms lined the other side. Opening the door wider, I poked my head out. To the right, all was clear. To the left . . .

"Well, hello there, gorgeous. Going somewhere?" a male voice drawled, startling the crap out of me. A tall blond guy peeled himself off the wall near my bedroom door, the same one who'd laughed at my dickhead comment earlier today.

*Griff*, Kolton's sister had called him.

When I froze in the doorway, he checked me out from head to toe, clicking his tongue as if in approval. I checked him out too, more to gauge his threat level. He was nearly as tall as Kolton but had more of a surfer's body, complete with board shorts and bleached highlights in his short spiky hair. He too had black tattoos on his arms, all the way to his biceps where they disappeared under his tight t-shirt. He was grinning broadly, and his puppy brown eyes . . . were twinkling with mischief.

Maybe not much of a threat. Unless he was a werewolf.

"I should warn you," he continued to drawl when I remained silent. "Kolton told me you might run. Which is completely fine by me. I love a good chase."

As that twinkling mischief turned a little feral, my heart thudded with panic.

Ah hell. Definitely a werewolf.

Before I could think better of it, I bolted down the right side of the hallway toward the stairs. I expected to hear pounding feet hot on my trail. Instead, all I heard was Griff's boom of laughter gradually fade behind me.

When the sandals slowed my descent, I kicked them off. Using the banister, I swung myself around the corners, taking the steps two at a time. The stairs led all the way to the ground level, where I paused to find the front door.

In that split second of time, something dropped down from above. Something *big*. A *boom* shook the marble floor as Griff landed right in front of me. With one hand splayed on the marble, he struck a pose like a superhero and grinned.

I backpedaled, but not fast enough. He rushed me like a linebacker. Before I could scream, he swept me clean off my feet. All the air left me in a violent whoosh when his shoulder dug into my stomach. Draped over him like a sack of potatoes, he spun me around with a booming laugh.

"Put me . . . down," I wheezed, uselessly beating on his back.

"What was that?" Griff said, spinning around again. "Nora? Nora, where are you?"

Not the least bit amused, I punched his back again. "Stop or I'm . . . I'm going to puke."

He spun again. "I could have sworn I heard something, but I can't tell if it's this way"—Spin—"or this way." Double spin.

I slapped a hand over my mouth as nausea swept through me.

"Griff."

With that single word, everything stopped. Griff slowly turned toward the sound, leaving me with nothing to see but the marble floor at his feet.

"Put her down."

Kolton. There was no mistaking his voice. Or the quiet command behind it.

Realizing he was getting an eyeful of my *butt* sticking up in the air, heat flushed my cheeks. When I started to squirm, Griff tightened his hold on my upper thigh.

A low growl cleaved the air.

I felt Griff tense beneath me, even as he chuckled and said, "Easy, Kol. She needed to be taught a lesson for running. It's not like I spanked her."

Wait . . . what?

"Griff," he said again, even quieter this time. "Don't make me repeat myself."

Goosebumps pricked at my skin. The quieter his voice became, the scarier it sounded.

Apparently, Griff thought so too. I abruptly slid backward. Before I could fall, he grabbed my waist to slow my descent. The second my feet touched the ground, I shoved his chest and broke his hold on me. Whipping my braid over my shoulder, I took a second to glare up at him. He answered my glare with a slow grin.

Huffing, I whirled around, only to come face to face with Kolton. At the intense look in his eyes, I almost cringed back, my earlier fear returning. But the look wasn't directed at me. Realizing his attention was still on Griff, I shuffled to the side—toward the front door—only to gasp as his hand shot out and captured my wrist.

Familiar heat licked at my skin. I pried at his fingers, demanding, "Let go."

His attention snapped to me and I froze, nearly swallowing my tongue. After a moment that lasted an eternity, he dropped my arm and said, "Come with me."

In a flash, he whirled and stalked off. Not up the stairs again, but deeper into the house. I watched him go, rooted to the spot with indecision.

When I cast a glance at the front entrance, Griff quietly said, "I would follow him if I were you."

At the seriousness in his voice, I peeked up at him and immediately frowned. Despite his words, he was still grinning. A highly suspicious grin, one that clearly showed how amused he was at the whole situation. Not an ounce of fear was in his eyes. When my frown deepened, his grin only widened.

"Nora," Kolton's voice rang through the air, making me jump.

I glanced at him, noting that he'd stopped just shy of an open doorway. Waiting for me.

"Someone's in trouble and it's not me," Griff softly sang, sticking his hands into his pockets before sauntering around me. Gently nudging my back with an elbow, he added, "Go on, gorgeous. He won't bite."

But when he brushed past to head back up the stairs, there was no mistaking his quiet laughter. Yeah, that wasn't reassuring. I was even more freaked out now.

Casting one last look at the front door, I squared my shoulders and marched after Kolton. I might be afraid of him, but I wasn't going to let *him* know that. I'd hear him out, then tell him I wasn't interested. Sure, he could keep me here against my will, but I wouldn't stop trying to escape. He hadn't harmed me yet—at least not physically—but I'd seen the darkness in his eyes.

He was dangerous. I would be stupid to willingly remain under his roof. No matter how desperate I was to free my wolf, I couldn't let him sway my decision to leave.

As soon as he saw me follow, he turned and led me through a

dining room containing the longest table I'd ever laid eyes on. Another crystal chandelier graced the high ceiling, twinkling brightly in the late morning sunlight. I almost stopped at the tall windows to sneak a peek outside, but Kolton was holding a swinging door open for me on the room's other end.

I felt myself tensing the closer I came. He watched my approach, noticing way more than I wanted him to. To his credit, he didn't say a word, his expression remaining neutral. When I brushed past him, I tensed even more, feeling his eyes follow me into the next room. But at the sight that greeted me, I abruptly stopped and gaped at my surroundings.

Several staff members were bustling about the cavernous kitchen, cleaning and wrapping up what looked like a mountain of leftovers. My stomach immediately growled at the scent of several different breakfast meats. The staff didn't notice me at first, too busy attending to their jobs. But when Kolton lightly cleared his throat, every single head whipped in our direction.

"Could we have the room, please?" was all he said.

Just like that, they were scurrying from the room. A few cast me curious glances on their way out and I did the same. When the last one left the room, I asked without turning around, "Are they human?"

"Yes."

I swallowed, suddenly sick to my stomach again. Before I could mask my expression, he came around me and saw. I ducked my head, but it was too late.

"If you have something to say, Nora, go ahead and say it."

Throwing caution to the wind, I blurted, "Are they safe here?"

"Yes."

I raised my chin to stare at him incredulously. "How? They're defenseless here and you know it. Do they even know what you are?"

He tilted his head to the side, watching me closely. "No, they don't. We're very careful not to reveal our true selves."

"And during the full moon?" I pushed, crossing my arms. "What then?"

"Every month, the staff is dismissed for three days when the moon's pull is strongest."

I stared at him. *Hard.* But couldn't detect any lie.

After a long beat of silence, he said, "I understand that you don't trust me—"

"Spot on again, Captain Obvious."

"—but I'm not the monster you seem to think I am," he continued as if I hadn't spoken.

Snorting, I simply replied, "You kidnapped me."

"Yes."

"Why?"

A muscle jumped in his jaw. "Because you needed help."

"Bull," I said, watching the slight shift in his expression.

His eyes narrowed. "I'm not lying."

"But you're not telling the full truth," I shot back. "Spill or I'm out of here."

When I took a step toward the exit, he jerked a hand through his hair and said, "Wait."

I shouldn't have, but I paused, curious to hear his explanation.

With a sigh, he moved toward the massive kitchen island and pulled out a stool. "Have a seat and I'll tell you," he said, rounding the island to open a drawer and cabinet. When he turned with a plate and fork, I cautiously approached. Flicking a glance at me as I slowly took a seat, he added, "Sausage and eggs?"

My stomach growled again and his lips twitched. Deciding that depriving myself was just plain stupid, I replied, "Yes, please."

He looked a little too satisfied with my response, but I kept silent as he moved to the stove and dished me up a second breakfast. Only when the plate was piled high with food did he return and set it before me.

"Coffee?"

I nodded, picking up the fork. I was just about to shovel eggs into my mouth when he dropped the bomb.

"I want you to marry me."

The eggs tumbled off the fork. "Excuse me?" I said, certain I'd heard him wrong.

He turned with a mug of coffee in hand. Then, with the most serious expression possible, repeated, "I want you to marry me."

I jumped off the stool so fast that it flew backward, tipping over with a loud clang. "Are you out of your mind? You want me to *MARRY YOU?*"

Yeah, I was shouting again. His words had that effect on me.

Setting the mug on the counter, he calmly replied, "Yes, I want you to marry me. In return, I will help you free your wolf."

There was a moment of perfect silence as I stared at him and he stared at me.

And then I was laughing. So hard that I curled forward and clutched at my stomach. He didn't look offended. Not even a little. As tears streamed down my face, he simply . . . waited. Expectantly. Like he knew—just *knew*—that I would say yes.

A fresh wave of anger simmered in my gut.

The moment I could speak again, I snapped, "You're insane."

He watched me for a beat. Then, "No. Just desperate."

I frowned. "What does that mean?"

A muscle feathered in his jaw again. "It means that I need a wife to further secure my position as alpha of Midnight Pack."

I scrunched up my nose. "But haven't you been alpha for awhile now?"

"Six years. But they've been a rough six years. As the leader of the largest pack in America, I have many enemies, something we seem to have in common."

At his raised eyebrow, I snorted and muttered, "I don't have *that* many."

"Because of my coveted position," he went on, "I'm often challenged. No one has bested me yet, but if I fall, my family will lose everything. The family estate, money, protection. The new alpha will force the pack to shun them. They will be left penniless and alone. Challengers are known to kill the fallen alpha's family to further secure their new position."

"What does this have to do with me?" I asked, my mind reeling with all that he'd shared.

"Marriage will ensure my family's safety if something happens to me," he continued, his gaze steady on mine. "An alpha's spouse gains full control over his assets when he dies. Your position as my wife would trump a challenger's victory. In essence, you would be considered the new pack alpha."

I swallowed. Hard. "And if the challenger challenges *me?*"

"You kill him."

"Oh, is that it? Have you *seen* me?" I sarcastically said, throwing up my hands. "I'm basically a human."

"Not if I can free your wolf," he quietly said, with such certainty—such *conviction*—that I paused to stare at him.

Ah hell, was I actually *considering* this crazy idea?

"But I'm a complete stranger," I pushed, searching his face. "Why me?"

"When I first met you at the club, I sensed a kindred spirit. I don't want love or a mate. I doubt you want those things with me either. But you're tenacious and resourceful, not to mention scrappy in tough situations. That's exactly what I need by my side. I also sense great power in your wolf. Once she's unleashed, you will be a formidable alpha female."

Hell, *yeah*.

Wait, no. He was totally stroking my ego, the manipulative dickhead.

"So, I would essentially be your life insurance policy," I said, not bothering to sugarcoat it.

"Yes," he replied without batting an eye. The guy had balls, I'd give him that.

"How do I even know you can free my wolf?" I said next, eyeing him carefully.

Instead of answering, he came around the island toward me. The move was so abrupt that I scrambled to place distance between us. Responding to my retreat, he slowed, enough that I paused to warily watch him approach.

My heart pounded as he eased into my personal space. This close, I had to tip my head back to maintain eye contact. As he lifted a hand, I instinctively flinched. He paused, studying me closely. When I stayed where I was, he erased the final inches between us and grasped my upper arm. His touch was firm yet gentle. Nonthreatening. Yet, I tensed all over.

"You feel that?" he quietly said, sweeping his thumb across my skin.

My wolf immediately stirred, filling me with heat. Overwhelmed, I simply nodded.

"Your wolf reacts when I'm near. Has that ever happened to you before?"

Swallowing, I managed to whisper, "No."

"I can only assume that my presence is encouraging her to awaken. If I touch you long enough," he said, sliding his hand down my arm, "what do you think will happen?"

My thoughts grew fuzzy as his touch produced more and more heat. Although uncomfortable, it wasn't altogether unpleasant. I even sort of . . . liked it. Crap, that wasn't a good sign. But even more unsettling was the realization that my wolf still responded without aid from the full moon.

It was almost as if Kolton *was* the full moon.

Swallowing with difficulty, I tugged my arm from his grasp. The heat immediately started to subside. "But what if you can't?" I questioned. "What if you can't set her free?"

"Then the marriage agreement will be annulled," he said, dropping his hand. "You can leave with no ill will from me or my pack. I will also make certain you're financially secure. And if you choose to remain within my territory, you will be protected—from the witches and anyone else who would cause you harm—for as long as I'm still alpha."

Oh. Oh wow.

No doubt about it, the guy knew how to talk a good bargain. But marriage? To *Kolton Rivers?* Saying yes could cost me everything. My family, my pack, my freedom. Then again, hadn't I already lost most of those things? He'd found me at my lowest. At my neediest. At my most *desperate.*

I narrowed my eyes at him shrewdly. What game was he playing? What about this arrangement did I still not know?

Before I could question him further, he raised his arm again . . . and stuck out his hand.

"So what do you say, Nora Finch?" he said, looking far too

confident for my liking. "Do we have a deal?"

# CHAPTER 7

I'd never been one to talk myself out of hasty decisions. Most of the time, I simply followed my gut and dealt with the consequences later.

So, when I realized that the deal before me was a win-win in my favor—regardless of the outcome—my resistance started to crumble.

Marrying Kolton would purely be a business arrangement. People did it all the time. I could live my life and he could live his. I doubted he would even care if I had a secret lover—not that I had any current prospects. Marrying him meant freeing my wolf. And even if he couldn't uphold his end of the deal, I would be leaving with everything else I'd always wanted: independence, protection, financial stability to pursue my dreams. I could move in with Brielle. I could get a *real* job.

The only downside to marrying Kolton would be if another wolf challenged and killed him, leaving *me* as pack alpha. But that was a concern for another day. Besides, he'd successfully ruled the largest pack in America for six years. I doubted he was easy to kill.

I stared at his hand for a solid minute. That was all it took.

"Deal," I said, locking eyes with him as I firmly grasped his outstretched hand.

He immediately gripped my fingers. Hard. Almost hard enough to hurt. Before I could panic—or change my mind—he muttered a single word under his breath. Something that sounded like "*connect*" in latin. A second later, a charge of electricity zapped my palm.

Startled, I jerked my gaze to our joined hands . . . and saw movement.

One of his tattoos—the black *snake*—was slithering off his skin and onto mine.

"*What the hell?*" I shrieked and tried to yank my hand away. Kolton gripped my fingers a moment more, then released me. I stumbled back, nearly falling on my butt. Righting myself, I thrust my hand out and bit back a scream.

There was a snake tattoo. On my *arm*. It coiled all the way up my right forearm, the head resting on my elbow. The tail circled my wrist and ended with a final curl around my thumb.

Too afraid to touch it, to even *look* at it, I set my sights on Kolton. "What did you do?" I bit out, my voice noticeably trembling.

His expression was firm, unyielding, as he replied, "Securing my insurance."

My hands started to shake and I balled them into fists. "Don't make me repeat myself. *Explain*."

At my choice of words, a warning flashed in his eyes. Yet he said, "It's a binding ritual. You're a flight risk, so I made sure you couldn't back out of our agreement. As long as you remain here, no harm will come to you."

Panic tightened my chest. I'd heard of supernatural bindings before, yet had never seen one performed. All I knew was that they were *permanent*, and breaking them held dire consequences.

Anger surged through me.

"I wasn't going to run," I spat, staring daggers at him. "Whatever you did wasn't necessary."

His gaze narrowed. "Oh? Then look me in the eye and say you didn't consider it."

At the challenge, I opened my mouth to deny the accusation. Only to shut it a moment later.

Smug satisfaction spread across his face.

My fists shook uncontrollably. "Take. It. Off."

His expression remained the same. "You agreed to the deal. There's no undoing it."

I took a threatening step toward him. "Bull. Remove the snake from my arm or I'll make your life hell."

Instead of being cowed by my words, he matched my step with one of his own, crowding his large body into my personal space. He bent his head and I stopped breathing as his deep voice rumbled in my ear, "Do your worst, sweetness, because I'm already in Hell."

And then, just like that, he left the room.

Vi found me an hour later, tucked in the corner of the walk-in kitchen pantry, a jar of half-eaten peanut butter propped between my bent knees.

"There you are," she started, then noticed the tattoo wrapped around my arm. "Is that a . . . ?" Her eyes widened in shock. "That *dick*. I'm going to kill him."

"Not if I kill him first," I mumbled, my mouth still crammed with peanut butter.

"I'm so sorry, Nora. I seriously have no idea why he's doing this," she said, leaning against the shelves near the door.

I stopped chewing. "You don't?"

"No. He's been very tight-lipped about the whole thing. We were all shocked when he brought you here."

A wicked idea formed. Before I could think better of it, I blurted, "He's forcing me to marry him."

The look on her face warmed my soul.

Maybe I wasn't above petty revenge after all.

"*Kolton Anthony Rivers*," she bellowed at the top of her lungs. Music to my ears. When she stormed from the pantry, I scrambled to my feet and followed, still clutching the peanut butter jar. She found him on the ground floor in a room near the foyer. His study, by the looks of it.

When Vi burst inside, already talking a mile a minute, he stood from his desk. One glance over her shoulder and his gaze found mine. Slowly pulling the spoon now licked clean of peanut butter from my mouth, I let a smile curve my lips.

*Gotcha*, I silently communicated, gleefully watching as Vi viciously lit into him.

"Dad would roll over in his grave if he knew about this . . ." she was saying, waving her arms in the air. "Forcing someone to marry you is practically *rape*."

Kolton's expression darkened. *You're going to pay for this*, his look promised.

*Game on*, I shot back, suppressing a shiver when black flames seemed to flicker in his eyes.

I was playing with fire by poking the big bad alpha, but it felt good. Like I was stealing back a little of his control over me. Instead of fear, excitement filled me.

When Vi finally paused to take a breath, Kolton opened his mouth. Probably to set the record straight about our deal. Not that it would make him look much better, especially with his *snake* still around my arm. Before he could utter a word, a sound from outside caught my attention.

One glance out the window and I was running. Hurriedly plonking the peanut butter jar on a side table, I raced toward the front door. Only to skid to a halt as Griff blocked my way.

"I thought we already went over this, gorgeous," he said, leaning against the door. "You don't leave unless Kolton gives the green light."

Annoyed at his choice of words, I stomped up to him and shoved my arm in his face. "Does it *look* like I'm going anywhere, *sputnik?* I just want to see my baby, so move aside."

His eyebrows hiked up impossibly high. "Sputnik?" he spluttered. "*Baby?* Wait . . ." He grabbed my arm, his expression switching to confusion when he saw the snake tattoo. Relieved when his touch didn't stir my wolf awake, I didn't pull away. After a moment, he flicked his eyes to mine, clearly alarmed. "Where did you get this?"

"Ask your dickhead alpha," I replied, right as I heard footsteps behind me.

"Let her go, Griff," Kolton said, that dangerous edge to his voice returning.

Griff immediately dropped my arm, but not before shooting Kolton an accusatory look. "She could have been hurt."

Well *that* caught my interest.

"But she wasn't. I know what I'm doing, Griffin."

A muscle ticked in Griff's jaw, but he stayed silent.

Vi didn't.

"That's crap. My brother has officially lost his mind. Nora has every right to leave this house if she wants. Anyone who stops her will have to deal with me."

I was *seriously* liking this girl.

"It's not that simple, Vi," Kolton quietly replied.

"Oh?" she snapped. "Then enlighten me."

Silence. Then, "Nora?"

Ah hell, he was *not* putting this on me to set the record straight.

Before I could think of some other way to get back at him, scurrying footsteps from outside paused the conversation. Griff turned and opened the door, just as a little body burst inside.

"Kol!" the girl squealed, streaking right past me. I caught a glimpse of dark pigtails and a pink tutu before Kolton bent and scooped her into his arms. When he tossed her in the air, she shrieked with delight, lapsing into giggles as he caught her again.

I froze solid, dumbstruck by the sight.

The girl, probably no older than six, showed no fear as she threw her little arms around Kolton's neck and squeezed.

And Kolton . . .

Kolton was smiling. *Grinning.* So openly that I forgot how to breathe.

"Uncle Jag let me ride up front like a big girl the whole way," the girl excitedly said, pulling back to beam at Kolton. "And he let me have two milkshakes. *Two.*"

"Oh, he did, did he?" Kolton replied, tugging on one of her pigtails. "Well, you shouldn't let him spoil you. You know better, Melanie."

Melanie rolled her eyes at him. *Rolled* them.

Kolton only chuckled and set her down, straightening to glance at the front door. "Is this true, Jagger? You encouraging my baby sister to break the rules?"

"You know Mellie," a new voice said, startling my surroundings back into focus. "She whines and whines until you give in."

"Hey," Melanie said with a huff, stamping her foot. But my attention was now on the new guy standing in the doorway.

Good grief, why were all the men here so *hot?*

This one was dressed head to toe in black, with shoulders nearly as broad as Kolton's. His skin was light brown and his eyes a blue gray, both showcasing his mixed heritage. Diamond studs glinted in both earlobes, and his black hair was shaved close to his head.

Surprisingly, ink covered his arms as well. Did they all get matching tattoos or something?

Realizing the room had fallen silent, I glanced up at his face again to find him staring at me. Crap. They *all* were. I was obviously the fish out of water here. The stranger. The *trespasser*.

And the guy staring bullets at me was making that perfectly clear.

"This her?" he said, giving me a once over. Unlike Griff, he didn't look impressed.

Before anyone could reply, he stepped forward and into my personal space. I stiffened, forcing myself to hold still as he slowly circled me. Now *this* reaction I was used to. It was like other werewolves could sense how broken I was. One look and they knew I wasn't like them. Most became a little excited when they realized I was practically human—and not the good kind of excitement. I was defenseless against their superior strength, which triggered their predator instincts.

When he paused behind me to inhale my scent, a low growl rumbled through the foyer.

"Jagger, stand down."

At Kolton's command, the guy behind me released a growl of his own. "She doesn't smell right."

The words shouldn't have offended me. I'd heard them dozens of times before. But I still flinched a little.

Kolton growled again, loud enough that goosebumps erupted over my flesh.

This time, Jagger backed off, stepping far enough away that I could breathe again.

A moment of awkward silence ensued.

I was just about to break the ice with a lame comment when a little voice said, "Your hair looks like *fire*. Can I touch it?"

All eyes went to me again.

Umm . . .

I looked over at Melanie. She'd glanced up at Kolton as if to ask for permission. His gaze remained fixed on me though, with an intensity that made me want to squirm. Not knowing what it meant, I focused on Melanie and replied, "Sure."

She grinned wide, revealing two missing front teeth. No one stopped her as she skipped over, as she looked up at me expectantly and tugged on my arm. Acutely aware of every eye on me, I crouched to her level. With wonder in her bright amber eyes, she reached out and pinched a curl that had escaped my braid. When she let go and the curl sprang upward, her eyes lit up like the sun.

Literally.

Every inch of me stiffened as her irises glowed a blazing yellow.

We suddenly weren't alone. Kolton's scent washed over me—a woodsy musk with hints of smoke and bourbon. He captured his sister's hand and gently lowered it. "You've had a busy morning, Mellie," he softly said, coaxing her attention back to him. "Why don't you check to see if Miss Gabby has some lunch ready for you?"

Her bottom lip poked out in a cute pout, but I noticed with relief that her eyes were no longer glowing. With one last longing look at my hair, she pulled away and scampered from the room. Kolton rose from his crouched position. When I saw him stretch out his arm to offer me a hand, I quickly shot to my feet. Feeling his gaze on me, I looked everywhere but at him. Attention didn't usually give me hives, but Kolton's was starting to make me itch.

Scanning the foyer, I made the mistake of looking at Jagger. His blue gray eyes were locked on my right forearm, on the tattoo there, and he didn't seem happy.

"Any problems on the trip up?" Kolton said, drawing Jagger's gaze over to him.

"None," he replied, giving my arm another quick glance.

"Thought as much. What's the prognosis?"

"Engine failure, among several other things. The piece of junk needs a complete overhaul."

My eyes flew wide. "Are you talking about my baby?"

"Oh, the *truck* is her baby." Griff loudly guffawed. "I thought she had an actual baby or something."

"Griff, *really?*" Vi groaned.

"Hey, how was I supposed to know? Chicks don't usually call their trucks 'baby.'"

"*Chicks?* We've talked about this, Griffin O'Neal. Girls don't like being referred to as baby chickens."

"Oh, but it's okay to call us names like *dickhead?* Sounds kinda hypocritical, Violet Rivers."

As they continued to bicker, I took advantage of the moment to slip outside. When no one stopped me, I took a step. Then another. Until I'd crossed the wide porch and descended the handful of stairs to the circular drive. A big white truck with dual rear drive was parked there. And hooked up behind it, looking sad and pathetic . . .

Was my truck. My *baby*. Banged up and rusted so badly that she looked more puke brown than yellow.

The sight of her familiar form brought tears to my eyes.

"Thought you would still want her."

Startled by Kolton's voice directly behind me, I quickly blinked the tears away. "Yeah."

"We can get her fixed up again if you want."

Hope soared in my chest, then plummeted when I remembered the tattoo on my arm. "Sure."

Uncomfortable silence stretched between us.

He drew in a breath. "Nora . . ." he began.

"Where do you want her?" Jagger suddenly interrupted, brushing past. He twirled a set of keys around his finger as he went. *My* keys. I balled my hands into fists.

"In the garage for now. It might take awhile for a new engine to come in."

"Got it, boss," Jagger said, pulling open the door to the white truck. As he started the engine, all I could do was watch. Watch as he drove away, taking my one last possession with him.

I'd never felt more helpless. More alone.

When the truck disappeared from view, I whirled and fled into the house.

# CHAPTER 8

For the umpteenth time, I scowled at the snake on my arm.

It was definitely permanent. I'd scrubbed at the tattoo for hours until my skin was raw, but the mark wouldn't fade.

If I wasn't so busy sulking, I would once again demand that Kolton remove it. But I refused to speak to him. In fact, I'd managed to avoid him for nearly two days now. A fairly easy task in a house—aka mansion—this huge. So far, I'd only seen him, Vi, Griff, Jagger, Melanie, her nanny Miss Gabby, and the human staff. But I knew that Midnight Pack was hundreds of wolves strong.

Would he invite them all to our wedding? Would we even *have* a wedding?

Since I'd spent the past day and a half either locked in my room or sneaking around the house to avoid attention, I didn't know when the marriage would take place. Probably soon, based on how fast things had progressed so far. As for freeing my wolf, I had no idea how he planned to do that. If he was going to force her out somehow, it would have to be during the full moon.

A whole *month* from now.

Which meant that I might get stuck in a marriage with him for at least a month. Longer, of course, if he freed my wolf.

I'd thought this deal would be a win-win, but too late, I realized how naive that was.

Kolton had trapped me with no way to get out. I really had made a deal with the devil.

Worse than being stuck inside his fancy mansion though was the lack of outside communication. I assumed he'd taken my phone from me while I was unconscious—which I still didn't know how he'd pulled off—but I hadn't asked for it back. Not yet anyway. I was about to though. Just as soon as I worked up the courage to break my self-imposed isolation.

"You can do this, Nora," I pep-talked myself, pacing the length of my room. "You have rights. *Demand* he give them to you. Take back control."

I'd never been the damsel in distress type and I wasn't about to start now. No one was going to rescue me from this situation. I'd gotten myself into this mess and it was my job to get myself out. If I didn't use my voice, nothing would ever change.

"Because you're *so* good at sticking up for yourself," I sarcastically muttered with an eye roll. Not that defending myself had ever gotten me anywhere in the past.

No matter. I'd spent the last day and a half inside my head, and if I didn't get out of it, I was going to explode. The inaction was driving me *crazy*. I'd rather face a cruel alpha than one more minute with my thoughts.

Sufficiently pumped for the trying task ahead, I marched to the door and ripped it open. No one greeted me on the other side. I hadn't needed a *guard* ever since Kolton had placed the snake on my arm. Technically, the snake *was* my guard.

"Stupid *snake*," I grumbled, glaring down at it again.

Fueled by my new friend "rage," I stormed down the hallway and stairs, heading straight for Kolton's study. It was late, but not too late. He should still be up—if he was a creature of habit, which I assumed he was. Skulking around the house had taught me his loose routine, as well as the others. So far, he was the only one who hadn't left the property at one point or another.

Well, except for me.

I hadn't even stepped foot *outside*. Which had been torture, since all werewolves craved nature. From my lofty viewpoint out the third floor bedroom window, I'd spotted a massive garden behind the house. It circled and twisted around a large pond like a maze. I ached to lose myself in it. To explore it. To *touch* it. Besides a plethora of hedges and bushes, I'd seen several species of herbs and flowers. I was itching to get my hands on them.

But I didn't know what this *snake* would do if I left the house. Then again, I almost didn't care anymore, I was *that* stir-crazy.

I'd just hit the ground floor when Vi came hurrying toward me. Without explanation, she grabbed my hand and dragged me toward the coat closet.

"Vi, what in the—?"

"Shh," she hissed, whipping the door open and shoving me inside. As with all the closets in this house, it was huge and not the least bit cramped. Still, I panicked a little when she shut the door and everything went dark.

"Mind explaining?" I said, quieter this time, sticking out a hand to find the light switch. When I found it and the space flooded with light, my panic faded.

Vi turned to me with an expression I'd never seen from her before. "Your pack is here."

I felt all the blood drain from my face. Ah hell, this wasn't going to be good.

"Kolton is outside talking with them," she went on, her intense expression starting to freak me out. "He won't let them see you, not if you don't want them to."

"What? No, I need to see them. I left without explanation and they're probably super pissed with me right now."

Her expression only intensified further. "Listen, Nora. I know they're your pack, but Kolton will protect you. I know he will. Just say the word and he'll send them away. They can't touch you here."

With a sigh, I reached for the door handle. "Thanks, but I've got this. Really. I'm used to them being mad at me."

She made a sound of protest but didn't stop me from exiting the closet. As I crossed the foyer, she trailed me, closer than was necessary. Before leaving the house, I took a moment to breathe, to steady my nerves, then thrust the door open.

The first person I saw was my mom. Then my dad. Then . . .

At the sight of Alpha Hendrix, I couldn't quite hold back a groan.

Kolton turned at the sound. Our eyes briefly connected and I quickly looked away, but not before I saw his surprise.

Refocusing on the others, I said, "Mom. Dad. Alpha Hendrix."

"Nora," they greeted, almost in unison. Oh boy. I was so in for it.

Drawing in another breath, I blurted, "I'm guessing you tracked my phone. I can explain why I didn't contact you. You see, I . . . lost my phone."

*Crap*. That was so lame.

"Oh, Nora," my mom sighed.

"You have a lot of explaining to do, young lady," Alpha Hendrix said in his booming voice. I cringed at the sound, not failing to notice how irate he looked, even through the darkness. His salt-and-pepper beard kept twitching, the way it always did when he was pissed. Before I could speak, he added, "Gather your things and say your farewells. You've imposed on Alpha Rivers far too long as it is. I'm surprised he hasn't punished you for the inconvenience you caused him."

When I hesitated, torn between obeying and explaining the

situation, he lost his patience.

"NORA!" he snapped, making me jump. "Obey me at once."

My spine went rigid. "Yes, sir," I replied out of habit. Then, "I mean, no, sir. I-I mean, I can't leave. I . . ."

Tongue-tied, I flicked a glance at Kolton, uncertain how to proceed. He was already watching me, his brow furrowed. When Alpha Hendrix started speaking—err, *yelling* at me again—the furrow only deepened.

"Nora, enough of this," my dad finally spoke, striding forward when Alpha Hendrix paused to take a breath. "Don't make this any more difficult or your punishment will worsen."

I winced as his boots made contact with the porch steps. He was halfway across the porch when Vi darted out and blocked his path.

"No, you can't take her!" she shouted, so loud that my dad jerked to a halt.

His startled expression quickly morphed into a frown. "This is none of your concern, miss. Now step aside."

When he reached out as if to bodily move her, a deep voice rumbled, "*Don't* touch her."

At Kolton's command, my dad immediately froze.

"Alpha Rivers, we mean you and your pack no harm," Alpha Hendrix said in the tense silence that followed. "We simply want to reclaim what is ours and be on our way."

Another beat of silence. Then, "Kolton, don't let them take her. *Please*." Vi again.

At the emotion in her voice—the *desperation*—Kolton looked at his sister, then at me. I didn't know what he saw, but he was suddenly turning toward Alpha Hendrix and saying, "You and your pack have entered my territory without permission. I request that you all leave immediately."

"But—"

"*Now*. If you wish to speak to my *guest*, then you will do so through the correct channels. Good evening."

With that, he swept up the stairs and ushered me and Vi inside, completely ignoring my dad still standing motionless on the porch. The moment Kolton shut the door, he said, "Vi, contact Griff and Jagger. Tell them to make sure our *intruders* find their way off pack land. When you're done, meet me in the study."

Still reeling from what had happened, I turned and retraced my steps from earlier. Kolton didn't stop me. Before I knew it, I was back where I started. In my room. The rage I'd built up had vanished, along with my determination to be heard. All I had left was . . . shock. And a growing numbness that should have concerned me . . . but didn't.

What the hell had happened? I didn't know what to feel. Or think.

Not knowing what else to do, I started getting ready for bed. I'd just tugged off my shorts when the bedroom door burst open. Startled by the intrusion, I whirled and gasped as Kolton stormed inside.

"Show me," he said in clipped tones, heading right for me.

Confused by his furious expression, I froze solid. Until he grabbed the hem of my shirt and yanked it up.

"*What the hell?*" I yelled, and wrestled to pull my shirt down. His grip only tightened.

I shoved him, but he didn't move an inch. He was angrier than I'd ever seen him before, his eyes laser-focused on my stomach. On my . . . on my . . .

My throat closed. "Let go," I rasped. He continued to ignore me, lifting his other hand toward my midsection.

"Who did this to you?" he said, his voice nothing more than a growl. When his fingers grazed my scarred skin, I jerked back with a hiss.

His eyes flew up to mine and held.

"Let. Go," I repeated, unable to stop my voice from quivering.

At the sound, he slowly released my shirt. Yanking it free, I scrambled over the bed and onto the other side. When I met his gaze again, his eyes were glowing bright yellow. Fear pumped through me. A second later, he audibly inhaled as if scenting the air. No, as if scenting my *fear*. His chest heaved and he squeezed his eyes shut. When he opened them again, they were no longer yellow.

"Tell me," he quietly said, watching as I fruitlessly tried to tug my shirt over my underwear. "Tell me who hurt you."

"No one," I blurted, scrambling to think of a believable explanation for the jagged scars spanning my stomach. Instead, my brain finally put two-and-two together. *Violet*. She'd thought I was being abused and told her brother. I wanted to be mad at her, but I was too busy fending off an enraged alpha. "It was an accident."

I could tell he wasn't convinced. And, for the first time ever, neither was I. Not after the awful way my pack had handled my most recent transgression.

I suddenly couldn't breathe.

"I need to be alone," I whispered, wrapping my arms around myself. Kolton tracked the defensive move. I yanked my arms to my sides, but it was too late.

He took a slow step toward me. "Tell me who did it, Nora. Tell me and I'll make sure they suffer."

His words only added to my misery. A hot tear slipped past my control. I furiously brushed it away and said, "I can't do that. Now please leave."

Frowning, he took another step.

"KOLTON," I barked.

He stopped dead in his tracks.

I didn't know who looked more shocked. Him or me. All I knew was that I'd said his name out loud for the first time. And it had been used to command him.

He should have put me in my place then. It didn't matter that I was upset. But he didn't. He simply stared at me. Then bowed his head and left.

The second the door snicked shut, I collapsed in a heap on the floor. I waited for the tears to come, but they didn't.

It was sometime past midnight when I finally got up. My body moved on autopilot, donning my shorts and a pair of sneakers without thought. All was silent as I cracked open the bedroom door and peeked into the hallway. I slipped from the room and closed the door, silently making my way down the stairs. Not a single soul was in sight as I passed through the dining room and entered the kitchen.

A light was on over the sink, just enough illumination for the task ahead of me. I walked to the counter near the stove and pulled a steak knife from the chopping block. Laying my arm on the counter, I curled my hand into a fist and positioned the knife at my wrist. Inhaling a deep breath, I dug the sharp point into my flesh and cut.

My skin parted like butter. Blood bubbled up and spilled over, darkening the granite countertop. The pain hit hard, stealing my breath. I didn't stop. I cut another line. Then another. Slicing the snake tattoo into ribbons.

The tears finally came.

They blurred my vision, making me lose my grip on the knife. It clanked loudly against the counter. I froze, straining my ears for any sound. A second passed. Two. Then a faint thumping noise from above caught my attention.

I bolted for the kitchen door.

No longer bothering with stealth, I fumbled to undo the lock.

My fingers shook, slick with blood. Clenching my teeth, I jerked hard and the lock sprang open. I was out the door in a flash, racing into the night. Ignoring the agony in my arm, I flew across the patio and down the steps, giving the pool a wide berth.

I'd scouted out the property's terrain earlier on and knew that the woods surrounding the estate were my best bet. They'd have to hunt me by foot, which helped even the odds of my escape. The only downside was the trail of blood in my wake. In my desperation to remove the binding ritual, I hadn't taken into account their keen sense of smell. Even without the full moon, a normal werewolf had heightened senses.

Whipping my shirt off, I quickly wrapped it around my arm, barely breaking stride. They no doubt knew these woods well, which was another point in their favor, but I was desperate. More desperate than them, that was for sure.

I made it to the treeline when the pain hit. Not just from the cuts but *everywhere.*

My stomach cramped and I stumbled, nearly plowing into a tree. Dragging in some air, I straightened and pushed on. Minutes passed. Agonizing minutes. The farther I got, the more crippling the pain became. Until my legs finally gave out and I crashed to the ground. Still not willing to give up, I crawled forward, groaning and panting as wave after painful wave pulsed through me.

A rustling in the woods broke through my haze and I raised my head, blinking hard to clear my vision. A moment later, yellow eyes flashed in my peripheral. Certain I was hallucinating, I blinked again and focused on the spot. A pair of glowing eyes stared back. *Wolf* eyes.

Of course. *Of course* I was going to die under the teeth and claws of a wolf. I'd always known it. I'd run so many times, but fate had finally caught up to me.

"Make it quick," I panted, squeezing my eyes shut as fresh pain pierced my skull. Clutching my head, I curled into a tight ball and waited for my gruesome demise.

Something nudged my injured arm. Something cold and *wet*. So consumed by pain, I barely flinched. A whine shivered through the air, followed by another. Warmth licked my cheek. A tongue? I was suddenly being nudged from all sides. More warmth lapped at my exposed skin. More tongues. More whines. Then a short howl. And another.

When I writhed on the ground, crying out from the pain, a *crack* rent the air. More cracks and pops followed, sounds I'd heard before but couldn't place. When the noises stopped, gentle hands touched me. Roving over my skin as if searching for injuries. Warmth licked at me again, this time internally. Growing hotter and hotter until I cried out once more from the added pain.

A familiar voice swore.

"Griff, go get a blanket," Kolton gruffly said. A whine answered him. "*Now*."

Feet scampered away.

Something wet nudged my injured arm again. A wolf nose. After a moment, hands joined in, carefully unwrapping my shirt. When it fell away, Kolton hissed through his teeth.

"Oh, sweetness, what have you done?" he roughly whispered.

Unable to answer, I continued to writhe and tremble from the pain. A large furry body laid down beside me, warming my back. Kolton used my shirt to put pressure on the wounds. Every few seconds, he whispered reassurances to me.

"Hold on, Nora."

"The pain will go away soon."

"You're going to be okay."

No, I wasn't. I wasn't okay. None of this was.

But he kept talking. Kept comforting. Until, sometime later, padding feet could be heard again. And then I was wrapped in a blanket and lifted. Higher and higher. Tucked against a hard chest. Held securely in a strong pair of arms. Kolton carried me all the way back to his house. I fell in and out of consciousness, more from blood loss than pain. The longer he walked, the more my pain faded.

But I didn't think my closer proximity to the house was what made the pain go away.

It was *him*. My closeness to Kolton.

The binding ritual hadn't been broken.

Which meant that I'd epically failed.

# CHAPTER 9

I woke to Vi's face inches from mine. The second my eyes cracked open, she threw herself at me.

Surprised more than anything, I grunted as she squeezed the daylights out of me.

"*Vi*," Kolton sharply said from somewhere nearby.

"Oh, relax, you big baby. She's fine," Vi replied, pulling back to narrow her eyes at me. "You scared the crap out of me last night. Were you trying to kill yourself?"

I blinked, trying to remember everything that had happened. Had I imagined the wolf thing? I must have. I'd been in so much pain. Unless they had pet wolves of the regular variety roaming their woods.

When I didn't answer right away, Kolton straightened from his spot near the windows. "No," I said, shaking my head. The action didn't cause me pain, which I was grateful for.

At my response, Kolton settled against the wall again. Although his expression was stoic, I could have sworn he blew out a quiet sigh of relief.

"Good. Because I would have killed you if you'd tried to kill yourself."

I snorted at Vi's cliche words. Feeling a twinge of pain, I frowned and raised my arm. It was now securely wrapped in white gauze, covering the damage I'd inflicted.

"Your wounds wouldn't heal, so Griff stitched you up," Vi explained. "He's kind of the pack healer." She chewed on her bottom lip for a moment, then blurted, "I didn't realize your wolf was stuck. I'm so sorry, Nora."

I flicked a glance at Kolton. One look and I knew he'd told her everything. I lowered my gaze, suddenly feeling pathetic again.

"Guess what?" Vi abruptly said, bouncing on the bed a little. "Kolton thinks we should get out today and have some fun. Which is basically code for going into town. Girl's day out, baby!"

I felt Kolton watching me closely but didn't look at him again. Was this his way of apologizing? Of making everything better?

"The guys are going with us, of course," Vi continued, making a face. "But they'll keep their distance."

Aaaand there it was.

I didn't complain though, because going into town—even under guard—sounded heaps better than sulking again. But getting out of bed, showered, and dressed took a lot more effort than anticipated. I must have lost a lot of blood. The fatigue made me feel even more human than usual. And my new stitches ached something fierce.

Deciding to take a peek at them, I slowly unwound the gauze. At the sight of my mutilated flesh—and the way the snake tattoo was puckered in several places—I froze and simply stared. Stared and stared.

A soft knock came at the bedroom door and I burst into action, scrambling to cover up the injury.

"Nora."

I froze again.

"Can I come in?"

My heart hammered inside my chest.

Not knowing what to say or do, I gawked at the door like it was about to eat me.

"Nora."

Silence.

The door burst open.

I jumped, meeting Kolton's equally panicked gaze. He searched me from head to toe as if afraid that I'd hurt myself again. When he saw the gauze tangled around my fingers, the panic bled from his eyes.

"Here, let me help you," he said, striding into the room.

I tensed, but didn't move a muscle as he approached. When he stopped in front of me, I looked down and held out my arm, too exhausted for defiance. He hesitated, then carefully grasped my arm, using the gauze as a barrier between our skin. Heat still flushed my insides though, his close proximity alone stirring awake my wolf. But his fingers were quick. Nimble. And surprisingly gentle.

"You ran," he said, breaking the silence.

"Yes," I simply replied, watching him work.

Another beat of silence. Then, "Why?"

I opened my mouth, then closed it. Opened it again. "I didn't feel like I had another option."

His fingers stilled. Silence stretched between us again. Then, "How can I make it better?"

My gaze flew to his. This close, I could see the flecks of gold in his deep amber eyes. This close, there was no denying the sincerity in them. Hope fluttered in my chest. "Don't imprison me. Let me make my own decisions."

I thought he would stare at me forever. The longer he did, the more my hope dwindled. I'd asked for the impossible. He was Kolton Rivers, after all. He was used to being *obeyed*, not questioned. I'd already defied him several times. Insulted him, hit him, ran from him. It didn't matter that I technically wasn't a member of his pack. I'd made a deal with him, and I should have known better. Should have known that he now owned me. Of course he wasn't going to let me make my own decisions. Of course he wasn't—

"I will give you more freedom, on one condition," he said, startling my thoughts into silence.

"What's the condition?"

"You promise to speak to me first if you feel like running again."

My eyes widened. "Is that it?"

"That's it."

I raised my bandaged arm. "And this? You'll remove the tattoo?"

His chest expanded. I braced myself, certain he would refuse me. Heaving a sigh, he finished wrapping the gauze before replying, "One week. By the end of the week, whether you've changed your mind about marrying me or not, I'll unbind you. Deal?"

Ah hell, another *deal?* Then again, he'd been right about me. I'd run, just like he'd suspected I would. Guess I couldn't blame him for wanting to test my commitment.

I could survive one more week like this. Knowing that it was only temporary made me feel less trapped and helpless. He obviously wanted this deal between us to work, and now that I'd met his sisters, I could understand why he so badly wanted to protect them.

One week.

One week to decide if I really wanted to bind myself to him in holy matrimony. As long as he freed my wolf, of course.

One week . . .

I stuck out my hand. "You've got yourself another deal, Mr. Rivers."

A smile curved his lips.

I couldn't stop grinning.

He'd given me back my *phone*.

The fact that Kolton had already honored our new deal was what kept the smile on my face, not the actual device. I'd actually groaned aloud the second I'd turned it back on to find several threat-filled texts from my parents and Alpha Hendrix. Apparently, being kicked off Kolton's property had wounded their delicate pride. They blamed the whole fiasco on me, of course, saying how ungrateful and selfish I was acting.

The only upside was my best friend Brielle's genuinely concerned messages. I quickly texted her back, saying all was well before refocusing on my surroundings. The trip into town had been spent listening to country music and trying not to freak out at Vi's crazy driving. She kept sticking her head out the Jeep's open side while she belted the song lyrics, her eyes on the sky more often than the road.

Knowing that the three guys in the truck behind us could no doubt hear everything, I threw caution to the wind and joined in. After the past few tense-filled days, it felt good to let loose again. By the time we reached town, I almost felt normal. Almost. Having three dominant werewolves watching my every move didn't exactly allow me to relax. When we parked in the downtown area, they kept their distance, but I knew they weren't far.

Thankfully, I had Vi to keep me distracted. She dragged me into store after store, buying pretty much everything I looked at for more than two seconds. Overwhelmed by all the free-spending, I trailed in her wake like a lost puppy, not quite knowing what to think.

Was this what it meant to be rich? Whipping out credit cards without a care in the world? I couldn't imagine ever doing that. I'd grown up feeling guilty for spending money on even the smallest of splurges.

"Want to hit up the movie theater after this?" Vi said as we left yet another store, our arms laden with bags. "You look like you need to sit down."

"Sure," I replied, struggling to balance my awkward load so that the handles wouldn't rub against my injured arm. My hometown was too small for a movie theater, and I hadn't been to one in ages. And she was right. A light sweat now coated my skin. I needed a break before I passed out.

We were headed back to her purple Jeep when I spotted the guys not far away on the sidewalk, talking to a young couple. Curious, I focused on the unfamiliar faces. One was a guy in his mid twenties with curly brown hair. He was talking to Kolton, Griff, and Jagger with familiarity, his arm draped over a blonde girl's slim shoulders. She was facing away from us, her head thrown back in laughter.

Vi groaned as she caught sight of them the same time I did. "Jasmine Deveron," she muttered. "That gold-digging hussy is at it again."

Confused, I refocused on the girl. And that's when I saw it. While she laughed, she reached out and touched Kolton's arm. Her hand lingered longer than necessary. A move that didn't go unnoticed by the guy she was with. Or Kolton.

My feet were suddenly veering off course, heading toward the group instead of the Jeep.

"Nora," Vi hissed, but I ignored her, my sights on the Jasmine girl. I needed to see her face. I didn't know why, but I couldn't shake the feeling of needing to know.

Kolton spotted me coming first. When his attention left the blonde girl, she turned to look over her shoulder. Oh. Oh wow.

She was gorgeous. Big blue eyes framed by impossibly thick lashes. Probably extensions. Plump pink lips and rosy cheeks. She wore a tight tube top that showed off her perky breasts and flawless skin. Her hair was professionally highlighted and fell in perfect barrel waves down her back.

I slowed, suddenly hyper-aware of my many imperfections. I didn't usually compare myself to other girls, but the one before me looked like a living breathing Barbie doll. A Barbie doll that was quickly sizing me up and finding me lacking. Before I could turn and walk the other way, she noticed Vi and smiled. Even her teeth were perfect.

"Violet," she called, waving her over.

Vi swore and grumbled under her breath, "I'm gonna need a stiff drink after this."

As we approached, it became more and more apparent that something was amiss. Kolton's posture was too stiff, as was Griff's. Vi was giving off "I'd rather die than be here" vibes, and Jasmine's smile was too bright. As for the guy she was with . . . he was staring at me far too intently—like a predator who'd spotted fresh prey.

"Who's this?" Jasmine said the second we joined their group, eyeing me with passing interest.

"Jasmine, this is Nora. Nora, this is Jasmine," Vi quickly said, clearly wanting this conversation to be over already. "Nora is staying with us for a while." When Jasmine's eyes widened, Vi added, "Or maybe a long while."

Jasmine looked at me again with renewed interest. Her gaze sharpened, taking in every inch of me.

"Vi," Kolton said, a warning clear in his voice.

"What?" she said, shifting the bags on her arms. "They're going to find out soon enough anyway. Might as well rip the bandaid off."

Alarm flashed in Jasmine's eyes. Only for a split second though. She quickly masked her expression, donning a look of polite curiosity as she turned to Kolton. "Find out what?"

A muscle jumped in his jaw. He was staring daggers at his sister, his gaze flashing dangerously. She stared right back with an almost bored expression, opening her mouth again before he could stop her.

"My brother and Nora are getting married. Probably before the month is over. Don't worry. I'm sure you'll be invited to the wedding."

Every single face lit up with shock. Except for Vi's. Hers looked rather smug. In contrast, Kolton looked two seconds away from strangling his sister.

Several voices were suddenly talking at once.

"You're *marrying* her?" Jagger said, definitely not pleased with the news.

"Bro, when were you going to tell me?" Griff said, sounding more hurt than anything.

"You didn't tell Griff and Jagger yet?" Vi said with an exasperated sigh.

But what really caught my attention was Jasmine. She looked at Kolton and whimpered, "But what about me? You know I need you, especially when I'm in heat."

The words were like a punch to my gut. Nausea abruptly whipped through me and I turned, walking away from the chaos as fast as my legs could carry me. Stunned by my body's visceral reaction, I tried to turn back around. To show them all that her words hadn't affected me. They shouldn't have. I'd already heard that Kolton was a womanizer. That he'd probably slept with dozens of females, if not more.

I didn't even *like* Kolton. His sex life was none of my business. He could help all the females in heat that he wanted. Alphas often did in order to keep fights from breaking out amongst the pack males.

Yeah, I might be marrying him soon, but it was a business arrangement. Who he slept with was none of my concern. Still, the thought of him intimately touching that perfect Barbie body filled me with heat. A heat I'd never felt before.

When I neared the Jeep, Vi caught up with me. "Nora," she said, trying to see my expression. I avoided her gaze, focused on removing the shopping bags from my arms. "Nora, I'm so sorry," she persisted, truly sounding remorseful. "I always lose my head around Jasmine. She's just so *fake*. And I hate when she simpers all over my brother, just so she can rise up in the pack. The only reason Rodney wants her is because she claims to be Kolton's favorite pack female. It drives all the beta males wild."

I stiffened all over.

"But she's nothing to Kolton," Vi continued, loading our bags into the backseat. "Yeah, she gets him to help her when she's in heat, but they aren't a couple or anything. I mean, Griff and I aren't together, but he's the one I always go to when I'm in heat."

Surprised, I finally turned to her. "You and *Griff*?"

She snorted. "You wouldn't think so, right? We're always fighting. But . . . he's an attentive male. *Very*."

I made a face and she laughed, effectively drawing me out of my funk.

Despite the not-so-pleasant run-in with more members of Midnight Pack, I found myself enjoying the afternoon in Vi's company. We nearly had the movie theater to ourselves, catching the only movie running for the day. It was a slasher film, my least favorite. Still, Vi made it better by making fun of the ridiculous scenarios.

"Why do they always go inside the building and say 'Hello? Is anyone there?'" she whispered, handing me the popcorn. "I mean, *duh*. Can't you smell them?"

At her werewolf slip, I suppressed a laugh, knowing she couldn't relate to a human's "dulled" senses.

The movie was halfway over when three more people entered the theater. At first, I thought the guys had decided to join us, but only one of them was the correct height. The other two were shorter, their silhouettes clearly feminine. Expecting them to sit down, I watched with confusion as they approached us. I squinted, trying to make out their faces, but the theater was too dark.

It wasn't until they turned into our row that I finally recognized the tall one.

*Fang.*

Ah hell, the witches had found me.

# CHAPTER 10

I didn't react at first, scrambling to decide what to do.

Vi was oblivious, eyes riveted on the movie as she sipped her drink. I didn't want to involve her, but I didn't see how not to. When the witches were halfway down the aisle, I whispered in her ear, so low that only her wolf-hearing could pick up the words, "Call your brother."

She turned to me but I was already standing, drawing the witches' attention. "Hey, guys, long time no see," I said. Loudly. Drawing even *more* attention. "Looks like you found me. Congratulations."

A few of the other viewers in the auditorium shushed me.

"As you can see," I continued, relieved when the witches slowed, "we have an audience. I bet there are even cameras in here. You wouldn't want to create a *scene*."

More shushing and grumbling.

"You don't think we know how to deal with a few humans?" Fang said with a sneer. And I'd thought he was hot. Pshh.

"Come with us peaceably, Nora," Keisha said, stepping beside Fang. "You have something that doesn't belong to you."

"And what's that?" I said, feeling my heart start to pound.

Instead of answering, she flicked a glance at Fang. "Subdue her."

Fiery magic sprang to his fingertips.

"Nora, *run!*" Vi suddenly screamed and lunged from her seat. I watched in horror as she threw herself at the witches. I expected Fang to take her out with a fireball, but he abruptly cried out, as if in pain.

"*Werewolf,*" Raelyn shrieked, scrambling back so fast that she fell.

Everything slowed as I took in the chaos, as I realized with a start that Vi had sprouted fur. *Wolf* fur. She lashed out at Fang again, raking her *claws* across his chest.

"*No!*" Keisha shouted. She whirled to protect Fang, only to leap back as Vi swiped at her next. The witch looked at me, then Vi, then Fang, clearly warring with herself. Cursing, she took a step back, then another. "You will pay for this. *All* of you," she hissed, dragging Raelyn to her feet.

"Keisha, please," Fang said, clutching his bleeding chest as he staggered toward them. "Don't leave without me. I'm still a Blackstone."

"Stop," she commanded and continued to retreat. "You know the rules, Fang. We do not protect vampires or werewolves."

"No. *No*, Keisha. I'm *not* a werewolf. It's just a little scratch!"

She shook her head. "Don't lie to yourself, Fang. Do *not* come back to the coven. You are no longer one of us."

An auditorium door suddenly burst open. Three tall figures stormed inside.

Spotting them, Keisha threw out her hand and a bright cerulean light exploded into existence. Several people in the theater cried out and covered their eyes, including me. When the white spots cleared from my vision, Keisha and Raelyn were nowhere to be found. People started scrambling from their seats and racing for the exit.

Realizing he'd been left behind, Fang threw back his head and roared. When he was finished, fury contorted his features. Focusing on Vi, he raised a hand and blasted her back with a fireball. I gasped as she crashed into the row of seats and flipped over the top.

More roars filled the auditorium, but they weren't from him.

I finally moved. Not to run away, but to help Vi. Before I could, Fang set his sights on me.

"YOU," he thundered, conjuring more magic to his fingertips. It blazed brighter and hotter with each passing second. "This is all your fault. You ruined *everything*, you wicked abomination!"

A fireball blasted toward me.

Knowing I didn't have time to dodge it, I squeezed my eyes shut and braced for the pain. Arms were suddenly around me. Pulling me close. Protecting me. A wall of flesh and muscle rose up between me and the magic's attack. The smell of smoke and bourbon teased my senses, right before the fireball hit.

Kolton's body jerked against mine. He grunted from the impact, further tightening his hold on me. Another fireball whistled through the air. Then another. And another. I cried out as every single one of them pelted Kolton in the back.

He suddenly moved. Faster than I could blink. I opened my eyes to find him gripping Fang by the throat. His other arm was still around me, holding me tightly to him. This close, I felt everything. Felt his muscles bunch. Felt his arm give a savage twist. Felt the *snap* of Fang's neck.

And then Kolton dropped him.

As he fell, I made the mistake of ogling the odd angle of Fang's neck. His head hit the seats before he crumpled to the floor.

Everything went silent for a beat.

Then sound rushed back in with a vengeance.

"Griff. Jagger. Phone Buck about the body."

"Got it, boss."

"Vi, you okay?"

"Yeah, fine. Just a scratch."

"Good. I need you to drive Griff and Jagger back. I'm taking

Nora."

With that, we were moving again. I didn't know how. I couldn't feel my legs anymore.

"Nora? I need you to focus. Can you walk?"

Instead of answering Kolton's question, I said, "You killed him."

"Yes. He tried to kill you, so I killed him. But you might want to keep that fact to yourself. We're leaving the auditorium now."

My legs gave out.

Kolton swept me into his arms.

"The people. The cameras," I said as Kolton strode into the hallway and toward the nearest exit. Someone stopped in their tracks to stare at me and I stupidly waved.

"No cameras. The humans ran out before they saw too much."

He shoved open the exit door and I closed my eyes against the early evening sun.

"Vi started to shift."

He paused this time. Then, "Yes."

*Yes?*

Three letters. Three little letters that blew my reality to pieces.

Memories filtered in. Kolton's and Melanie's glowing yellow eyes. My failed escape attempt last night. How *easy* it had been for them to find me, because . . .

Because they'd shifted into wolves.

I'd been surrounded by *werewolves.* They could have torn me to shreds. *Killed* me.

But they hadn't.

"How?" was all I could think to say.

"Not all werewolves are bound to the full moon."

I blinked rapidly in disbelief. "Since when?"

"Since forever."

He said it so matter-of-factly, like I should have *known.*

Starting to hyperventilate, I blurted, "She's gorgeous. Your girlfriend."

"She's not my girlfriend," Kolton immediately replied, pausing to unlock the truck. Somehow, he managed to get the door open and tuck me inside without dropping me. When I sat there like a limp noodle, he grabbed the seatbelt and reached around me to buckle it.

Seconds later, he was jumping into the driver's seat and revving the engine.

I flinched at the sound, suddenly feeling a familiar itch. An itch to— "I'm freaking out," I said, remembering our deal. "I want to run. I need to."

Laughter pushed at my throat, but I shoved it back down.

"Nora, look at me."

I shook my head.

"Nora." He captured the back of my neck and turned me to face him. Heat flushed through my body, dispelling some of my panicked haze. "It's going to be okay."

I shook my head again. "Someone died."

He tilted my face up, forcing me to meet his eyes. "He tried to hurt you, and I couldn't allow that. I protect what is mine."

At the conviction in his voice, all the air left me. "I'm not yours," I whispered.

He searched my face for a long moment. Then quietly said, "I think you and I both know that's not true."

The drive back to the mansion was spent in silence.

I had so many questions. So many theories that demanded

answers. But my mind was stuck on the last thing Kolton had said.

*I protect what is mine.*

I wasn't his. And yet, his tattoo was inked on my arm. I wasn't his, but I was staying in his home. I was planning to *marry* him. I was becoming good friends with his sister. I was *jealous* of his "not my girlfriend."

Everything had become so messed up so quickly.

All because I'd wanted to be "normal."

But I *wasn't* normal.

The witches knew it. My pack knew it. Even Kolton knew it.

Maybe Fang had been right about me.

I ruined everything.

And yet, Kolton had protected me. Even after my very presence had put his sister in danger. I was still waiting for him to realize that I wasn't worth the trouble. He could marry anyone. *Anyone.* There must be dozens of females better-suited for him than I was. Strong ones. Unbroken ones. Maybe even one he could fall in love with.

I suddenly felt small again. Small and wholly inadequate.

It wasn't until we were parking in front of the house that I managed to quiet my thoughts. The first thing I noticed was the back of Kolton's shirt as he jumped from the truck. I scrambled out after him, nearly falling on my face in the process.

"Let me see," I demanded, coming around the truck toward him. He slammed the door shut and turned to me with a confused frown. I twirled my finger in the air impatiently. "Turn around."

His expression cleared. "It's fine. The wounds have already healed."

Pursing my lips, I stalked around him to see for myself. As I grabbed the hem of his ruined shirt, I abruptly paused, recalling the way he'd done this to me. Blinking the memory away, I said, "May I?"

He turned his head to side-eye me. "You may."

I hesitated again, suddenly wondering what was wrong with me. Why wasn't I running for my life? He'd just killed someone. *Murdered.* Proving the rumors were true about his violent nature. And yet, true to his word, he'd protected me. He'd kept me safe. One moment, I saw him as cruel and ruthless. The next, caring and gentle.

The puzzling question was, which one was he?

Flustered, I threw caution to the wind and followed my instincts. Instincts that demanded I check him for injury. I lifted his shirt, careful not to touch him. But when all I found was smooth skin and no injuries, curiosity got the best of me. I splayed both hands on his broad back, searching for even the smallest cut. He tensed beneath my touch, his muscles becoming rigid like stone.

I froze, realizing how forward I was being. I'd never touched him like this before. Never . . . explored. Familiar heat pulsed through me and I jerked my hands away.

Before I could flee, he caught my uninjured wrist and faced me. Our eyes locked and I froze again, forgetting how to breathe. His irises were glowing yellow, brighter than I'd ever seen before. When I sucked in a quiet gasp, they only intensified. Still holding my wrist, he slowly stepped into my personal space, making my heart skip several beats. As if reacting to the sound, he audibly swallowed and focused on my lips.

Holy hell, I wasn't prepared for this. Not in the least.

I should push him away. I should *really* push him away. He might be comfortable with helping females in heat, having sex with lots of women, and kissing girls he barely knew, but I had no intention of becoming one of his conquests.

Mixing business with pleasure was *not* a part of our deal.

But as his head lowered inch by inch, I remained rooted to the spot. My heart raced out of control. The heat simmering in my veins built to a fiery inferno. I parted my lips. Anticipating. Dreading. Hating. Hoping.

"Kol. Nora. You're back!" a little voice squealed, jerking me back to reality.

I tore my wrist from Kolton's grasp and quickly put space between us, struggling to catch my breath.

Melanie bounced up to her brother, then abruptly paused to give him an odd look. "You smell weird," she said and wrinkled her little nose.

Kolton cleared his throat. *Loudly.* As if he were uncomfortable. "It isn't nice to tell people they smell weird, Mellie," he chastised, softening the words with a mock scowl.

She stuck out her bottom lip. "But it's true. Miss Gabby told me to always tell the truth."

He smothered his laughter with a cough. "Let's talk about it over some milk and cookies, okay?" He veered toward the house, nudging her along with him.

"But I already had a snack," she replied, skipping ahead. "Miss Gabby says it's almost dinnertime."

Kolton did laugh this time. "Well, I wouldn't want to spoil your dinner. What is Cook making tonight?"

As she tried to remember, fumbling over her words, an emotion tightened my chest. One I couldn't quite place. Watching them together—seeing how much they adored each other—made me realize how broken my own family was.

I couldn't remember my parents ever looking at me the way Kolton looked at his baby sister.

My chest tightened to the point of pain.

Realizing I hadn't followed, Kolton turned to eye me. He studied my face for a long moment, probably seeing far more than I wanted him to, then tilted his head as if to say, *You coming?*

I hesitated, feeling some of the tightness in my chest ease. Then lifted an eyebrow as if to say, *Well, duh*, and moved to join him.

# CHAPTER 11

A caller arrived bright and early the next morning.

"I knew this would happen," Kolton muttered with a clipped sigh, watching the middle-aged woman climb the porch steps.

After he'd allowed her entry through the front gates, we'd all abandoned breakfast to spy on her approach through his study windows.

"Way to go, Vi," Griff whispered. He let out an *ooph* as Vi jabbed her elbow into his ribs.

"Would you let it go already? I've apologized like a million times."

"No can do. Knowing someone screwed up and it wasn't me has been way too satisfying."

"Sadist."

"Wedding crasher."

She gasped. "I did not—"

"Would you two quit?" Jagger grumbled, stepping back from the window. "Mrs. Bailey can hear you."

Vi gasped again and ducked when the woman outside glanced toward the windows. Caught staring, I awkwardly raised my hand and waved. I really needed to stop doing that.

"Let's get this over with," Kolton said, turning to stride from the room. When the others followed, I hesitated, uncertain if I was supposed to join them.

During an impromptu meeting last night, Kolton had caught

Griff and Jagger up to speed on our deal. They'd seemed skeptical at first—especially Jagger—but at least they knew why I was here now. I'd also told them about the stupid deal I'd made with the witches and why they were hunting me—even if I still didn't understand why they wanted me so badly.

They'd become suspiciously quiet after my explanation, but I hadn't felt comfortable questioning them. I still wasn't one of them. Sure, we were fellow accessories to *murder*—which they didn't seem all that concerned about—but that didn't mean they'd accepted me into their inner circle. Griff was friendly enough, but Jagger still remained standoffish where I was concerned.

It was Griff who noticed that I hadn't moved to join them. He turned and gave me a mock scowl. "Don't make me throw you over my shoulder again, bride-to-be. Get your cute little butt out here."

"*Griff*," Kolton and Vi barked at the same time.

I stiffened at the term "bride-to-be," but hurried after them when Griff stepped toward me as if to make good on his threat.

The second Kolton opened the front door, the visiting woman launched into an excitable greeting. "Oh, Alpha Rivers, good morning! I came as soon as I heard the news. I'm so beside myself with joy. I've been impatiently waiting for this day. Your parents would be so *thrilled*."

"Good morning, Mrs. Bailey," Kolton evenly responded when she paused to take a breath. "I'm pleased you're happy, but your excitement is a little premature, I'm afraid. Nothing has been decided yet."

I peeked over Vi's shoulder just as the woman's face crumpled. "But I heard you were betrothed."

Ah hell, *that's* what this was about? I slowly started to back away.

Kolton cleared his throat. "Not exactly. I—"

At that moment, the woman caught sight of me. Excitement lit her expression again. "Is this the lucky female? Oh, my dear," she said, bustling right through the door and past Kolton, "you must marry this wonderful boy. He's a catch, I'm telling you. I used to be his nanny, you know. Oh, the stories I could tell. I—"

Only feet away from me, she froze in her tracks. An odd expression crossed her face as she lifted her nose into the air . . . and sniffed. I braced myself, already knowing what would happen next. I'd seen that look countless times before.

"Oh dear," she whispered, looking at me as if seeing me for the first time. "Oh dear, oh dear. What's wrong with you, child?"

I opened my mouth, but nothing came out. It didn't matter how many times I'd heard the words. They still stung.

Awkward silence followed. I shifted on my feet, feeling a desperate need to run.

A presence suddenly warmed my back. Before I could see who it was, a large hand gripped my hip. Almost possessively. I stiffened in surprise but didn't pull away. Not when Kolton opened his mouth and said, "Nothing's wrong with her, Mrs. Bailey. You should apologize to Nora for saying such a rude thing."

At the slight bite to his words, I shivered.

Mrs. Bailey's eyes widened comically. "Yes, Alpha," she hurriedly said, lowering her head in submission. "I spoke out of turn. I profusely apologize for my poor manners, Nora. I meant no disrespect."

Shocked at the turn the conversation had taken, words continued to fail me.

"Thank you, Mrs. Bailey," Kolton said when I didn't respond. "You may take your leave now."

She nodded and backed toward the door, completely cowed by his words.

When she was gone and safely out of earshot, Griff let out a low whistle. “Well, the cat’s out of the bag now. If Jasmine and Rodney don’t tell the entire pack about Nora, Mrs. Bailey certainly will.”

Kolton’s hold on my hip tightened, then fell away. “Let them talk. It’s what they do.”

“Yeah, but if other alphas catch wind of this, you could be facing an increase in challenges,” Jagger cautioned. “They’ll want to make their move before the union further strengthens your position.”

“Let them come. Their failure will only serve as a warning to future challengers.”

The words were matter-of-fact, devoid of pride or arrogance. Still, I suddenly couldn’t take it anymore. The pressure. The stakes. Knowing he could get hurt again, which would then put his sisters in danger. I barely knew them, but I’d already begun to care. To worry about what happened to them.

Up until now, I’d been responsible for one person’s welfare. Mine.

But now?

The consequences of accepting our deal had just become real and utterly terrifying.

“Excuse me,” I quickly said, and hurried out the front door without explanation. No one stopped me, so I picked up speed and jogged around the side of the house. By the time I reached my destination, I was puffing and sweating, a vivid reminder of just how “wrong” I was.

I hadn’t planned to come here, but it made sense. I’d been ogling this stretch of land for the past few days, desperate to explore it. The garden was well cared for, but I spotted a section right away that could use a little TLC. With a Bachelor’s degree in Environmental Science, plants were sort of my thing. Actually, all living things were, but Botany was my passion. I’d always had a green thumb, and finding ways to help plants flourish in their environment satisfied my itch.

It didn't take long before I stumbled across the estate's groundskeeper. He seemed surprised to see me, then pleased when I could speak "plant." In no time, he allowed me the great honor of tending to his babies, showing me where the gardening tools were.

I was on my knees, my hands buried wrist-deep in soil, when Kolton found me. With the late morning sun beating down on my bare neck and my hair tied back in a messy bun, I was no doubt a sight for sore eyes.

"Well, this is unexpected," he said, stopping feet away. I saw his shoes first, shiny and expensive. They didn't belong in this little world I'd cocooned myself in. For once, *he* was the one who didn't fit in. Not me.

That fact brought a small smile to my face. Without looking up from my task, I replied, "I didn't run. I just needed some space."

"I know," he easily said. "But you were upset earlier. I wanted to make sure you were okay."

I paused, unused to this kind of attention. Besides Brielle, no one had ever really cared if I was upset. Stabbing my spade into the soil, I replied, "I'm fine. I just got a little overwhelmed."

Which was putting it mildly.

"About?" he questioned, making me pause again. Did he really care? Or was he simply looking after his *insurance?*

Sighing, I decided to confess one of my worries. The simpler, less scary one. "A lot has happened in a short amount of time. To say that I feel like a fish out of water is an understatement."

He was silent for a beat. Then, "It'll get easier."

I snorted and rocked back on my heels to finally look up at him. Wiping the sweat from my brow, I said, "Not if your pack sees me as a strange parasite."

Wow. I hadn't meant to confess *that.*

Before I could duck my head in embarrassment, he crouched to my level. "Nothing's wrong with you, Nora," he quietly said, his gaze steady on mine.

A lump formed in my throat. I shook my head, swallowing with difficulty. "Thanks, but you don't have to say that."

His brow furrowed. "Say what?"

"A lie to make me feel better."

He studied me for a moment, long enough that I dropped my gaze. "It's not a lie," he finally replied. "Once I free your wolf, the others will see what I saw the first day I met you."

My eyes flew back up to his. "And what did you see?"

Reaching forward, he gently tucked a daisy into my hair. "A rare flower ready to bloom."

Four days later, it happened.

I was in the garden again, as had become my morning ritual, when Melanie came running up to me. "Nora, Nora," she sang, uncontrollably bouncing up and down. "Hurry, quick. Kol has a surprise for you!"

Not reacting swiftly enough for the over-excited girl, she grabbed my hand and hauled me to my feet with her supernatural strength.

"Come on, come on!" she cried, dragging me behind her.

I sputtered out a laugh, allowing the six-year-old to lead me toward the house. Not that I had much choice. The girl was *definitely* stronger than me.

"Where are we going?" I said, pausing to kick my shoes off before entering through the kitchen door.

"It's a surprise. Hurry, hurry!"

Laughing again, I surrendered to her excitement, shrugging at the kitchen staff as we rushed past. When we reached the foyer, she let go and gleefully clapped her hands.

"What—?" I began, then stopped as Kolton sauntered from his study.

"Close your eyes," he said, slowly grinning at the confused look I gave him. "Do it or no surprise."

Rolling my eyes, I gave in and shut them. Ever since Mrs. Bailey's visit, everyone in the house had gone out of their way to make my life easier. I couldn't remember a time when I'd been this relaxed. After all the stress I'd been through since meeting those crazy witches, the past few days had felt like a vacation.

Despite their threats, neither my pack nor the witches had tried to make contact again. A tiny, unrealistic part of me had started to think they'd given up on me, which I was totally okay with. I'd spent most of my time in the garden or with Kolton's sisters. Melanie didn't currently have school and Vi had taken the week off to spend it with me.

I knew Kolton was no doubt encouraging the closeness, hoping the new friendships would convince me to stay and marry him. I didn't feel manipulated though. If anything, I was grateful for the opportunity to interact with fellow werewolves, something that had always been off limits to me in my hometown pack.

This past week, I'd slowly started to learn what it felt like to be a *true* pack member. I wasn't actually a member of Midnight Pack. At least, not yet anyway. But the acceptance within these walls had done wonders for my self esteem.

"Are they still closed?" Kolton said, coming up behind me.

"Yes, Mr. Rivers," I sarcastically replied, nearly leaping out of my skin when he placed both hands on my hips. He hadn't touched me since tucking that flower into my hair, and the rush of heat that immediately filled me stole my breath.

"Good," he said, lightly digging his fingers into my hip bones. "Then all you need to do is step forward."

Trying my best to ignore the way my body and wolf reacted to his touch, I took a tentative step. "Like this?"

I heard the smile in his voice as he replied, "Yes, just like that."

Guided forward by light pressure from his fingers, I blindly shuffled toward the front door. When he reached around me to open it, his arm brushed against mine, flaring awake more heat.

After a few more shuffling steps across the porch, he stopped me and said, "Okay, you ready?"

"Bro, the suspense is killing me," Griff groaned from somewhere nearby. "Just let her see it already."

"Yeah," a chorus of familiar voices said, drawing a grin from me.

"Yes, I'm ready."

"Then open your eyes," Kolton said, clearly amused at the others' impatience.

Still grinning, I opened my eyes and immediately froze solid.

Because there, parked in the roundabout, was my baby.

And she'd never looked better.

I bit my trembling lip. "Is she fixed?"

"She's fixed," Kolton said and dropped his hands.

"How?" I dumbly asked, tearing my eyes from the truck to glance at the others.

"It's pretty much the only thing the guys did *all* week," Vi said with an exaggerated eye roll.

"Hey, she was in rough shape," Griff said defensively, crossing his arms as he leaned against a porch column. "We almost had to completely take her apart to find all the problems."

"Yeah, sure," Vi shot back. "You were probably goofing off and drinking beers most of the time."

"I mean, some of the time."

"Can I drive her?" I abruptly asked, drawing all eyes my way. When silence greeted me, I tensed. Did they think I was going to take her and run? As the silence stretched, my palms began to sweat. This was it. This was the moment when they showed their true colors and locked me away. It's what my pack would do. I was going to lose any semblance of freedom again, this time for good.

Just as panic tightened my chest, Jagger stepped toward me and pulled something from his pocket. "She's all yours," he said, tossing a jangling set of keys my way.

I caught it and gaped. My keys. He'd given me back my *keys*. I gripped them tightly, blinking back sudden tears.

"Go ahead, gorgeous," Griff said, grinning widely at me. "Give her a test spin."

I realized then what was happening. They had decided to trust me. Trust me not to run.

Too overwhelmed for words, I silently walked across the porch and down the steps toward my truck. My hands noticeably shook as I opened the door and climbed inside, sliding the key into the ignition. Grabbing the wheel, I turned the key. The engine started with a mighty roar. At the glorious sound, I threw back my head and belted, "Yes, baby, *yes!*"

Cheers and whistles reached my ears. I looked out the window to see my new friends sharing in my excitement. Even Jagger fist-pumped the air. Laughing, I threw the truck into drive and gunned it. The tires squealed as she leapt forward like a young colt, raring to go. I peeled around the circle, marveling at how beautifully she responded. Whipping onto the long drive toward the front gates, I shot down the road at breakneck speed.

"Woohoo!" I crowed, rolling the window down to inhale the air as it hurtled past. I stomped on the gas, driving faster, faster, *faster*. The wind screamed at me, whistling through the cab. As the front gates loomed before me, I slammed on the brakes. The truck skidded to an abrupt halt.

The only sound that filled the cab was the idling engine and my rapid breathing. I sat and stared at the gates. As if, by staring at them long enough, they would magically open. And then, just like that, they did. The steel gates slowly swung wide on greased hinges, allowing my exit. Beckoning me onward. Giving me a choice.

My freedom.

I stared and stared, tightening my grip on the wheel.

Kolton was releasing me, just like he'd promised. And the week wasn't even up.

I glanced in the rearview mirror, then at the open road ahead. After a solid minute, I looked down at my forearm, at the tattoo that was slowly yet surely healing. I studied it. Then reached out and gingerly touched it. The skin was still slightly puckered in places, still held together by stitches. But I assumed Kolton could remove the binding ritual despite the damage. With a final parting word, I could have our connection severed and be on my way. I could leave this all behind—the stress and responsibility that came with staying. It would be easy. So easy.

I glanced in the rearview mirror again.

After a long moment, I heaved a sigh and lightly pressed on the gas, easing the truck around. Driving back the way I'd come, I slowed my pace, watching as the house grew larger and larger. It wasn't long before I saw shapes dotting the front porch. Five of them. Standing exactly where I'd left them.

I pulled into the roundabout, smoothly sliding to a stop in front of the house. As I opened the door and jumped out, no one said a word. They simply watched as I climbed the steps and walked across the porch to stand directly in front of Kolton. I looked up at him, unable to read his expression. He waited. Simply waited for me to announce my decision.

Instead of holding out my arm, demanding he remove the tattoo, I shoved my hands into my pockets and said, "I'm ready to uphold my end of the deal."

He didn't react at first.

And then . . .

He slowly grinned. Wider and wider until it stretched across his entire face.

I grinned back.

The moment was interrupted by a loud *whoop* as Griff rushed over and swept me off my feet. Twirling me around, he hollered, "We've got a wedding to plan, baby!"

"*GRIFF*," several voices shouted at once.

I threw my head back and laughed.

# CHAPTER 12

The day before the wedding, I woke up screaming.

Seconds later, Kolton charged into my room. Then Jagger and Griff, followed by Vi. They searched for the invisible threat, looking nearly as panicked as I felt.

"It was just a nightmare," I quickly assured them, shoving back a tangled mass of curls. "Sorry to wake you all."

I watched as, one by one, they relaxed. Except for Kolton. He still didn't look convinced. Ever since our wedding had officially been announced five days ago, he'd been nonstop busy. We all had, scrambling to pull together a last-minute event that actually looked planned. I'd tried on dress after dress, trying to ignore the price tags and the fact that they'd been *airlifted* here.

But I'd seen Kolton's usually pristine appearance grow less and less polished as the wedding day approached. I was pretty sure he hadn't slept in days—he still wore yesterday's clothes, and his usual five-o'clock shadow had grown thick.

I'd been warned that the announcement would stir up unrest. That we'd have to marry quickly before challengers could line up outside the door. But if Kolton had received any complaints or challenges this past week, I wouldn't know. He was keeping me in the dark, probably so I wouldn't change my mind at the last minute. I'd heard him pacing in his study though. Heard the late-night phone calls. The agitation in his voice. But I hadn't dared eavesdrop or disturb him. We weren't married yet, and I had no business being in his business.

Still, I'd picked up on his stress, enough to carry it into my dreams. This latest dream had been a doozy. I'd dreamt that it was our wedding day. Everything looked beautiful. The entire Midnight Pack was there to celebrate the occasion. I was halfway down the aisle when the pack rose as one from their seats and pointed at me, hissing, "She doesn't smell right. Something's wrong with her. You can't marry this parasite."

When Kolton hadn't listened to them, every single one of them had challenged him. They'd charged him en mass and killed him, then set their sights on me. I'd tried to run, but my frail human body was no match for the ravenous pack of werewolves. They'd torn me to shreds with their teeth and claws, viciously biting and ripping until I was nothing more than bloodied chunks of meat.

I unconsciously placed a hand over my stomach, trying to shake the awful dream. But, as the day wore on, I grew more and more paranoid. We'd all sat down to an early dinner when Kolton finally confronted me.

"What's wrong, Nora?"

I looked up from my steak, blinking until the dining room sharpened into focus. "Huh? Oh. Nothing's wrong."

He slowly set down his fork. "You haven't touched your dinner. Or lunch. Or breakfast."

I glanced down at my full plate again. At the thin trail of blood pooling beneath the steak. I swallowed, fighting back a wave of nausea. "Pre-wedding jitters, I guess."

"Getting cold feet?" Griff said, popping a huge chunk of meat into his mouth. As he noisily chewed, nausea surged up my throat.

Without a word, I scrambled from my chair and fled the room. Kolton found me five minutes later, still dry-heaving into the downstairs toilet. I stiffened at the intrusion, ready to tell him off for barging in uninvited. But when he handed me a cool washcloth, I gratefully accepted it without comment.

As I shut the toilet lid and sat, pressing the cloth to my flushed neck, Kolton leaned against the doorway and waited. He knew something was up. I wasn't exactly good at masking my feelings. Then again, I wasn't used to talking about them either. They were currently a tangled jumble in my brain, and I didn't know how to express them verbally.

Opting for the usual unscripted approach, I blurted, "I think we should postpone the wedding."

Holding in a wince, I waited for him to blow up. I'd unfairly sprung this on him last minute, after all the trouble he'd gone through these past couple of weeks. I deserved his wrath.

But all he said was, "Why?"

Not anticipating such a calm reaction, I finally looked up at him. He didn't seem angry at all. More like . . . resigned. As if he'd been expecting this.

"I-I don't mean indefinitely," I hurriedly stammered, wanting that expression on his face to go away. "But maybe for another week or two. Just until . . . until . . ."

Ah crap. Too late, I realized my mistake. He would never go for it. Not after everything I'd—

"Until I free your wolf?" he finished for me, making my eyes widen with shock.

"Well, yes," I said, flushing even more under his steady gaze. "I know that wasn't the deal, but I don't want your entire pack to see me for the first time like this." I lamely gestured at myself. At the weak and pathetic human that his pack would no doubt despise.

I was used to being rejected, but this was different. I was marrying an *alpha*. One who needed a strong female by his side. My glaring weaknesses would make *him* look weak. Would make his enemies that much more keen to challenge him. And if he fell, I was next. Without a single supernatural ability to aid me, I would lose. And no one would be left to protect his family from suffering the same fate.

Not knowing how to tell him this, I bit my lips hard enough to draw blood. But I didn't have to say a thing. His expression suddenly cleared, as if he completely understood.

"Okay."

I blinked, certain I'd misunderstood him. "What?"

"Okay," he calmly repeated. "Let's go free your wolf."

My eyes widened again, until I felt them start to bug out. "What, like right now?"

His lips twitched. "Yes, like right now."

I nearly fell off the toilet seat in my haste to stand. Straightening, I sputtered, "But the full moon isn't for another week and a half. I couldn't possibly shift right now."

He gave me a "do you really believe that?" look, one that sent my pulse through the roof. No way. No freaking way. Was this really happening?

"And the wedding?" I said, nervously wringing the washcloth.

"Will still take place tomorrow. Unless you need more time."

"No, no, that should be fine," I replied, my mind reeling. Before I could think better of it, I blurted, "How can you be okay with this? What if you free my wolf and I run?"

On second thought, I *really* shouldn't have asked that.

In response, he slowly lifted an eyebrow. "Guess I'll just have to trust you."

I froze, realizing he was once again giving me a choice. He may have kidnapped and supernaturally bound me to him, but he'd spent the last couple of weeks making up for those errors in judgment. Which was why I didn't even hesitate to say, "I'll stay bound to you. Until after the wedding."

We'd been so busy that I hadn't asked Kolton to remove the tattoo yet. And since neither of us had left the estate all week, it hadn't been an issue.

Until now. Until my greatest wish was inches away, nearly within my grasp.

In my excitement, who knew what I would do. I'd always been rather impulsive, which was why I decided to offer him some insurance in return. It was only fair.

"Deal," he said, graciously accepting my offer, then pulled out his phone. "Griff, I need the estate and grounds cleared for the evening. That means everyone. Can you manage it? Good. See that it's done right away, please."

He slipped the phone back into his pocket, his expression still calm, like he'd simply ordered a pizza. We listened as the others moved about the house, alerting the staff that they needed to leave. Feet pounded up the stairs. A few minutes later, they came back down.

"All clear!" we heard Griff holler, right before the front door slammed shut.

Silence descended. Ear-splitting silence.

Then, "Meet me out back when you're ready," Kolton said and pushed off the doorway. He left without a sound, leaving me alone to face a hurricane of emotions.

It was a full five minutes later before I managed to move. To untangle the thoughts whirling around in my brain. Dropping the washcloth into the sink, I strode into the hallway and began to pace.

This was it. I'd waited my entire life for this moment. I couldn't be any more excited. At the same time, I was terrified. More terrified than I could ever remember being. Despite the countless years I'd waited for this moment, I hadn't mentally prepared myself for it yet.

Could Kolton really free my wolf without the full moon? If he could, what did that make him? A *superwolf?* And what did that make *me?*

"Come on, Nora," I muttered to myself, glancing toward the back doors. "Get out of your head and go for it."

After all, what's the worst that could happen?

I really needed to stop asking myself that.

Before I could do something stupid like chicken out, I threw back my shoulders and marched toward the back doors. Whipping them open, I deeply inhaled the evening air and strode across the patio. As I descended the steps, I spotted Kolton standing beside the pool. The sun had just set, triggering the pool lights to flicker on. The glowing blue highlighted his profile as he turned at my approach.

When I was feet away, I stopped and said, "I'm ready."

He searched my face for a long moment before nodding his approval. "Good," was all he said, then reached for the top button of his shirt. When he undid it, then the next, and the next, I gave him a deer-in-headlights look.

"Wait, what are you doing?"

"I don't make a habit of jumping into the pool with my clothes on," he replied, continuing to unbutton.

My lungs seized with panic. "Th-the *pool?* Why are you jumping into the pool?"

He looked at me like I was a few eggs short of an omelet. "The water will help with the shifting process. You're going in too, so unless you want those clothes ruined, I suggest you undress."

With that, the last of his shirt buttons came undone. I nearly swallowed my tongue when he shrugged off the shirt, allowing me a clear view of his naked torso for the first time. My poor eyes didn't know where to look first. There was just so *much* to look at. For one, he was ripped. Which shouldn't have surprised me. But his dress shirts had safely hidden that fact.

I knew I was staring, but my eyes wouldn't obey me when I told them to look away. They hungrily devoured every inch of his deep olive skin, tracing the swells and dips, exploring the ink that traveled all the way up both arms to his shoulders.

I'd always thought he was hot, but that word was too small to describe him now.

Just as I unglued my eyes from the thin trail of dark hair beneath his navel, he went and did the unthinkable.

Without the slightest warning, he unbuckled his belt and unzipped his pants. Before I could look away, he tugged off his pants—and *underwear*—in one swift move.

"Kolton!" I shrieked, covering my eyes. But it was too late. I'd already seen his penis. His *humongous* penis.

At my reaction to his strip tease, he had the audacity to laugh. *Laugh*.

"Relax, Nora. Nudity is an unavoidable part of being a werewolf. Might as well get used to it."

"Well, I'm *not* used to it," I said far too loudly, still covering my eyes. "I was never allowed to be around when the clothes started to come off."

He was silent for a moment. Then, "Where did your pack put you during the full moon?"

Ah hell, I did *not* want to have this conversation right now. Especially with his giant *penis* hanging out.

"In the farm cellar," I blurted anyway, unable to stop my nervous babbling. "They locked me in when I was younger. Usually only a day or two. Sometimes three. But when I got old enough, I locked myself in."

I felt him slowly approach, his bare feet silent on the concrete. When his hands cupped mine, I jumped, swallowing a startled squeak. His fingers were firm yet gentle as they carefully pried my hands from my face. Heat flared up at the contact, then fizzled out when he let go. My arms fell to my sides.

"Those days are over, Nora," he said, the softness of his voice coaxing my eyes back open. "I don't know what other horrors you've experienced at your pack's hands, but once you're an official member of Midnight Pack, you never have to see them again. Their rights to you will be severed."

Swallowing past the sudden lump in my throat, I nodded, too overwhelmed for words.

He stared at me a moment more, then turned and jumped into the pool. Holy hell, his backside was equally scrumptious. I had no idea how I was going to do this.

Popping back up, he slicked his hair back like one of those models in a cologne commercial and glanced at me questioningly. *You coming?*

Oh boy. Oh boy, oh boy, oh boy.

I wasn't a shy person, but I wanted nothing more than to wrap myself in a blanket right now. Or two. Or three. A mountain of blankets would do.

At my obvious reluctance, he turned around and called back, "Is this better?"

No.

"Yes," I said, pausing to make sure he wasn't peeking before whipping my shirt off. My shorts quickly followed. Toying with a bra strap, I chickened out and left it on, along with my panties. Instead of jumping in, I sat at the pool's edge and slid in. The water was surprisingly cool, immediately soothing my overheated skin. I removed the tie from my wrist and secured my hair into a messy bun before saying, "Okay. You can look now."

He turned, not looking surprised that I'd kept my underwear on. When he moved toward me, I panicked and backpedaled, hitting the pool's edge.

"Wait, hold on." I held up my hands to ward him off. "Tell me what the plan is first before you come at me with all of that."

He paused, a wicked gleam entering his eyes. "Simple. Your wolf responds to my touch, so we need to be close. *Really* close."

I stopped breathing. "How close?"

He moved again, watching me carefully as he approached. My heart thundered, nearly leaping from my chest, but I didn't stop him. Even when he eased into my personal space, I held perfectly still.

"This close," he whispered, reaching around me to place a hand on my spine. I inhaled sharply as he reeled me forward and pulled me flush against him.

Heat immediately blasted through me, my wolf going wild at the intimate skin contact. My body did too, lighting up like a Christmas tree. Unable to hold in my reaction, I released a shuddering breath and gripped his arms.

"That's it," he continued to whisper. "Hold onto me, sweetness. This is going to hurt."

I whimpered at his words, in fear but also excitement.

In response, a growl rumbled in his chest. His other hand grabbed my upper thigh and lifted my leg, fitting our lower halves together. At the feel of his thick shaft against my stomach, I sucked in a startled gasp and gripped his arms harder. The shaft noticeably swelled, making me tremble with a sudden need.

He quietly swore.

Surprised, I looked up at him and froze. His eyes were blazing bright yellow.

My lips parted at the sight and his gaze zeroed in on my mouth.

Swearing again, he slid his hand up my spine to possessively grip the nape of my neck. The action drove my wolf into a frenzy and I cried out as heat slammed into me.

"It hurts," I gasped, squirming to escape the pain. "I can't . . . I can't do it."

"Yes, you can," Kolton said, firming his grip on my neck when another heatwave blasted through me.

I screamed this time and dug my nails into his skin. When I could speak again, I groaned, "Ah hell, that *sucks*."

Despite my misery, Kolton quietly chuckled. "I know it does, but the pain means your wolf is emerging."

"Yeah. Great," I panted, suddenly questioning why I'd wanted to free her so badly.

Over the next several minutes, heatwave after heatwave pounded through me, stealing my breath and sanity. I cried and screamed, writhing against the pain. Kolton kept me firmly in place, murmuring soft words of comfort. Words that barely registered as I fought to stay conscious.

After an exceptionally painful heatwave, one that left me limp and trembling, Kolton said something. Something that broke through my haze.

"Let me help ease your suffering, Nora. Please."

Struggling to breathe, I gasped, "H-how?"

"Like this," he said, and released my thigh to slide his hand inside my panties. My eyes flew wide and I met his gaze, utterly frozen in shock. He froze too, waiting for me to pull away. To demand he stop. I did neither, too weak, too *desperate* to ease the pain. He slid his fingers lower. And lower. When they found my clit, I choked out a gasp.

He paused again, allowing me to adjust. To accept the intimate touch. But only for a moment.

His fingers started to move, in a way that sent pleasure jolting through me. My hips violently bucked in response. He pinned my thighs against the pool's side with his, stilling my movements. Heat flushed through me once more, but this heat was different. I liked this heat. Hell, I *really* liked this heat.

In the back of my mind, I was hyper-aware that Kolton Rivers, the renowned womanizer, was *pleasuring* me. But I couldn't seem to care right now. The heavenly sensations shooting through my body allowed a slight reprieve from the terrible pain and heat.

As his fingers continued to touch me in all the right places, I shuddered against him and let my eyes roll shut. A pleased growl rumbled in his chest and he stroked me harder. The water allowed his fingers to smoothly glide over the sensitive flesh, further adding to my pleasure. When I moaned, shaking uncontrollably, he breathed in my ear, "Has a man ever touched you like this before?"

Too overcome with pleasure, I simply shook my head.

"Bloody hell, Nora," he groaned, increasing his pace. "You're going to be the death of me."

Stars burst behind my eyelids. I was pretty sure *he* would be the death of *me*.

In no time, I was panting and writhing against his fingers, desperate for release.

"Bloom for me, sweet flower," he crooned, adding more pressure until I gasped his name and arched against him. "Come," he persisted, the word rumbling with authority. "Come *now*."

Just like that, the command shoved me over the edge. Throwing my head back, I screamed as ecstasy whipped through me. Screamed and screamed. Until the screams became howls. *Wolf* howls. Before I could freak out at the sound, snaps and cracks filled the air.

Bones. My *bones* were breaking.

The bliss from moments ago was replaced by blinding agony as my body began to shift. To *change*.

"Shift, Nora. *Shift!*" I heard Kolton roar over the pain and howls and breaking bones.

I suddenly couldn't breathe. Couldn't breathe as something new. Something foreign. Something *huge* rose to the surface of my consciousness. I knew it was my wolf. Knew that she'd finally awakened. Knew that she was slowly yet surely coming out of her shell. Out of *me*.

A final deafening *crack* rent the air as my spine snapped.

Then blissful darkness dragged me under.

# CHAPTER 13

*My awakening brought agony.*

*The kind I'd been hiding from for the past two decades.*

*I tried to curl back inside my den, but the male who'd forced me awake crouched to my level.*

*He was naked, but that didn't bother me.*

*What bothered me was the hand he slowly held out, as if he expected me to sniff it. Like an animal.*

*The audacity.*

*I shook my head, suddenly aware of the water weighing down my clothing.*

*No, it was fur. I had fur now.*

*I glanced down at my feet—or rather, paws. They were mostly white, but one had a bright patch of orange. Like fire.*

*"Hello, beautiful," the male quietly said, drawing my gaze back up to his. My ears, large and furry, swiveled forward in recognition. "Don't take off yet. I'm going to shift first."*

*When he stood and slowly stepped away, I became aware of other things.*

*The chirp of crickets. The drip, drip of water plopping onto the cement. The wind stirring the air, teasing another of my heightened senses awake. A strong one. A visceral one.*

*Smell.*

*All on its own, my nose lifted into the air and scented it. Tasted it.*

*The world around me suddenly burst into life.*

*Despite my dread at being awakened, the intoxicating smells hitting me from all sides sharpened my focus. I continued to sniff, noticing the way my black nose flared as I inhaled the rich aromas.*

*Until now, I had no idea smells could be like this. Colorful. Intense. Exciting. My pain receded as a tiny spark of pleasure shivered through me.*

*I tensed, ready to explore. To bolt. To run.*

*Before I could, several loud pops and cracks blasted my sensitive ears. I glanced over at the male again to see him on all fours, his bones awkwardly moving and changing. Fur sprouted over his skin. Dark fur. Almost black. Sharp claws shot from his fingertips.*

*I watched, curious as his human body morphed into an animal's. A wolf's. Paws formed. Large pointed ears. A tail. His lips pulled back in a grimace, revealing wicked sharp fangs. When the transformation was over, a massive wolf stood before me. Close to five feet tall at the shoulder.*

*He shook out his sleek fur, pausing a moment to sniff the air, then froze.*

*It was at this same time that I too sniffed the air, drawing the dark wolf's scent deep into my lungs.*

*His huge head whipped my direction and our eyes locked.*

*Recognition once again shivered through me, but not the same as before. Not even close.*

*Before I fully knew what was happening, the hackles on my back raised and I bared my teeth. An unearthly growl tore from my throat.*

*And then . . .*

*I charged.*

*Kill, kill, kill, my instincts screamed at me.*

*My claws scrambled for traction on the slick cement, my newly formed legs wobbling unsteadily. Still, I charged full steam ahead at the dark wolf with glowing yellow eyes.*

*My nemesis.*

*My mortal enemy.*

*Within feet of him, I opened my maw wide, prepared to bite and rip and maim. Before I could sink my teeth into his throat, he moved. Just enough that I shot past him. My claws skidded across the cement as I desperately tried to correct my course. But I ran out of room.*

*Splash!*

*I fell head first into the pool, fully submerging. By the time I dragged myself to the surface again, the wolf was nowhere to be found.*

*Coward! I screamed, but only a growl emerged. Still, I kept on screaming. Kept on trying to be heard. Come back and fight me, you yellow-bellied snake!*

*My senses picked up another presence in the pool a moment too late. Thick, muscled arms wrapped around my throat and squeezed. I thrashed against the ironclad hold, but without the aid of arms, I couldn't break free.*

*"Shift!" a familiar voice thundered in my ear. "Shift back, Nora."*

*But I suddenly didn't want to.*

*I needed to kill that wolf first. It was my life's calling. My sacred duty. My redemption.*

*But, no matter how hard I fought, the world started to slip away.*

*Soon, darkness swallowed me whole.*

I woke to the sound of birds chirping in the trees. They were loud. *Really* loud.

Other sounds slowly filtered in. These too were loud. The

wind rustling in the grass. Bees buzzing in the flowers. A squirrel scampering in the woods.

"Squirrel!" I blurted, jerking my eyes open.

At how clear and *bright* my surroundings were, I sat up in alarm, slapping a hand over my eyes. Why was it morning already? Had I slept out by the *pool?*

As something fell and plopped onto my lap, a throat cleared. I peeked through my fingers and spotted Kolton sitting on a lounge chair not far away, his forearms braced on his knees. His eyes were carefully averted, as if he was trying not to look at something.

I glanced down and gasped, scrambling to cover my bare breasts with the fallen towel.

"What the hell?" I said, wincing at the sound of my own voice. Lowering the volume a notch, I added, "Why am I naked?"

Kolton's gaze slowly returned to me. "It's kind of what happens when you wolf out."

My jaw dropped. I stared at him, waiting for his words to sink in. When they did, I squealed and did a little butt jig. "My wolf came out? What does she look like? What color is she? Why can't I remember anything?" My eyes widened. "Did she eat something gross?"

I clutched the towel to my chest, suddenly feeling nauseous.

When Kolton didn't respond to my questions, I paused to study him more closely. Whoa. I could hear his heartbeat. I could hear his *heartbeat.*

Tears of relief, of *joy,* pricked my eyes.

"You did it," I whispered, my lips quivering. "You freed my wolf."

I was finally normal. *Normal!*

Kolton's gaze dropped to his folded hands, as if my happiness was too much for him to bear.

My smile slipped. "What's wrong?" Alarmed when his knuckles

slowly whitened, I pressed, "Kolton, what is it? Did something happen? Did my . . . did my wolf hurt someone? A human?"

A heart started to frantically pound. Mine.

He quickly looked up. "No, she didn't hurt anyone."

I waited for a beat. Then, "But?"

His shoulders rose and fell as he heaved a tired sigh. It was then that I noticed his haggard appearance. His shirt was buttoned wrong, the sleeves carelessly shoved up his arms. Hair fell limply into his eyes, eyes that looked dull, surrounded by dark circles. Concern filled me. He hadn't slept again?

Finally, he spoke. Four little words. "Your wolf hates me." If not for my newly heightened hearing, I might have missed them.

Still, I stared at him as if I'd heard wrong. "What?"

"Your wolf hates me," he repeated, louder this time. "Well, maybe not *me* exactly. My wolf. She hates my wolf."

I blinked, still not comprehending. If only I could remember my time as a wolf. "How do you know? What did she do?"

"The minute I shifted, she attacked. She would have ripped out my throat if I hadn't subdued her."

Stunned, I shot off my chair, nearly losing my grip on the towel. "But . . . but no. I'm not a violent person. I would never . . ." I swallowed, desperately trying to recall the memory. Even a phantom feeling of it. But there was nothing. It was as though I hadn't even shifted. Frustrated, I growled, "Why can't I *remember?*"

He slowly stood, but kept his distance, sticking his hands inside his pockets. "It's normal to not remember the first few shifts. Until you learn how to control your wolf, they're in charge for most of the time."

I frowned in confusion. "You make it sound like my wolf and I aren't the same being. Like she's a completely separate entity."

"She is."

I gaped at him like he'd lost his mind. "Look, this might have been my first shift, but I'm not ignorant. I was born from werewolves. Raised by werewolves. I *am* a werewolf. There isn't an actual wolf stuck inside me like a . . . a *parasite*."

I'd raised my voice, desperate to defend my beliefs. My *reality*. What he said didn't make sense. My wolf wasn't separate from me. My wolf *was* me.

He took in my panic for a moment before saying, "You're right. Werewolves are essentially one-and-the-same with their human counterparts. A supernatural toxin is what made werewolves into who they are. Whether you're a created or natural-born werewolf, this toxin is what drives our animalistic urges and instincts. It's what forces werewolves to shift during the full moon, spurred on by a magical link with the moon's cycle." Relief filled me. These facts I knew. "But those rules don't strictly apply to us, Nora. I'm sure you've started to suspect that we aren't normal werewolves."

*Not all werewolves are bound to the full moon.*

I'd ignorantly convinced myself that Kolton's alpha abilities had something to do with it. That being around him allowed other werewolves to shift on command. But he'd said "us." *We* were different. Not just him.

All the air fled my lungs.

Before I could come to grips with the bomb he'd just dropped on me, I distinctly heard a door open. "Hello? Kolton? Nora? We're back."

Neither Kolton nor I responded to Vi's greeting. We simply stared at each other, caught in an impossible stalemate. As we listened to the others return, moving through the house in search of us, a realization slowly dawned on me.

"Do they know?"

Kolton nodded.

My eyes widened. "Are they . . . are they like us?"

A slight pause. Then a single nod.

Ah hell. So much for being *normal*.

For a moment, I thought Kolton was going to call off the wedding. I mean, my wolf *hated* him. Or rather, she hated his wolf. He didn't seem too happy about that fact. But it wasn't like I had any *control* over how my wolf felt about him—according to his theory that my wolf wasn't me.

Did I believe him though?

I hadn't decided yet. I needed more information. More *proof*. What made us different from normal werewolves, and why?

But my questions would have to wait. The wedding was still on and Kolton had made himself scarce, attending to last-minute details. The guy was doggedly determined to see this marriage through, that was for sure. Then again, I couldn't forget what he'd told me. That he didn't want love or a mate. This was strictly a business arrangement to him. *Insurance* for his family's safety.

Whether my wolf hated him or not shouldn't matter.

Unless he thought she was a liability. A *threat* to him and his family.

I still couldn't believe she'd tried to attack his wolf. But why? I had so many questions, but my ticket to answers was nowhere to be found. I half wondered if he was avoiding me. Guess I couldn't really blame him. His future *wife* had just tried to kill him.

Despite my burning questions, one thing kept me thoroughly

distracted. Now that my wolf had been freed, I had supernatural *abilities*. There were so many things I wanted to try. Even in human form, my agility and strength had noticeably increased. I'd hurried up to my room to change earlier without even getting winded. I'd been half-tempted to jump over the railing on my way down like Griff had the first day we'd met, but managed to restrain myself.

As for Kolton's broody attitude, it couldn't seem to touch me. Even his news that I wasn't a normal werewolf couldn't dampen my good spirits. Because I *felt* normal. For the first time in my life, I truly felt like the being I was meant to be. I clung to that feeling as the day wore on, as I prepared to uphold my end of our deal.

"You're awfully chipper today," Vi observed, patiently wrestling with another section of my hair. We'd been in her bedroom for two hours after she insisted on taming my wild curls for the wedding. Her funeral. I knew how impossible the task was and had given up trying years ago.

"My wolf isn't stuck anymore," I said by way of explanation. I'd said the words countless times today, but they still brought a smile to my face. "Oh, and look," I added, holding up my arm. "My cuts have completely healed! I even pulled out the stitches."

"Ew, gross," she said, making me laugh. She worked in silence for a minute, then, "So, you know?"

"That we aren't normal werewolves?" Excited that I might have found a new source for answers, I tried to face her.

"Hold still," she scolded, tugging on my hair as punishment. "And, yes. We're different. Sorry I didn't say anything before, but it's not really my secret to tell. I'm only mentioning it now because Kolton confirmed this morning that you're the same as us."

"Did he tell you that my wolf tried to attack him?"

"*What?*" she shrieked, accidentally yanking some of my hair out when her fingers caught on a snarl. "Is that why he's been so moody today? I was wondering what got him all testy. Do you know why she attacked him?"

"Not a clue. I was hoping *you* would have some answers."

"Ah, girl. I wish I could talk to you about this, but Kolton is very strict when it comes to this subject. If you want answers, you'll have to ask him."

My shoulders drooped. "I would, but I think he's avoiding me."

"Maybe, but he can't avoid you forever. I mean, you're getting married today, and I doubt he'll be keeping his distance *tonight*. Also gross, by the way. I don't want to imagine what my brother will be doing on his wedding night."

I went poker straight at the insinuation, immediately recalling our time in the pool. I'd been half-delirious with pain, but I could still remember what he'd done to me. What his *fingers* had done.

When I was too flabbergasted for speech, Vi leaned over the chair I sat on to peek at my face. "Hey, I was just teasing. Whatever arrangement you and my brother have made is none of my business."

I relaxed a little. But, at the same time, worry niggled at the back of my mind. We'd never discussed this part of our arrangement. He didn't want love or a mate, but that didn't mean sex was off the table. I sat up straight again as a sudden thought formed. What if . . . what if Kolton wanted children? What if one of my duties as his wife was to give him an heir?

Ah *hell*. What had I gotten myself into?

# CHAPTER 14

I felt strong. And prepared.

Well, as prepared as I could be, considering how fast everything had happened.

But, as I faced the entire might of Midnight Pack, I wanted nothing more than to run like a terrified rabbit.

My wolf had been quiet all day, almost as if she was sleeping. If not for my newfound abilities, I could almost believe she hadn't even emerged. But, despite her silence, my heightened senses allowed me to hear whispered snippets from the large audience.

"Look at that flaming red hair."

"Her dress is rather simple, don't you think?"

"I can't smell her yet, can you?"

"She doesn't seem all that special."

"One of our own pack females would have been a better choice."

"Do you think the rumors are true about her condition?"

At that, I almost tripped over the hem of my dress. *What condition?* I wanted to turn and ask. But taking my eyes off the path before me required courage I didn't currently possess. Surrounded by this many wolves, it was all I could do not to hyperventilate. I'd been raised to keep my distance from wolves. To hide. To *run*.

The saying was true. Old habits died hard.

I might feel strong, stronger than I'd ever felt before. But with so many eyes judging me right now, I still felt different. Inadequate.

*Wrong.*

I tightened my grip on the white calla lily bouquet, suddenly wishing I'd invited my parents to the wedding. I'd never gone this long without seeing or talking to them before. But I hadn't known. I hadn't known Kolton would agree to free my wolf before the wedding. They hadn't even heard the good news yet.

But . . . would they even care?

I'd read all of their text messages. Listened to all of their voicemails.

They'd never been more disappointed in me.

But maybe all of that would change if they *knew*. I was no longer a liability. My wolf had emerged. I was marrying the most powerful alpha in *America*.

They would forgive me then. *Accept* me then. Right?

Realizing that stressing over my parents wasn't going to make this any easier, I firmly focused on the present. On the white runner below my feet. On the white satin dress swishing around my legs. On the brilliant golden sunset to the left. On the wall of green oaks and pines to the right. On the two-hundred-plus guests boring holes into my skin.

My brain chose that moment to remember my nightmare from yesterday.

*Okay, scratch that. Don't focus on the guests. Focus straight ahead. Focus on your goal. Focus on . . .*

Kolton.

Up until now, I'd been too nervous to look at him. Ever since my startling revelation about an *heir*, my stomach had been in knots. We should have voiced our expectations *before* the wedding. But now, it was too late. There was no changing things. No backing out. Kolton had upheld his end of the deal, and now, it was my turn.

As I slowly lifted my gaze to him, my heart started to pound. The guests could no doubt hear it. Even *he* probably could. But when our eyes met for the first time since early this morning, my worries and doubts started to fade. Because he was staring at me with a look I'd never seen before. At first, I couldn't define it. But, as he took in my hair and face and dress, his eyes drinking in each and every detail, I suddenly knew.

Awe.

He was in awe.

Flustered, a blush stole up my neck. His throat bobbed, drawing my gaze to the rest of him. He wore an immaculate black suit that accentuated his olive skin tone. Every line was perfectly pressed, not a stitch out of place. His hair was neatly swept back, and his face freshly shaven. Even the eye circles from earlier were nowhere to be found.

He'd never looked more polished. More defined and ruggedly handsome. And his moodiness from earlier had completely vanished.

But as I neared, as I joined him under the arch dripping with white roses and ivy, I inhaled a scent. One that I instinctively knew how to define.

*Fear.*

Cold fingers of dread raked down my spine.

Although his face didn't show it, there was no denying what I'd smelled.

He was afraid.

Kolton Rivers was *afraid.*

Of me.

Shocked by the revelation, I tore my gaze away, looking everywhere but at him. The priest—who I assumed was a werewolf—began the ceremony, but I could barely focus. Not that I needed to.

The wedding was traditional, not unlike many human weddings. Simple yet tastefully done. Kolton had decided to hold both the ceremony and reception at the family estate, only yards away from where he'd freed my wolf—and given me the best orgasm of my life.

My cheeks flamed, my mind going places it shouldn't.

*Focus, Nora, focus!* I chastised myself, hoping Kolton didn't pick up on my influx of emotions. I could no longer smell his fear, but I was still too nervous to look at him again. How was this marriage going to work if he was *afraid* of me?

Too soon, the time came to recite our vows.

This was it. The time for running had come and gone.

Or had it?

I hadn't said my vows yet. Maybe I'd be doing us both a favor if I just—

Kolton suddenly reached for my hand. Oh no. Oh no, oh no, oh no. As his fingers grasped mine, I squeezed my eyes shut, waiting for the *heat* to flare up. Except, all that stirred was a faint warmth—like my wolf was simply cracking an eye open. Seconds later, the warmth fizzled out, as if she'd fallen back asleep.

Shocked, my eyes flew up to Kolton's. He looked equally surprised, as if he'd sensed the same thing I had. We simply stared at each other, my hand in his, until the priest cleared his throat.

"Do you have the rings?"

Rings? Oh crap. This was really happening. I tucked away thoughts of my wolf's underwhelming reaction for later.

Kolton nodded, his expression suddenly dead serious. He held out his other hand and Jagger stood up to place something on his palm. Rings. Two gold rings.

A slight tremor shook my hands as Kolton slid the thinner band onto my ring finger and began to recite his vows. They were scripted, nothing new or original. Still, each and every word sank deep into my bones.

When it was my turn, I didn't think my legs would support me. But they did. Even though my entire body trembled like a leaf and my voice shook, I stood tall and recited the vows back to him, placing the thicker band on his ring finger. As the last word fell from my lips, I exhaled a relieved sigh, glad that the hard part was over.

But my relief was short-lived. I'd forgotten about one last ceremonial tradition. One that I didn't think we could ignore.

Sure enough, when the priest said, "You may now kiss the bride," Kolton moved toward me.

*Okay, don't panic*, I tried to pep-talk myself, holding still as Kolton slid an arm around me. *You can handle a quick peck. It's not like he's going to—*

Before I could finish the thought, he dipped me backward. Caught off balance, I gasped and threw my arms around his neck, meeting his eyes to fiercely whisper, "What are you doing?"

"Making this believable," he whispered back, then captured my lips in a searing kiss. *Searing*, being the key word.

Heat that had nothing to do with my wolf surged through me, shooting straight down to my core. Holy *hell*. Startled, I inhaled sharply, only for his mouth to swallow the sound. The kiss was possessive. Almost rough. His lips were firm and unyielding, but also surprisingly soft. He briefly pulled back to nip at my bottom lip, drawing a gasp from me. Then sealed his mouth over mine again.

I didn't know how long the kiss lasted. Only that, by the time it ended, I was breathing heavily and my body ached with need. And there hadn't even been *tongue*. His breaths were ragged too, and judging by the boner in his pants, we were feeling the same ache.

Wait.

My eyes flew open when I realized that at some point during the kiss, Kolton had grabbed one of my thighs. It was currently hiked in the air, pressed against his hip. Which meant that my gown slit was probably open, allowing a clear view of my entire leg. As for his boner, it was pressed tightly to my aching center. Throbbing to the beat of my racing pulse.

Holy hell, I was in so much trouble.

The world around us suddenly exploded with noise. My eyes widened even further, horror filling me when I heard several wolf-whistles and a few suggestive howls. Kolton continued to stare at me, as if reluctant to end the moment. Then, he abruptly chuckled and threw his pack a megawatt grin, still holding our position. When I started to squirm, he straightened, but took his time releasing my thigh. I sucked in another gasp as his fingers briefly slipped inside the gown slit and brushed the edge of my panties.

The crowd roared their approval.

Okay, I'd been wrong. This ceremony was *not* of the traditional variety. I'd heard of werewolf weddings where the couples made out and even *claimed* each other in front of their guests, but I'd never actually been to one. Kolton was obviously not shy about a little PDA in front of his pack, but *I* sure was. My face was probably beet red, which clashed horribly with my hair.

Still, I didn't dare pull away. The mood might seem light as the pack celebrated their alpha's marriage, but it could turn dark in a split second if I dared to openly defy him in public. I might be embarrassed by all the attention, but this moment was a thinly-veiled test of my loyalty. Of my *submission* to my new husband. My actions were a reflection on him, on his leadership and dominance. To tip that balance would be to destroy our marriage before it even began.

When he finally released my leg, I started to breathe easier, glad for the much-needed space between us. But I doubted it would last. Kolton was clearly trying to win over his pack by showing them how much he desired this union. Desired *me*. Which didn't bode well for our "strictly business" arrangement.

My thoughts flew to sex and children and heirs again. I'd really messed up this time. I'd really *really* messed up. If I didn't find a way to stop this trainwreck, I'd be knocked up within a month. Maybe sooner, if the huge tent in Kolton's pants was any indication.

Brielle would be laughing her head off at my situation.

*"You're married to a hot as sin billionaire, Nora Bora,"* she'd say. *"If you don't want to be impregnated with his babies, then I will."*

Yeah, until she realized they would be *werewolf* babies.

She would have loved to attend the wedding, but there was no way I'd let my *human* best friend be surrounded by so many werewolves. I'd tell her about the marriage as soon as I could though. Maybe even in person, now that my deal with Kolton was officially completed.

Oh. Oh wow.

I was married now. Well and truly married.

Even though the marriage was a business arrangement, it suddenly felt terrifyingly *real*.

The next part was a blur of faces and well-wishes and sensory overload. Even my wolf stirred a bit, no doubt picking up on my stress. I actually welcomed the flare of heat, grateful for her presence. She made me feel strong. Normal. Reminding me that I no longer needed to hide from the predators surrounding me.

I was now a predator too. A fierce one. A *powerful* one, according to Kolton.

He remained close beside me as his entire pack filtered by, eager to personally meet their alpha's new bride. Every time a male approached, Kolton's hand found my hip. The gesture was subtle enough, but it spoke volumes all the same. He might as well be shouting, "Back off. She's taken."

Males and their territorial nature.

Most of his pack was congenial enough, no doubt for Kolton's sake, but several eyed me shrewdly. Among them were Jasmine and Rodney. The blonde-haired Barbie doll barely deigned to glance at me, smiling only when she looked at Kolton.

"Congratulations on your marriage," she said in a breathy voice, flicking her hair back to better display the cleavage busting from her tight pale-pink dress. "I can only hope your new wife is up for the challenge of meeting your every need. If she isn't, you know where to find me."

At the barely-concealed insinuation, an unearthly growl tore from my throat. I didn't know who was more startled at the sound: me, Jasmine, or Kolton. My wolf was fully awake now, rising up as she took note of the threat before us. She urged me to stake a claim, so I did, pushing forward to wedge myself between her and Kolton.

Something in my eyes caused her to gasp and stumble back. Rodney steadied her, even as he keenly watched me with open curiosity.

Hands were suddenly turning me around. Firmly yet gently. I growled again, but stopped when I realized it was Kolton. He gripped my chin and tipped my face up, staring deeply into my eyes. "Calm down," he quietly said, yet his voice dripped with command. When my upper lip slowly curled, revealing a hint of teeth, a low growl vibrated his chest. "Calm. Down."

After another few seconds of tense silence, the heat pulsing through me faded, as if my wolf was retreating. *Submitting.*

I blinked, slowly coming back to myself.

"There you are," Kolton whispered and stretched his thumb along my jaw.

I blinked again, suddenly realizing what I'd just done. Mortified, I whispered, "I'm sorry. I didn't mean to."

"Don't be," he said, releasing my chin to tuck me against his side. "It's exactly what they needed to see."

Still shocked by what I'd done—what my *wolf* had done—I nervously peeked at our guests. Several mouths were open, many as shocked as I was. It wasn't uncommon for wolves to stake claims or assert dominance, so I could only assume their stunned reactions were due to rumors they'd heard about me. About my *wolf*—or lack of one.

*Well, she's here now, suckers,* I wanted to shout at them, putting their gossip to rest once and for all.

When I finally focused on Jasmine again, she was looking between me and Kolton with horror. When she noticed me watching her, she curled her hands into fists and stormed off.

Oops?

Nah, I didn't feel the least bit sorry.

"You are my *hero*," a familiar voice breathed in my ear moments later. Vi gave me a quick squeeze before pulling back with a conspiratorial wink. "You're doing great."

I smiled at her, feeling some of my tension ease. If I couldn't have Brielle here, then I'd gratefully lean on my new friend's open support.

Griff hugged me next, completely ignoring Kolton's warning growl. "Save that fire for later, gorgeous," he whispered, but loud enough for Kolton to hear. "It could lead to some kinky bedroom fun."

Ah hell.

"Griff, let go of my wife before I make you," Kolton muttered, clearly annoyed.

With a chuckle, Griff immediately stepped back, but I barely noticed. Not when I was still focused on what Kolton had said.

Wife.

He'd called me *wife.*

I didn't know why that made my heart skip a beat, only that it did.

Melanie and Jagger were next in line, the latter more subdued in his approach. He still hadn't warmed up to me like the others, but I couldn't detect any animosity coming from him—unlike the first time we'd met.

"Are you my new *sister* now?" Melanie said, turning in Kolton's arms to face me. She looked adorable in a blue flower-print dress, with a big poofy bow in her curled hair.

When I hesitated, unsure how to answer her, Kolton replied, "Yes, Mellie. Nora's a part of our family now."

Melanie squealed and leaned over to wrap one of her little arms around my neck. I laughed in surprise, allowing her to tightly squeeze me. Overwhelmed, tears sprang to my eyes.

Was this what it felt like to be accepted? To be *wanted?*

Realizing Kolton was watching me, I quickly averted my gaze, relieved when Melanie let go. By the time the last guest filtered past, I was desperate for a break. But the reception was next, only yards away under several large white tents. Night had recently fallen, allowing twinkling lights, chandeliers, and candles to illuminate the space. I marveled at the beauty, taking in the elaborate flower centerpieces on the dozens of tables draped in white cloth.

Before I could spy on the guests like they'd spied on me for the past couple of hours, Kolton swept me into his arms without warning. "Here we go," he murmured, inhaling a deep breath before striding into the tents.

Hoots and hollers greeted us, and I waved awkwardly as Kolton carried me to our table. It was raised above the others, of course, as was tradition. Kolton climbed the platform steps and made for our seats. Expecting him to put me down, my eyes widened when he claimed his chair and sat.

With *me* on his lap.

"Get it, bro!" Griff shouted from nearby, spurring several others to loudly voice their approval.

I stiffened, realizing that we were the only two up here. Which meant that all eyes were on us.

And, apparently, our audience was hungry for a show.

# CHAPTER 15

"Have I told you yet how lovely you look?" Kolton said, shifting me on his lap so that I was facing forward. So that I couldn't *hide* from his ravenous pack.

The compliment warmed my insides, even as I tensed when he raised another morsel of food to my lips. He'd started the show by hand-feeding me my dinner. Not with a spoon or fork, but with his *fingers*. I had resisted at first. But knowing that everyone was watching, I quickly gave in and accepted the food.

The act of feeding me wasn't purely for entertainment. Kolton was clearly delivering a message to his pack. He intended to provide for and take care of my needs, just as he did for his pack.

It was kind of sweet, really, but I still felt like a spectacle on display. At least we no longer had *everyone's* attention. Most were enjoying their own dinners, freely talking amongst themselves.

Instead of responding to Kolton's compliment, I said, "Aren't you afraid my *wolf* will tell me to bite off your fingers?"

When his hand paused halfway to my mouth, I hid a wicked smile. It was mean of me to bring up his fear. At the same time, it gave me a perverse sense of power over this awkward situation.

"I'm not afraid of your wolf," he finally said, his hand resuming its path to my lips.

I stared at the cluster of pomegranates he was waiting for me to accept, annoyed at his quick brush-off. I hadn't expected him to openly confess, but an outright lie was just rude. Wanting him to feel my annoyance, I opened my mouth and savagely bit into the seeds. And his fingers.

He jerked his hand back with a hiss, cursing under his breath.

A small smile curved my lips. "Thought you weren't afraid," I goaded and chewed the sweet seeds with gusto.

"I'm not."

"Bull."

"Does it *feel* like I'm afraid?" he said, grabbing my hips and pushing me down on top of him.

At the feel of his rock-hard shaft pressed against my backside, I nearly choked on the seeds. Swallowing carefully, I shifted on his lap to put some much-needed space between me and his dick.

"Don't," he growled, tightly gripping my hips to still my movements.

The action only pressed me against him harder. Annoyed again, I retaliated by wiggling my butt against his stiff cock.

He groaned, so loud that my core heated in response. A new scent tickled my senses. It was sharp. Cloying. Seductive.

Ah hell, it was my *arousal.*

Now it was my turn to curse.

Mortified, I tried to escape. Before I could, Kolton slipped a hand inside the slit of my dress and said in my ear, "So you want to play, wife?"

My eyes flared wide. I started to shake my head, but it was too late. His fingers touched my clit through my panties, drawing a sharp gasp from me.

"You're soaked," he rumbled, clearly pleased with the discovery. Heat filled my cheeks.

"Kolton," I hissed in warning, my eyes locked on the crowd.

Despite the tablecloth hiding his actions, I was certain they could sense what was happening. Maybe even *smell* it.

"You can always stop me," he said, slowly spreading his thighs, which spread *my* thighs.

*Heaven help me.*

"You know I can't."

I'd already acted out once today. A second time could garner negative attention from his pack.

"I'm sure you could find a way if you really wanted to," he breathed, caressing the shell of my ear with his lips.

I shuddered, both from his lips and the feel of his fingers sweeping over my panties. I tried to think. Tried to find a way out of this. It was one thing to let him ease my pain, but letting him publicly touch me during a *wedding* was insane. And yet, when I didn't move a muscle, Kolton began pleasuring me in earnest.

As his fingers expertly worked my center, sliding over my panties with practiced ease, I lost the battle. His touch felt so *good*, and I was helpless to resist it.

Gripping the table's edge for dear life, I struggled to keep my eyes open. To keep my expression neutral. As long as no one caught wind of what we were doing, I could survive a public orgasm.

Yeah, right. Who was I kidding?

The longer Kolton stroked me, the harder it was to control myself. In no time, I lost the fight with gravity and slumped against him, my head falling back on his shoulder. He growled his approval, pausing to press a knuckle against my clit. My eyes rolled back and I whimpered as pleasure rolled through me. Losing sight of our audience, I struggled to keep quiet. To hold still while his touch filled me with bliss.

"Good girl," he purred, his warm breath fanning across my cheek.

"But let's see how well you handle this next challenge."

Wait, he was *challenging* me?

Something sharp nicked my inner thigh and I flinched in surprise. Before I could fully realize what it was, my panties started to tear. Slowly, ever so slowly, Kolton ripped them.

With his *claws*.

My whole body began to tremble with excitement and anticipation. The table creaked as my grip tightened further. With one final tug, the panties severed.

For one agonizing moment, he made me wait.

And then his claws found my center, stroking up its length.

I bit my tongue to silence a scream, stiffening as ecstasy shot through me. I could barely breathe, utterly overwhelmed by the foreign sensation of his claws gently scraping my sensitive flesh.

Responding to my reaction, familiar heat stirred.

"Calm," Kolton crooned to my wolf, sensing her alertness.

Shockingly, she paused and once again listened to his voice. After a moment, the heat faded, as if she knew I wasn't in danger.

Kolton resumed stroking me, using his claws to flick and tease in a way that drove me wild with need. I softly whined, begging him for release. His lips against my cheek curved into a wicked grin.

For an unbearable moment, he made me wait again. But when I whined once more, he chuckled and murmured, "Shhh, I've got you, sweetness."

Then he gave me what I wanted. So hard and fast that euphoria exploded through me. For several seconds, I couldn't see or hear. The pleasure was so intense that everything else ceased to exist. I could be screaming and shaking uncontrollably, alerting his entire pack to my explosive *orgasm*, for all I knew.

But when I finally came back down and opened my eyes, the

pack's attention wasn't on me. It was on the table I was still gripping. I glanced down, stunned to see that the table was now entirely split in two.

Kolton took me to the middle of nowhere.

I doubted it even showed up on a map.

We'd left the ceremony early, shortly after the table incident. Apparently, he'd seen how mortified I'd been and had taken pity on me. But now that it was just him and me, miles and miles from the nearest living soul, I suddenly wanted to be surrounded by his pack again.

Who cared if they'd seen me break a table with my newfound strength, all because I'd experienced another mind-blowing orgasm at Kolton's hands. Who cared if they'd scented the air, realizing seconds later what had happened.

I'd take humiliation over *fear* any day.

And I was. As Kolton drove his truck up the last winding stretch to our destination, I was terrified.

We were alone.

*Alone.*

And it was our wedding night.

The drive had only taken an hour, but it might as well have been a lifetime. After we'd packed our bags—Vi had sneakily packed mine—and said our farewells, Kolton had lapsed into silence. All of his alpha bravado from the wedding had vanished the second we'd driven off. I'd tried to break the tension, but after receiving a few distracted responses, I'd settled into silence as well.

Watching him white-knuckle the steering wheel for an hour

had frayed the last of my nerves. Either he was second-guessing his decision to marry me or he was afraid too. Not for the same reason I was though. I doubted there was anything for him to fear in *that* department.

Another thought came to me. A much darker one.

What if he'd brought me out here to kill me? After what happened last night with my wolf, maybe he'd realized this marriage couldn't work. Maybe the wedding had just been for show. Now that his pack had seen me, they could spread word of the union, which would effectively deter future challengers. Kolton could go *years* pretending to still have a wife, even if no one was allowed to see her.

He could bury me out here and no one would ever know.

Ah hell. Now that I'd had the morbid thought, I couldn't get it out of my head. Sure, he'd protected me from the witches, but that had been *before* my wolf had attacked him. She'd behaved at the wedding, but who knew what would happen the next time she emerged.

When the truck jolted to a stop, I nearly leapt out of my skin.

For the first time since we'd left his estate, Kolton turned to look at me. "Okay, Nora. What's wrong?"

I sat ramrod straight, looking everywhere but at him. "What? Nothing. Nothing's wrong."

Sighing, he put the truck in park and killed the engine. At the absolute *silence* that descended, my heart frantically hammered.

"Nora."

"Hmm?" I replied, wincing when my voice squeaked.

"Is this about the wedding?"

Nervous laughter pushed at my throat. "The wedding? No. The wedding was fine."

"So you were fine with everything that happened?"

"Sure. Why wouldn't I be?" I really needed to get out of this truck before my voice became any more shrill. But when I reached for the door handle, Kolton laid a hand on my arm. My body violently reacted. With a muffled shriek, I tore my arm away and scrambled from the cab.

The moment my feet touched the ground, the hem of my dress tripped me up. Before I could right myself, Kolton was there, lending me a hand.

"I'm fine, I got it," I hurriedly said, evading his touch. Desperately trying to cover up my nervousness, I opened the back door of the truck to grab my packed bag. "So, where are we, exactly?"

Kolton watched me for a moment before finally responding, "We're near Ampersand Lake. I bought a secluded cabin up in the mountains for this occasion, thinking that I'd be releasing your wolf for the first time here. Less chance of running into humans."

I paused at his explanation, then swung my bag from the truck. "And now?"

Might as well rip the bandaid off.

He reached for my bag, but I swept right on by him, heading for the two-story cabin built into the mountain. With my newly-enhanced vision, I could make out every detail. At my approach, the outside lights flicked on, giving me an even better view. "Cabin" was too small a word for this place. It was bigger than my farmhouse back home. One side was completely made up of windows, the top ones forming a triangle shape.

I quickly glanced over to take in the mountain view and nearly gasped. We were at the top. The *very* top. Far below was a valley and what I assumed was Ampersand Lake. Well, if I was going to die, at least the location was beautiful.

"And now," Kolton said from behind me, answering my question, "we get to know each other better."

I stiffened. Without turning around, I asked, "How come we couldn't do that at your family estate? Why did we have to drive way out here?"

"I think you know why, Nora."

A chill worked its way up my spine.

Dropping my bag onto the front porch, I whirled to face him. "No, I don't. Why don't you spell it out to me?"

A muscle feathered in his jaw. He slammed the truck doors shut and approached me. When I noticeably tensed, he stopped just shy of the porch. Searching my face, he blew out a breath and said, "We're married now."

Crossing my arms over my chest, I forced myself to maintain eye contact. "Yes, we are, Captain Obvious. I've upheld my end of the deal."

Frustration flashed in his eyes. "You should know it's not that simple, Nora."

"No, I *don't* know, Kolton," I shot back, feeling my hands begin to shake. "You didn't tell me I had to do anything more than marry you. I did that. I said my vows. I let you kiss me. Even *touch* me. But you didn't say I had to have *sex* with you."

*Crap*. I snapped my mouth shut, wishing I could take back the words.

Kolton's chest heaved. He looked away, clearly upset by what I'd said. "Nora . . ."

"No," I interrupted, needing to say my piece before I lost the nerve. "This wasn't a part of our deal."

"I know we never discussed it, but an unconsummated marriage will never stand. Any wolf who gets within a dozen feet of you will know—"

"Will know what?" I interrupted again, feeling my face flush scarlet. "That we haven't had sex?"

He paused, then slowly looked up at me. "That you're still a virgin."

My insides turned to ice. Struggling to breathe past the panic tightening my chest, I whispered, "How do you know?"

"Females smell different when they haven't . . . been with a male."

Ah hell. How come no one had told me? I'd been warned about my menstrual cycle. Even about females going into heat. How come I hadn't been warned about *this*?

"Great," I said, wishing the mountain would crack open and swallow me whole. "So I'm basically a walking "I'm a virgin" billboard. Good to know."

Kolton huffed a humorless laugh. "Basically."

I studied him for a moment. "How much of a problem will this be?"

"The pack will suspect my motives for marrying you," he truthfully replied, sliding his hands into his pockets. "They'll assume the union is a farce and will question my leadership. I could end up losing their support and respect. If I'm put on trial and the truth comes out, they could even challenge me with the intent to elect a new alpha."

I blinked. "Oh, is that all?" I said a little too shrilly, throwing my hands in the air. "So, if we don't have sex, your family's safety could end up being worse off than if we hadn't married. This is really screwed up, you know."

He grimaced. "I'm not happy about this any more than you are."

My jaw dropped. "Seriously? This was *your* idea. Besides, it's not like you haven't had sex before. I was saving my virginity for the right guy . . ." At the shift in his expression, I pointed at him and snapped, "Don't look at me like that."

He stiffened. "Like what?"

"Like I hurt your feelings. The only thing that's hurt is your *ego*, because you can't imagine why a female wouldn't want to have sex with you."

His expression darkened. "What's that supposed to mean?"

Too incensed, I didn't even hesitate to blurt, "It means your reputation has preceded you. I've heard about your exploits with women. You're a ladies' man. A *womanizer*."

When he took a step toward me, my heart leapt into my throat. "And what other *rumors* do you believe about me?"

"They're not rumors," I said, standing my ground. "I've witnessed them firsthand. I know you've been with Jasmine. You've even taken liberties with me and we barely know each other."

His lips pulled back in a silent snarl. "You know those weren't ordinary situations, Nora. I'm an alpha. I have responsibilities."

I curled my hands into trembling fists, feeling my chest tighten to the point of pain. That shouldn't have hurt as much as it did. But hearing me lumped in with the rest of his *responsibilities* was a sucker punch to the gut.

"And will you continue your *responsibilities* now that we're married? There are a lot of unmated females in your pack, Kolton. Ones still desperate for your *help*. Will you continue to service them? Or am I your sole *responsibility* now?"

He clenched his jaw, trembling with barely restrained fury. If I wasn't so mad myself, I would have cowered at the sight. Instead, I met his angry stare with one of my own, daring him to refute my words.

After a long moment, he quietly said through clenched teeth, "This conversation is over."

"You bet your blue balls it is," I shot back, feeling tears stab my eyelids. "Screw your responsibilities. You are *not* touching me again."

Before he could see my tears, I brushed past him and stormed off into the night.

# CHAPTER 16

There was nothing more painful than knowing that you weren't wanted.

That you were nothing more than a duty. A *responsibility*.

Kolton had all but admitted that touching me, *kissing* me, had been nothing more than his responsibility.

Knowing this made me feel used. *Dirty*. Not to mention weak and pathetic.

I'd been so focused on freeing my wolf that I hadn't stopped to think of how *deeply* this marriage would affect me, both physically and emotionally. I'd been naive to think that saying "I do" would be enough. That nothing more would be required of me.

What would his pack do to *me* if they knew our marriage was a lie? I doubted they'd let me go without facing consequences. My pack had always disciplined harshly for secrets and deceit. I understood why though. We only had each other for protection in a world that would cage us or kill us if they knew what we were.

Trust was everything. Which was why I so often got into trouble for making reckless decisions.

And here I was, causing strife yet again.

I didn't blame Kolton for wanting to consummate the marriage. Not really. I blamed myself for being stupid enough to think that I wouldn't have to. That his pack would be perfectly accepting of their alpha's little "business arrangement."

Deep down, I'd known better. Every decision a pack member made affected the whole, *especially* the alpha's. The pack relied on their leader for protection. If they knew Kolton had chosen this marriage for the sake of his immediate family, they might even feel betrayed. Like he cared more about his *family's* welfare than the pack's.

And, to a pack, every member was family.

The problem could be easily rectified if I just had sex with Kolton, but the thought of doing so felt too much like losing my freedom all over again. Like giving up yet another piece of myself simply to please the pack.

Maybe that made me selfish to think such things, but I'd already given up so much. I was married to someone I barely *knew*, for heaven's sake. Wasn't that enough?

"You know it isn't," I muttered at myself, slowing to unsnag my dress from a prickly bush. The skirt was now in tatters, but I couldn't seem to care. In fact, I secretly wanted it destroyed. The thing reminded me too much of the public orgasm Kolton had given me. Of his hand sliding inside the skirt's slit. Of his *claws* tearing my panties.

The underwear was still dangling from my waist, a constant reminder of what he'd done. What I'd *allowed* him to do. All to please his pack.

"Well, that was the *last* time," I seethed, tromping through the woods without direction. I'd been aimlessly walking for at least half an hour, allowing my instincts to lead the way.

Thankfully, Kolton hadn't followed me. If he had, I would have no doubt chewed him out some more. I couldn't go far though. Every time I traveled too far away from him, pain lanced my body, reminding me that I was still *bound* to him. So, I'd essentially been walking in a circle, testing the limits of my invisible *leash*.

"That isn't fair," I chastised myself, unconsciously rubbing at the snake tattoo. I'd told him to keep it on, after all. As *insurance.*

I should have taken off in my truck while I had the chance.

As soon as I had the thought, guilt jabbed at me. Even though my relationship with Kolton was rocky, I'd grown close with his sisters. Leaving them now almost felt like abandonment. They hadn't asked their brother to marry for the sake of their own safety, but they needed protection all the same. The thought of something happening to them if Kolton was challenged and killed . . .

"Ah hell," I groaned aloud, throwing my head back. I totally didn't need a reminder of why Kolton had wanted to marry me in the first place. His willingness to sacrifice for his sisters was *not* making me reconsider.

Slumping against a tree, I closed my eyes and breathed in the night air, trying to clear my thoughts. A handful of minutes passed before a light *snap* caught my attention. I stiffened, thinking it was Kolton. But, as I continued to listen, it became more and more clear that the noise had come from an animal. And not just any animal.

*Prey.*

At the realization, excitement shivered through me. And something else too. A sudden flash of *heat.*

My wolf was awakening.

Before I knew what was happening, she surged up. Just like that, my body began to change. To *shift.* I stifled a scream as agony whipped through me, forcing me to my knees. Heat engulfed my senses, baking me alive. Everything was fire, fire, *fire.*

And then my bones began to break. The pain robbed me of air. I shook uncontrollably, unable to do a thing as my body slowly transformed. My arms sprouted white fur. Claws painfully shot from my fingertips. Fangs pushed through my burning gums. I opened my mouth to scream, only for an agonized howl to emerge.

When the transformation was complete, I struggled to stay conscious. To remain alert as my wolf took control. I felt the moment when my body became hers. She shook out her fur as if shaking off the transformation. As if shaking off *me*. But I stuck to her like a tenacious burr.

Lifting her nose into the air, she sniffed. Scenting. *Searching*.

So focused on her singular task, she didn't seem to notice that I was still with her. We were suddenly moving. Slipping through the woods as she continued to sniff. Her tread was light. Silent. Pure predator.

She was on the hunt.

At the first whiff of her prey, excitement rushed through me again. Through *her*. Her focus sharpened even more. She slid forward like a ghostly shadow, remaining downwind from the animal. When the scent grew strong, she slowed and searched our surroundings.

There. A *deer*.

Her keen eyesight zeroed in on the creature. She crouched, watching its movements closely.

I knew what would happen next. Knew, but couldn't do a thing about it. She was fully in control, her only thought on hunting. On catching. On *devouring* her prey.

Crap. I was *not* going to enjoy this.

Before I was ready, she burst from her hiding spot and raced toward the deer. The animal startled and leapt forward, but my wolf was *fast*. I almost lost myself to the thrill of the chase then, marveling at her speed and agility. But as she gained on the creature, my trepidation returned. Was I really going to kill and *eat* this thing?

Faster than I thought possible, my wolf covered the remaining distance and sprang. Her claws dug into the deer's hide, sinking in deep. The poor animal bleated in terror, struggling to escape. When my wolf wrestled the deer to the ground and lunged for its vulnerable throat, I screamed and shut my eyes.

Except that my eyes wouldn't *shut*.

I screamed again as my wolf clamped her jaws over the creature's throat and bit down *hard*. Blood gushed into her mouth. *My* mouth.

*YUCK!* I bellowed.

My wolf suddenly flinched and jerked away, releasing the animal. Wounded but still alive, the deer thrashed in my wolf's grip. A hoof caught my wolf in the ribs and she yelped. I cried out too, startled by the flare of pain.

As the deer stumbled upright, blood streaming from its neck, a growl cleaved the air. We glanced over just in time to see a massive dark wolf jump onto the deer's back. The animal collapsed under the weight, thudding to the ground once again. As the dark wolf latched onto its throat, my wolf abruptly exploded into action.

With a ferocious snarl, she leapt to her feet and bared her fangs at the wolf. Glowing yellow eyes fixed on her. On us.

*Kolton.*

Somehow, I knew she didn't see him that way though. All she saw was the dark wolf, and the very sight of him made her blood boil. She loathed him. Hated him. Not only that, she wanted to *kill* him.

Holy hell, Kolton had been right.

Even as my wolf prepared to attack him, he remained where he was, his hold on the deer slowly draining its life. Furious that he was claiming *her* kill, she growled again in warning. He only tightened his hold and stared at her, unblinking. At the blatant challenge, she roared and charged.

*NO!* I shouted, but there was no stopping her. She ate up the distance between them and lunged, her mouth opened wide. At the last second, Kolton's wolf released the deer to face her attack. They met in a clash of claws and flying fur. My wolf snapped at his neck, missing his throat by inches. Spitting out a patch of his dark fur, she lunged for him again. In a flash, he bowled her right over and pinned her beneath his greater weight.

She snarled up at him, scratching at his underbelly as she fought to break free. He growled back, so loudly that she froze. *We* froze. His mouth full of razor sharp teeth was inches away. At any moment, he could rip out our throat. My wolf didn't seem to care. She continued to thrash, boldly snapping at his face.

He opened his maw wide and lunged for our neck. When his jaws clamped down on our windpipe, she finally stilled. Finally realized who the stronger wolf was. Still, her lips pulled back in one last defiant growl. He growled back, tightening his hold. I whimpered at the uncomfortable sensation, but no sound left my wolf's mouth.

When she stopped fighting, Kolton's wolf slowly released his grip and stepped back. My wolf lied still for a moment more, then rolled to her feet and faced him. They stared at each other for a solid minute, neither of them moving a muscle. Kolton moved first. One step back. When my wolf bared her fangs and tensed as if to attack him again, I shouted, *NO!*

She paused and tilted her head to the side, as if in confusion.

Surprised, I tried speaking again. *Don't attack him, wolf.*

She flattened her ears back and whined.

Holy crap, she could hear me?

Kolton's wolf watched us as if he knew. Knew that I was communicating with her. When she didn't attack, he retreated another step, then another.

Giving us space.

My wolf tracked his movements, her ears still flat against her skull. A quiet growl rumbled in her throat as Kolton's wolf shuddered and began to shift. I watched with open fascination, taking in the cracking bones and receding fur. Within minutes, the dark wolf was gone.

When Kolton slowly rocked back on his heels, revealing his naked form, I tried to look away. Tried and failed. My wolf unflinchingly stared at him, not the least bit embarrassed by his nudity. Meanwhile, I was getting an eyeful. I saw everything. *Everything.*

*Look away*, I scolded my wolf, even as I marveled at his sculpted body. He was gorgeous. Every last inch of him. If I was forced to stare at a naked male, at least he was ridiculously hot.

My wolf ignored me, never once taking her eyes off him. Until he looked over at the deer. Her gaze snapped to it as well, noting the absent rise and fall of its chest. Dead. Kolton had killed it.

My wolf didn't seem to care *who* had killed it. Only that the deer was now *hers*.

She prowled toward it, keeping close tabs on Kolton. He remained where he was, still in his crouched position. Still very much naked. When my wolf reached the deer, she paused to sniff it. To inhale its delectable scent.

*Noooo*, I wailed, knowing all too well what she planned to do next. *Please don't eat it.*

Ignoring me once more, she threw one last warning look at Kolton, then bit into her prize. I continued to wail and scold her, but she completely tuned me out. Saliva rushed into our mouth as the rich and savory meat hit our tongue. Suddenly realizing how empty our belly was, she tore into the meat like a starving animal. Well, I supposed she was. This was her first live kill, even if Kolton had technically finished the job.

She zealously fed, painting our muzzle red with the blood of our prey. I should feel disgusted. *Nauseated.* But I didn't. The raw meat slid wonderfully down my throat, settling pleasantly in my stomach.

All the while, Kolton patiently watched. He didn't approach. Didn't move a muscle. I knew very well that he could claim the deer for himself. Knew that he could feed and make *her* wait. She knew it too. Knew that, despite her strength, he was more dominant. More *alpha.*

But he stayed where he was. Almost as if . . .

As if he was *gifting* her the deer.

A wedding present. To his wolf bride.

That shouldn't please me, but it did. It pleased me *greatly.* Or maybe that was my wolf's reaction.

Either way, we accepted the gift, only drawing away when our belly was full. She licked her muzzle and glanced over at Kolton again.

He slowly shook his head. "No. You've explored enough tonight. Give back control to Nora."

The hackles on her back raised.

I, on the other hand, perked up. *Yeah, give me back control, wolf. Listen to Kolton.*

Her lips pulled back in a silent snarl.

*Hey,* I snapped, suddenly done being in the passenger's seat. *Don't give me that attitude. Shift back, wolf. NOW.*

Annoyance filled my head. *Her* annoyance. A female voice abruptly barked, *My name isn't WOLF.*

Startled by the voice—a voice that was *definitely* not mine—I didn't even realize I was shifting back until pain splintered my vision. I lost sight of the world around me, blinded by the agonizing transformation back into human form. When it was finished, I curled up on the forest floor, panting and trembling with fatigue.

Moments later, a warm hand touched my arm. I flinched and

scrambled away. Or, at least, tried to. My body protested the move, completely giving out on me. I slumped back to the ground and whimpered as pain racked me from head to toe. Everything felt wrong. Like my bones hadn't shifted back into the right spots.

"Easy," Kolton crooned above me, once again laying a hand on my arm. "Let me help you, Nora."

"Don't. Want. Your help," I gasped, even as I allowed him to carefully gather me into his arms. When he stood, I buried my face in his neck to stifle an agonized moan. "Hurts. So much."

"I know, sweetness," he said, his voice still soft and soothing. "You were shifted for a long time. It'll take longer for your body to recover."

As he began to walk, I tried not to cry. Or pass out. Every inch of me felt pieced back together with *tape*.

"I remember everything," I said against his skin, drawing comfort from his warmth. His scent. "I was awake."

"I wondered about that," he replied. "She obeyed my command to shift back way too easily."

I was silent for a beat. Then, "You were right. She's not . . . she's not me."

He tucked me more securely against his chest. "No. She's not."

# CHAPTER 17

Kolton carried me all the way back to the cabin. While we were both *naked*.

I would have been traumatized, if I wasn't so exhausted.

By the time we made it inside the cabin, I could barely stay awake. The interior was lowly lit and . . . cozy. *Too* cozy. Reminding me once again that this was our wedding night. My thoughts went haywire and I struggled to wake myself back up. To prepare myself in case he decided to force himself on me.

"You're safe," he said, even as he started to climb the stairs to the second floor. To the *bedrooms*. I scrambled to think of a way out of this mess, acutely aware of my naked skin pressed to his. All he had to do was glance down to see my bare breasts and, well, everything *else*. A sigh fled his nose. "Really, Nora. You can relax. I won't touch you. Not unless you want me to."

My eyes widened and I finally looked up at him. "But what about your pack?"

He studied me for a moment, then focused straight ahead as we reached the second floor. "It's my fault for not making the specifics of our union clear. I won't force myself on you. Whether you decide to consummate the marriage or not, the choice is yours."

Not exactly an answer to my question, but I breathed easier all the same.

When he carried me into a bathroom and flicked on the light, I became hyper-aware of our naked state once again. All he had to do was look in the mirror and—

He set me on the counter between the double sinks, then reached for a towel and handed it to me. All without sneaking a peek. I gratefully accepted the towel and covered myself while he turned to wrap a towel around his waist. I should have felt only relief, but a tiny part of me sighed in disappointment.

I mean, I wasn't *completely* immune to him. In fact, as he leaned over to turn on the bathtub faucet, I secretly hoped the towel would slip so I could have one last look at his sculpted backside.

No such luck.

When he turned to face me again, he noted the question in my eyes and said, "A soak in the tub will help with the healing process. There's some Epsom salt on the ledge."

I nodded, clutching the towel to me. A bath sounded heavenly. As long as I didn't fall asleep and drown.

Expecting him to leave then, I blinked in surprise when he approached the counter again and grabbed a washcloth. "What are you doing?" I warily asked, watching while he dampened the cloth.

Without answering, he stepped into my personal space and murmured, "Hold still."

Before I could prepare myself, he swept the cloth over my chin. I flinched back and gasped at the streak of red that now coated the white cloth.

"Your wolf's a messy eater," Kolton explained with mild amusement, reaching up to lightly grasp the nape of my neck. I tensed as he invaded more of my space, nudging my legs apart so he could stand between them.

Holy hell, that was too close. *Way* too close. Especially since I didn't have underwear on.

Still, I didn't move a muscle while he thoroughly cleaned off the blood, his expression set in lines of concentration. This close, I could see every single facial detail. Every freckle. Every fleck of gold in his dark amber eyes. And his *scent.* It was everywhere. I could barely breathe, overwhelmed by the way my body reacted to it.

"How are your ribs?"

I blinked, struggling to clear my hazy mind. "Huh?"

His mouth twitched. "Your ribs. I saw the deer kick you."

"Oh. Fine, I think. Healing."

I squeezed the towel, wishing he would stop talking. Wishing he would stop *caring.* I was supposed to be keeping my *distance* from him, not wanting to be closer.

When the cloth brushed across my bottom lip, my thoughts emptied. I focused on the cloth. On the sensation of it caressing my sensitive skin. Gently. *Intentionally.* Warmth rushed through me, settling in places it shouldn't. The cloth abruptly stopped. Kolton's eyes rose to mine, then fell to my lips.

My heart started to pound and I felt my body sway forward. Drawn to his silent invitation. More like *pulled.* My lips yearned to taste his again. To explore. To consume and be consumed.

Crap. *Crap.* I wasn't thinking properly. I wasn't thinking at *all.*

"You don't need to take care of me," I blurted, hating how breathless my voice sounded.

He swallowed and slowly lifted his gaze to mine again. "You're my wife," he said, as if that explained everything.

The words did crazy things to my insides, but I shoved the feelings aside before they could scramble my brain further. Any female would swoon over being tended to by Kolton Rivers, and that was the problem.

His actions weren't entirely innocent. I knew what he was doing.

What he hoped to gain from this encounter.

Instead of anger, sadness filled me. Sadness for us both.

Before I could lose my nerve, I replied, "Yes, I'm your wife. But you should have a choice too, Kolton."

I watched as my words slowly sank in. As he realized what they meant.

No matter his responsibilities, he shouldn't feel forced to consummate our marriage either.

His eyes suddenly shuttered. Clearing his throat, he stepped back, looking everywhere but at me. "I should . . . I should go. Enjoy your bath."

With that, he was gone, leaving me to wonder if I'd done the right thing.

The next morning, I awoke to the smell of food.

Scrambling out of bed, I grabbed the white satin robe Vi had packed for me and hurriedly covered my skimpy nightgown—*thanks, Vi.* Not even bothering to tame my bedhead hair, I wrenched the bedroom door open in search of the delicious smells.

My body moved on autopilot, my stomach growling louder and louder with each step. I was famished. *Starving.* It felt like I hadn't eaten in days.

Skipping several stairs in my eagerness to find the food source, I hit the ground floor at a run. Only to swing around the banister and come to a screeching stop at the sight of *him.* Kolton. Standing in the kitchen with an *apron* tied around his waist. Combined with a dark t-shirt, I'd never seen him look so casual. So . . . domestic.

The cabin's open floor plan allowed me a clear view of him, but it also allowed him a clear view of *me*. The second I jerked to a halt, his eyes found mine. They immediately dropped, taking in my apparel. When he froze, I glanced down and silently cursed. The robe had fallen open, revealing the lace and satin nightgown. The skirt's hem barely covered my underwear, and the lace top was semi-transparent.

Worst of all, I wasn't wearing a bra.

Cursing again, I quickly closed the robe. Vi had no doubt picked out the sexy nightwear thinking she was doing me a favor. Yeah, not so much. Especially when I looked back up at Kolton and saw that he was still staring at me. In a way that sent heat rushing to my face.

Needing a distraction, I blurted the first thing that came to mind. "You know how to cook?"

Tearing his gaze from my body, he replied, "You sound surprised."

His voice was deeper than usual. Huskier. And when I looked closer at him, his posture was noticeably stiff. Was he tense from seeing the lingerie intended for our wedding night? Or was he still upset about the last conversion we'd had? I couldn't tell. He wasn't looking at me anymore, focused on turning sausages in a frying pan.

My mouth began to uncontrollably water.

Swallowing, I said, "I mean, you have a cook and kitchen staff at the estate. I just assumed . . ."

"That rich people can't take care of themselves?"

When a smile curved his lips, I huffed a laugh. "Yeah. Guess I kind of did."

"My mom taught me when I was younger," he replied, turning from the island's cooktop to grab two plates from a cabinet. "She loved to cook."

Oh.

Now I *really* felt bad for my flippant comment. Like I'd insulted his mother's memory or something.

"I'm sorry," I lamely said, not knowing what else to say. I really needed to stop blurting out the first thing that came to mind.

He faced me again, watching as I crossed my arms over my chest. Setting the plates on the counter, he said, "You have nothing to be sorry for." An awkward silence followed while he switched off the burner and started to dish up the plates. My eyes tracked his every movement, fixated on the growing piles of tantalizing food. "Hungry?"

I wrenched my gaze from the food, only to see his knowing expression. I wordlessly nodded, afraid that drool would escape if I opened my mouth.

He nudged a heaping plate across the island's surface.

My feet were moving before I could stop them, making a beeline for the food. I barely took time to accept the fork Kolton offered me before digging in. At the first bite of mouth-watering goodness, I shut my eyes and moaned. Holy hell, the guy knew how to *cook*. Or maybe I was so hungry that *everything* tasted amazing. Either way, I scarfed down the sausage, bacon, and eggs like a thing possessed, only pausing to take an occasional breath.

When buttered toast and jelly appeared before me, I gobbled that up too. Along with a tall glass of orange juice. Finishing it all, I looked around for more. I'd always had a healthy appetite, but this was excessive. My werewolf metabolism must have kicked in full throttle.

More food miraculously appeared on my plate, and I didn't question it. Only when I'd polished that off too did my stomach sigh with contentment. "Dude," I finally said, licking my fingers clean. "That was incredible. If you cook like this for me every day, I'll be your biggest fan for *life*."

Right at that moment, I glanced up at him and saw the way he was looking at me. I stopped talking. Stopped moving. Stopped *blinking*.

He looked . . . starved.

His food lay before him untouched. Unnoticed. The only thing he seemed to notice . . . was me.

"Biggest fan?" he said, his voice rough. Almost guttural. "For life?"

My throat closed. "It was a figure of speech," I managed to whisper, but he didn't seem to believe me. Or even hear me.

He started to move. Rounding the island, he slowly approached. My heart wildly fluttered inside my chest.

*Run. Run!* I screamed at myself, but I was frozen. All I could do was stare as he came closer. And closer. And closer.

He stopped, near enough that I felt the heat emanating from his body. Placing one hand on the counter, he raised his other toward my face and murmured, "You have a little something"—his thumb brushed the edge of my mouth—"right here."

He pulled the thumb away, now smeared with jelly. And slid it into his mouth.

I swallowed. *Hard.*

Holy hell. That was *hot.* My knees threatened to buckle, so I leaned against the counter.

This wasn't good. This wasn't good at *all.*

Apparently, my little speech from last night hadn't left a lasting impression on him. He was still actively trying to break down my barriers, and, boy, was it working. The man oozed sex. Combined with his exceptional culinary skills, I was practically putty in his hands.

As he slid his now clean thumb from his mouth, my gaze fixated on his lips. I was suddenly hungry again. Not for food. For *him.*

My breathing sped up.

"Kolton," I said, my voice tight with need. Crap, crap, *crap.*

"Nora," he replied, reaching up again to grasp an errant curl. He slowly stretched the curl taut, then let go. My heart beat double time when he watched the curl spring upward with rapt fascination.

"Kolton, I need . . ." I began again, desperately trying to slow my thundering pulse.

"You need . . ." he parroted, his eyelids falling to half mast as he leaned forward, filling my world with only him. I shivered when he placed two fingers beneath my chin and tilted my face up toward his. "What do you need, Nora?"

Our lips were a hair's breadth away, so close that his warm breath caressed my mouth. Teasing me. Taunting me to erase that final inch. To press my lips to his. To kiss him. To *give in*.

And I almost did. I wanted to. He was sinfully sexy and my body ached for his kiss. His *touch*. I had no doubt that he could make me feel things I'd never felt before. Not to mention do things I'd never done before. He was making it easy. *So* easy to give in and have sex with him. All I had to do was give him the green light.

My body begged for me to do it. Just one inch. One little inch and Kolton would fill my world with pleasure. And would that be so bad? My body would get what it wanted and Kolton would get what he wanted. Our marriage would be consummated and his role as alpha would be secure.

A win-win for both of us. Right?

But I'd done this before. Fallen for a deal that ended up with strings attached. I *still* had his snake tattoo wrapped around my arm.

He was too good at this. Too wickedly cunning and convincing.

All he had to do was lay on the charm and I was panting all over him like a female in heat.

The thought suddenly reminded me of Jasmine. Of the countless women he'd no doubt charmed into his bed.

Picturing him with them, having *sex* with them, immediately brought me back to myself. Like being splashed with ice water, I snapped out of it and remembered why I didn't want to have sex with him. This was business to him. A responsibility. A *duty*. I might be his wife, but he didn't love me. I didn't expect him to, but I couldn't give him my virginity simply to appease his pack. I respected myself too much for that.

There *had* to be another way to convince his pack that our marriage was legit.

And so, instead of giving in to a moment of passion, I blurted, "I need answers."

# CHAPTER 18

It was awkward sitting on a stool in only a nightie and thin robe.

But my need for answers was greater than any discomfort I felt.

"Coffee?" Kolton asked from a safe distance away. After I'd successfully diffused another heated moment between us, he'd returned to his side of the kitchen island. If he was disappointed that I hadn't given in to his advances, I couldn't tell. The guy had a good poker face.

"Sure," I replied, feeling a sense of déjà vu as I remembered the last time we'd had a serious conversation in a kitchen. Maybe breakfast conversations were our thing.

He seemed hesitant to answer my latest question though.

*Why are we different from other werewolves?* I'd point-blank asked him, my need to know coming back full force. I'd been patient long enough. Despite my skimpy apparel, I wasn't going to leave this spot until he gave me answers.

He didn't respond to my question until each of us held a steaming cup of coffee. Then, leaning against the kitchen sink, he finally said, "Has your wolf communicated with you yet?"

I sat up straighter, trying not to appear overeager. "I think so, yes. Last night, when I was trying to take back control, I heard a voice in my head say, 'My name isn't Wolf.' Do you think that was her?"

A smile tugged at his mouth. "That was her. She's a difficult one, just like you."

The comment should have offended me. Instead, it made me want to laugh. I'd actually heard my wolf *speak.* "How is she not me? Where did she come from? Do you know why she hates your wolf so much? She doesn't seem to hate *you* though. How come I never knew that there were wolves like us? Are we even werewolves?"

At my rapid-fire questions, he held up his free hand with a laugh. "Hold on. One question at a time. Yes, we're werewolves, but our wolves aren't. At least, not metaphysically." At my confused look, he continued. "Have you ever heard how witches get their magic?"

I slowly nodded. "They're gifted with magic at birth by spirits."

"Yes. And those spirits are celestial beings. Spirits who wish to join the corporeal world must sacrifice a piece of themselves. Witches have always believed that they and they alone were gifted this sliver of spirit, which allows them to wield magic. Do you know what a witch's familiar is?"

"A spirit in animal form."

"Correct. The spirits will sometimes seek out the missing piece of themselves, which is why some witches and warlocks have familiars. It's the closest the celestial being can get to being whole again."

"And what does this have to do with us?" I took a sip of my coffee.

"Our wolves are celestial beings."

I spat my sip of coffee across the counter. "*What?*"

That wasn't possible. *No way.*

Kolton casually turned to grab a dishcloth. Too busy gaping at him, I didn't even realize he'd begun to clean up my mess. "At birth," he said while he cleaned, "we were given a sliver of spirit. But, unlike witches, our parents were werewolves. Because of our pre-existing DNA, we have the ability to experience something witches can only dream of."

"And what's that?" I whispered, feeling my heart begin to race.

He paused in his cleaning to look me in the eye and say, "We can transform into our familiars."

All the blood drained from my face. "Are you saying what I think you're saying?"

"That we have an entire celestial being residing inside of us? Then, yes. That's what I'm saying."

If I was the fainting type, I'd be out cold on the floor.

"Wait," I said, feeling my hands start to shake. "Let me get this straight. My wolf is a *spirit?*"

"Her consciousness is, yes. Because you're a natural-born werewolf, she was able to not only place a piece of her spirit inside you at birth but place the rest of herself inside the animal part of you. Essentially, she's your familiar."

My jaw dropped. "So what does that make me? A werewolf *witch?*"

He shrugged, as if he hadn't just blown apart my reality. *Again.* "I call us hybrids. I don't know if there's an actual name for what we are though."

"Wait, wouldn't we be *tribrids*, then? Because we carry a familiar inside us too?"

He paused to look at me. "Tell your wolf to settle, Nora. She's responding to your stress."

I frowned, suddenly realizing how *hot* I was. Setting my coffee down, I shrugged off my robe. "It feels like a *sauna* in here. How can you tell when my wolf starts to emerge anyway?"

*Settle, girl. Settle,* I tried telling my wolf, surprised when I could have sworn I heard her growl in annoyance.

"For starters, your eyes start to glow—"

Kolton's words were suddenly interrupted by a loud *crash.* Startled, I glanced over to see that he no longer held a coffee cup. It must have fallen to the floor, but he didn't seem to notice. He was too busy staring at my—

Ah crap, I'd totally stripped in front of him. He could no doubt see my nipples through the nightgown's sheer lace top.

Before I could cover up again, he tore off his apron. Then his shirt. "Put this on, Nora." He tossed the t-shirt at me.

I caught it, sputtering, "B-but I can just—"

"*Now*, Nora."

I bristled at the command, until I noticed how agitated he looked. How *desperate*. And his eyes . . . they'd started to glow yellow.

Wordlessly, I obeyed his command and put on the shirt. Then sat and waited for *his* wolf to calm down. As he gripped the counter, clearly still struggling, I murmured, "Better?"

He stared at the shirt, then quietly swore and squeezed his eyes shut. "No. Seeing you in my shirt does *not* make it better."

I continued to wait in silence, trying my best not to ogle his pecs. Apparently, he wasn't immune to *me* either. I bit my lip to hide a pleased smile. I might still be a responsibility to him, but at least he found me attractive.

After a long moment, he opened his eyes and released the counter. "I need some fresh air," he stated, looking everywhere but at me. "I won't be far."

I watched him leave through the front door, wishing I'd kept my cool. Several questions still brimmed on the tip of my tongue. I couldn't believe my wolf was a *celestial being*. But what kind? I'd heard stories about witch familiars. That many of them were malevolent and self-serving. My wolf *had* been rather cranky since she'd woken up. And she absolutely hated Kolton's wolf.

Crap. Did I have a *demon* inside me?

Trying not to freak out, I decided that asking was the best

approach. Clearing my throat, I said out loud, "Hey. So I know we got off on the wrong foot, but I'd like to start over, if that's okay. I'm Nora. Nora Finch. And you are?"

Silence.

Not even the slightest stirring of heat.

Pursing my lips, I tried again, this time inside my head. *Look, I know we're not technically the same person, but we do sort of share the same body. I'd like to know you better by asking some questions. Can you please respond?*

Nothing.

"Ugh!" I groaned, throwing my head back. Add stubborn and ornery to my wolf's character traits. Hopping from the stool, I got to work cleaning up the kitchen, careful not to cut my feet on Kolton's shattered mug. While I cleaned, I kept up a running dialogue with my wolf, certain that she could hear me despite her silence. "I'm a really great listener, you know. If something's bothering you, feel free to speak up. I'd love to at least know your name. Sorry for calling you wolf earlier. Up until now, I had no idea an entirely separate *being* lived inside me."

I sputtered out a laugh, unable to hide my nervousness. I had a *spirit* living inside me. How freakishly amazing was that? If only she'd talk to me—

*Storm.*

At the sound of my wolf's voice, I nearly dropped the pan I was washing. Excited that she'd spoken, but not wanting to spook her, I calmly responded, *Is that your name?*

*My chosen earthly name, yes.*

I grinned a mile wide. "It's pretty. Nice to officially meet you, Storm."

She didn't respond, but I didn't let that squash my excitement.

Quickly finishing up in the kitchen, I bolted upstairs and got dressed, then went in search of Kolton. Almost an hour had passed since I'd last seen him. Plenty of time for him to cool down. Right? I hadn't dwelled too long on his reaction to my little strip tease, too busy trying to communicate with my wolf.

With *Storm*.

But now, as I used my newly heightened sense of smell to track him, I couldn't help but remember the heat in his eyes. Even though he'd probably given that same look to countless women before me, it still sent a thrill up my spine. I'd been so focused on my studies in college that boys had fallen to the wayside. Combined with my required trips back home every weekend and zero interest from the males in my hometown pack, I'd been in a perpetual dry spell.

Until Kolton.

Now that he'd given me a taste of passion, it was hard to ignore my awakened libido. Plus, he was my *husband*. Despite the vow I'd personally made not to consummate our marriage, the temptation was growing stronger with each encounter we had. Maybe it was time to set some boundaries. For starters, I couldn't let him cook for me again.

Seeing Kolton in an apron surrounded by food was an *instant* turn-on.

Just thinking about it sent a jolt of heat straight to my core. Cursing under my breath, I shoved the image aside and focused on tracking his scent. It was the hints of bourbon that gave away his location. When I caught sight of him through the trees, more excitement rushed through me. I briefly paused to assess my reaction, telling myself that it was because I'd successfully tracked him down. *Not* from seeing him again—or the fact that he was still shirtless.

His back was to me, but at the sound of my approach, he turned.

Light glinted off his phone as he lowered the device and slid it into his pocket.

"Guess what?" I called from several yards away, too eager to keep silent a moment longer. "My wolf told me her name. It's . . ."

Spotting his expression, I ground to a halt. The angry look cleared a second later, but I'd already seen.

"What's wrong?" I asked, worry filling me. His hair was completely mussed, falling onto his forehead as if he'd run his fingers through it several times. When he didn't respond right away, I pressed, "Kolton, what happened? Who was on the phone?"

A muscle jumped in his jaw. Then, "Pack your stuff. We're leaving."

My eyes widened in alarm. "Why? What—? Kolton, what are you—?" Flustered when he strode toward me and grabbed my arm, I let him turn me around without comment. But when his agitated steps forced me into a light jog, I demanded, "Kolton, speak to me."

His grip on my arm tightened. "Your *alpha* called. He wants to meet."

I nearly lost my footing as my limbs went numb with shock. Kolton noticeably slowed but didn't glance my way. "Wait," I said, trying to digest the news. "Aren't *you* my alpha now?"

"No. You haven't officially been initiated into the pack yet. Until that happens, your old pack still has visitation rights."

My stomach soured. "You make it sound like I'm a child without a say in the matter."

His hold on my arm gentled, as did his voice. "I'm sorry, Nora, but those are pack rules. They've been in place for decades. Maybe centuries."

"Stupid pack rules," I grumbled under my breath, then winced, remembering who I was talking to.

Kolton ignored the complaint, saying, "Even as your husband, I can't deny their request to see you. But I don't have to leave you alone with them. If you want me to stay, I will."

I chewed on my bottom lip, feeling smaller and smaller with each step we took. After a long moment, I said, "Is it just Alpha Hendrix who wants to see me?"

"I don't know. I only know that he called in his rights to see you and I have no choice but to let him. Now that he's following proper protocol, we only have twenty-four hours to comply."

When my heart gave a hard thud, Kolton finally glanced at me. Hoping he couldn't see the turmoil brewing inside, I met his stare and replied, "Well, let's not keep him waiting then."

# CHAPTER 19

The drive to Underhill, Vermont took three hours. During that time, I barely spoke a handful of sentences.

It was our last car trip all over again, except in reverse.

Kolton tried to coax conversation out of me, but I could tell he was tense too. His tension only further amplified mine, until the itch to run overwhelmed me. To keep myself from jumping out of the truck, I twisted my gold wedding band. Round and round and round. Until I caught Kolton watching and stopped.

Minutes from our destination, he spoke again, asking a question I couldn't help but answer. "What's your wolf's name?"

I stopped biting my lip to say, "Storm."

"Fitting."

I huffed a quiet laugh. "Yeah. What's yours?"

"Shadow."

"Also fitting."

"Spirits seem drawn to descriptive names for their animal forms. Usually visual ones."

Right when I felt myself relax a little, the truck slowed, turning into a familiar driveway. *My* driveway. Or rather, my parent's. My mouth dried and I went poker straight. The mailbox had been repaired since I'd plowed into it. Everything else looked exactly the same. The only thing missing was my truck. In its place was a big black Hummer.

Alpha Hendrix's vehicle.

My palms began to sweat.

No one greeted our arrival as Kolton parked the truck. But if Alpha Hendrix had given Kolton this address, then my parents were no doubt inside as well. Waiting. Waiting for their prodigal daughter's return.

When the engine died, Kolton turned to me. I tried meeting his stare, but couldn't quite manage it. Before I could reach for the door handle and make a hasty exit, he said, "They can't know about our deal."

I nodded my understanding. "What should I tell them?"

"Anything you want, as long as they believe this marriage was your choice."

I flicked a glance at him. "It was."

He gave me a pointed look. "You know what I mean."

"Okay, fine. And what about my wolf? They'll sense something's different about me."

"The moon will be full in a week. If they question you, just say you've been experiencing changes lately. They'll assume your wolf is finally starting to emerge."

I nodded again, so fast that my brain rattled. "So, don't mention that I've already shifted."

"No."

"Why not?"

"Because I don't trust them with that information."

I finally focused on him, noting the hard line of his jaw. "Do they even know that werewolves like us exist?"

"Maybe, but it's not common knowledge. I keep it a secret for good reason. Many in Midnight Pack don't even know."

My eyes slowly widened. "And why's that?"

His expression turned dead serious. "Because we're different. And different in our world means dangerous. Our own kind would turn on us if they thought we were a threat, not to mention humans and other supernatural beings."

The blood slowly drained from my face. "Is that . . . is that why the witches wanted me?"

"I believe so, yes. And I also believe they would tear you apart if they got their hands on you."

A swallow got stuck in my throat. Well, that explained why he'd gone to such extreme measures to keep me safe. It almost made everything he'd done—everything *bad* he'd done—seem heroic.

Wow. Was I actually justifying his actions? The kidnapping? The *murder?* Crap. Maybe I was.

He was violent, no doubt about it. Even cold and ruthless at times. But not in the way I'd first assumed.

Inhaling a deep breath, I blurted before I could change my mind, "I want you to come in with me."

He searched my face for a long moment. "You sure?"

"Yeah," I said without hesitation, reaching for the door handle. "I mean, my parents should probably meet my husband."

I'd meant to say the words flippantly. *Teasingly*. But, as I said the word "husband," heat filled his gaze. Holy hell. I felt its warmth to the tips of my toes. At the abrupt mood shift, I scrambled out of the truck like my tail was on fire. Slamming the door shut, I paused for a moment to calm my erratic pulse. To make sure my trembling legs would carry me.

I tried to pass off my reaction as nerves for the upcoming meeting. But that would be a lie. This one was *all* Kolton's doing. Which only got worse when I rounded the truck and he joined me. Before I could prepare myself, he reached between us and threaded our fingers together. At the intimate contact, a buzzing electricity shot through my hand and up my arm. I stifled a gasp, throwing him a questioning look.

"Gotta make this believable, right?" he said, firming his grip on my hand when my steps faltered.

"Right," I said, way too breathlessly. Despite the tingling sensation surging up and down my arm, I squared my shoulders and strode toward the front door of my parent's farmhouse. I always used the back door, but today felt different. Like I was just visiting. Like I was a *stranger* to my home of twenty-two years. The feeling settled in my gut like a lead weight.

*You can do this, Nora*, I inwardly coached myself, cringing when I realized Kolton could probably feel my sweaty palm. *They're still your pack. Your family. What's the worst that could happen?*

Suddenly second-guessing my decision to bring Kolton with me, I opened my mouth to tell him to wait outside. Before I could, the front door swung open. I swallowed the words, forcing a smile on my face as Alpha Hendrix's broad frame filled the doorway. At the deep scowl he wore, one I'd seen a million times before, I felt my shoulders curve inward.

"Alpha Hendrix," I greeted, keeping the smile on my face despite his withering glare.

"Nora. Alpha Rivers," he said, his scowl only slightly lifting when he acknowledged Kolton. Until his gaze shot to our joined hands. The scowl returned, his face noticeably reddening. Still, he stepped aside and added, "Please, come inside."

Oh boy. This was going to suck.

I tried pulling my hand from Kolton's, only for him to tighten his hold and nudge me forward. Okay, then. He really wanted to sell this marriage thing. I could do that. As long as he didn't try to cop a feel in front of my parents. Suddenly nervous that he *would*, I barely made it inside the house without laughing. This situation was getting worse and worse every second.

Moving past the entrance hall, I turned the corner to see my parents sitting in the living room. At the sight of me, they both started to rise from the couch. Only to sit again when they focused on a point over my shoulder. I stiffened, sensing Alpha Hendrix behind me.

"Why don't we all sit down," he said, moving into the room to claim a chair. He didn't sit though, waiting expectantly for me and Kolton. The only other available spot was the loveseat across from my parents, so I moved toward that. Without letting go of my hand, Kolton joined me. When he sat so close that his thigh pressed against mine, my face heated.

For an uncomfortable moment that felt like an eternity, no one spoke. Alpha Hendrix sat in the armchair near the couch, studying us as if trying to read our thoughts. My dad stared at our joined hands and touching thighs. My mom was looking at my arm, her eyes nearly bugging out.

"Nora," she started, pointing at the snake tattoo. "When did you—?"

"Pamela," Alpha Hendrix interrupted her. "Please offer your guests some refreshments."

Kolton's thigh, still pressed against mine, went rigid. I glanced sideways to see his eyes superglued to Alpha Hendrix.

"Oh, of course," my mom said, starting to rise again. "Would you like tea or coffee? Water?"

"We're fine, Mom. Really," I said, needing this interrogation to get underway. "I'm not a guest. I'm your daughter. We can skip the formalities and jump straight to scolding me."

Across from us, Alpha Hendrix noticeably bristled. "Hold your tongue, young lady. I've had enough of you and your sass."

Kolton squeezed my hand, so hard that it started to hurt. When I flinched, he released my hand. Only to reach over and place his hand on my bare thigh. The possessive move didn't go unnoticed. My dad looked about ready to have a conniption.

"Nora," my mom gasped, pointing at me again. My other arm this time. "Is that a wedding ring?"

"Oh. Yeah." I looked down at the ring, then at my shocked parents and lamely finished, "Surprise."

I didn't expect them to jump up for joy and congratulate me or anything, but I also didn't expect my dad to hiss, "Nora Elizabeth Finch, what have you *done?*"

As I winced, Kolton's hand on my thigh started to tremble.

Before I could speak, Alpha Hendrix turned to Kolton and said, "See, this is why I was so adamant that Nora be returned to us. The girl is always causing trouble and disobeying the rules. Whatever she's gotten herself into this time, I'll take full responsibility for and make sure she's properly punished. I've been too lenient with her recently. I'll make sure she doesn't—"

"Doesn't what?" Kolton finally spoke, so deathly quiet that a chill crept up my spine. "Doesn't escape again? And what will you do to ensure that? Lock her in the cellar?" My mom gasped, but Kolton's gaze remained fixed on Alpha Hendrix. "Or maybe you'll try to kill her again. Let your wolf handle the problem. Because that's what Nora is to you, right? A *problem?*"

Ah hell, he did *not* just say that.

I went rigid like a frozen popsicle when Alpha Hendrix's face darkened with outrage. I braced for the explosion and didn't have to wait long.

"Is *that* what she told you?" he bellowed, shooting to his feet.

Kolton shot to his feet at the same time, squaring off with him. "No, she didn't tell me anything. I saw the scars and had to guess the rest. And, based on your reaction just now, I guessed correctly."

"That's preposterous," Alpha Hendrix continued to shout, throwing me a death glare. *You'll be punished for this*, his eyes promised, making me feel ten inches tall.

"Don't look at her, look at *me*," Kolton quietly seethed and took a step toward him. "Do you enjoy terrorizing your pack members, or just Nora? Because what I see is a petulant bully, not a leader. An alpha *protects*, even the weakest of his pack. He doesn't tear them down, all to make himself look strong. He doesn't disrespect them in their own home. He doesn't make them feel small and helpless. He doesn't *break* them."

Every word he said struck me like a bullet. I remained in my seat, frozen with shock. My parents were equally frozen, their eyes wide with horror. No one had ever spoken to Alpha Hendrix this way before. His face had darkened to an ugly shade of purple. He trembled with fury, his beard twitching like crazy as he opened his mouth to retaliate.

Before he could utter a sound, Kolton spoke again, saying words that chilled me to the bone. "I want you to apologize to Nora for mistreating her."

Now it was Alpha Hendrix's turn to look shocked. He silently shook for a moment, then burst out, "I will do no such thing. I'm an *alpha*. Alphas don't apologize, especially to the lowest member of their pack. Nora's lucky I kept her alive when she should have been put out of her misery years ago. She's caused me nothing but trouble, and I—"

Kolton suddenly lunged at Alpha Hendrix. He had the older man by the throat before he could think to defend himself. "Don't make me challenge you," he said in the man's purple face, his voice nothing more than a guttural growl. "If I do, I will kill you and claim your pack without a shred of remorse. Now, I will rephrase this in a language you'll understand. *Apologize* to Nora."

Holy. Crap.

Kolton let go of Alpha Hendrix and stepped aside, giving the older man a clear view of me. I looked up at my alpha, pretty certain his face was now blue. The man was *furious*. The entirety of his wrath hit me like a battering ram, forcing all the air from my lungs. The urge to run, to *hide*, was stronger than I'd ever felt before.

But I couldn't move. Couldn't do anything but stare.

So much for being a strong alpha female.

Alpha Hendrix's lips pulled back in a trembling snarl. "Nora, I—"

"On your knees."

Alpha Hendrix shot Kolton an incredulous look. "Excuse me?"

"You heard me," Kolton said. "Apologize to her on your knees."

Wow. *Wow*. He was trying to humble my alpha before me. To downright *humiliate* him. I stopped breathing, certain that Alpha Hendrix was going to lose it. There was no way. *No way* he would lower himself. Not for me.

The air crackled with tension as Kolton and Alpha Hendrix stared each other down. Neither of them blinked, wholly focused on breaking the other's will. On proving who the more dominant alpha was. The staredown lasted less than a minute. Then, the impossible happened.

Alpha Hendrix dropped his gaze and lowered himself to the floor.

My mom's hand flew to her mouth as she smothered a gasp. My dad nudged her into silence, just as Alpha Hendrix raised his eyes to mine.

The moment our eyes connected, I wanted to throw up. Hatred.

Hatred burned in his gaze. He'd been angry at me plenty of times, but not like this. I almost couldn't bear it. Almost looked away. But I didn't. I needed to see. Needed to witness with my own two eyes a moment I never thought in a million years would happen.

"Nora," he began, his gritty voice like sandpaper against my skin. "I apologize for any mistreatment you endured while under my care."

The words settled in my stomach like bricks. Because I knew this wasn't how the meeting would end. He wasn't in control right now, and he *always* ended a conversation with him firmly in control. I waited for the other shoe to drop, and it came swiftly.

Still on his knees, he said, "It's clear to me now that you don't belong in the Underhill Pack. I've tried to accommodate you and your disabilities, but we're obviously not a good fit for you. So, from this day forward, you are no longer welcome in my territory. I will ask you and Alpha Rivers to leave straight away. Say goodbye to your parents, because you won't be returning here to visit them again."

I couldn't breathe. I was pretty sure an elephant had sat on my chest. I stared at him, unable to grasp the full meaning of his words.

It was my mom who broke the silence, saying, "Alpha Hendrix, please. We'll make sure she never leaves again. Just tell us what to do and we'll do it."

"My word is final," Alpha Hendrix said, still staring at me as he rose to his feet. "Nora is no longer a member of Underhill Pack."

I expected the statement to hurt like a knife to the chest, but I was suddenly numb. Numb and detached, like I wasn't even here. Not really. When my mom left the couch to approach me, I watched without expression. She tugged me to my feet and drew me into a hug, sniffling loudly. I patted her back, offering her empty comfort.

"I'll be fine, Mom," I heard myself say, but it didn't sound like me. "You can always text and call me."

She said something in return, but I couldn't understand it. My dad approached next, giving my shoulder a quick squeeze. He'd never been a hugger. At least not with me.

"Behave yourself," was all he said, then urged my mom to let go. And, just like that, she did, leaving me standing. Alone.

But I was only alone for a second.

A presence suddenly warmed my side. Kolton. When he placed his hand on my lower back, some of the fog lifted. Enough that I heard him clearly say, "I'll send someone to collect her things tomorrow morning."

With that, he steered me from the living room. We were nearly to the front door when I finally regained some sense. What was I *doing?* I couldn't leave like this. They needed to know first. Know how strong I was now. How *normal.* They didn't need to be disappointed in me anymore. I wasn't weak and pathetic!

As I started to turn, Kolton's arm slid around me. "Don't do it," he breathed, firmly gripping my hip. "Don't give them something they don't deserve."

I opened my mouth to protest, then shut it. Even though I was still desperate to prove myself, I listened to his words. They didn't fully make sense to me, but they felt . . . right.

As we got into the truck and started to pull away, no one left the house to bid us farewell. Still, my eyes stayed glued to the front door. Waiting. Hoping. When we turned onto the main road, I kept watching, until the farmhouse faded from view. No one came out.

My heart sank.

Feeling my eyes start to burn, I dropped my gaze. Only to find Kolton's hand resting on the middle console. Palm up. Fingers splayed wide.

An invitation.

Without hesitation, I placed my hand in his.

In return, he gripped my fingers tight.

# CHAPTER 20

Everything was too much.

Lights. Voices. Faces.

I was relieved that Kolton had returned us to his family estate, but I couldn't socialize right now. I didn't have the strength. In fact, all I could think about was curling up in bed and sleeping. Maybe forever.

As if he could read my thoughts, Kolton redirected all conversation his way the moment we stepped through the front door. It wasn't long before the others picked up on his silent cues.

*Nora has checked out for the evening.*

It was around dinnertime, but I didn't have an appetite. So, murmuring a lame excuse, I headed up to my bedroom on the third floor. Kolton let me go. They all did. I could feel their eyes on me as I trudged up the stairs, but couldn't seem to care. My mood was officially in the gutter. I didn't experience burnout often, but when I did, it hit me *hard*. Usually from months and months of repressed emotions all pouring out at once.

Except that I was still in the too-shocked-to-feel-anything stage.

When I closed myself inside the room, I kicked my shoes off on the way to the bathroom. After a quick pee break, I washed my hands and splashed water on my face, too tired for anything else. But, as I reached to switch the light off, I paused.

*No. Don't do it.*

Clenching my teeth, I turned back around and faced the mirror again. This time, I looked. Looked at the girl with wild flame curls and aqua eyes. Eyes that looked . . . dead. I studied her impassively, as if she were a stranger. Took in her lightly tanned skin and high cheekbones. The faint smattering of freckles and full lips. I tried to make her smile and couldn't.

My gaze abruptly dropped to her stomach. High-waisted shorts and a cropped top covered her skin, so I reached down. Reached down and grabbed the shirt's hem.

*Don't do it, don't do it.*

With trembling fingers, I lifted the shirt and exposed her midsection. A ghastly scar greeted me, stretching from one side to the other. The first line started at the top of her ribs and ran all the way across. The next two cut across her middle, barely avoiding her navel. And the last was lower. I pushed down the shorts so I could view the entire scar in the mirror.

So I could see the *claw marks* Alpha Hendrix had given me.

As I beheld the full damage he'd inflicted on my body, the memory came hurtling at me. I'd only been ten when it happened. By that point in my life, my whole pack knew that something was wrong with me. All natural-born werewolves started to shift around the age of six. When I hadn't, my parents had begun locking me in the cellar for my safety.

*You're too weak*, they'd told me. *The other wolves will see you as prey.*

I hadn't minded at first. Until they'd leave me down there with no food, water, or electricity for two, sometimes three days at a time. Still, I'd convinced myself that starving was better than being torn to shreds by a wolf.

But one full moon during my tenth year, my parents had

accidentally forgotten to secure the cellar lock. I'd been sleeping on my half-deflated air mattress when a huge gray wolf got inside the cellar and attacked me. I hadn't realized who it was until years later, when I'd snuck outside and actually saw Alpha Hendrix transform into his wolf.

I'd never confronted him about it, but I'd always wondered. Always wondered why the most powerful wolf in the pack with the most control had practically disemboweled a little girl.

And now I knew. Knew that it hadn't been an accident.

But that meant . . . maybe the unsecured lock hadn't been an accident either. Maybe my parents had allowed him to attack me. Had *wanted* him to attack me.

Because they were ashamed of their wolfless daughter.

The image in the mirror suddenly grew blurry. I blinked, desperately trying to staunch the flow of tears. No, I wouldn't cry. I *wouldn't*. I was too hurt. Too mad. Too *furious*. Could my mom and dad have really wanted me dead? Was I *that* much of a burden and disappointment?

When the tears persisted, scalding my cheeks as they fell in droves, I yanked down my shirt and glared at the girl in the mirror. *Hard*. Her eyes were no longer dead. They were glowing blue fire. I gasped at the sight. Not because my eyes were glowing *blue* instead of the typical yellow. I gasped because Storm could have stopped this from happening. She'd been there all along. Slumbering like a lazy hound dog.

"Why didn't you help?" I hissed at my reflection. At *her*. "Why didn't you *save* me?"

When the blue fire dimmed in response, announcing her retreat, I screamed. Screamed and punched my reflection. The mirror exploded into a million shards, shattering against the counter. I drew my fist back and saw blood coating my knuckles. With morbid fascination, I watched my split skin slowly start to repair itself. I continued to stare until I heard rushing footsteps and a door burst open.

"Nora. *Nora*," Kolton called, hurrying through the bedroom. He jerked to a halt in the bathroom doorway, inhaling sharply when he saw the mess I'd made.

I looked up at him, at the shock on his face. My anger abruptly drained away. Holding up my injured hand, I said, "They wanted me dead. All of them."

He stared at my hand, then at me. Realization slowly dawned. "Nora . . ."

"I no longer have a home," I continued, more to myself than him. My pack had shunned me. My own *parents* had let me go without a fight.

When Kolton moved toward me, my eyes flew wide.

"If you touch me, I'll cry," I managed to say, my throat already closing up.

But he came anyway and wrapped me up in his arms. Blood-stained hand and all. The instant I felt his strong embrace, I burst into tears. Great sobs racked my body. So great that my knees buckled. Kolton lowered us both to the floor, sitting with his back against the counter. He held me tightly to his chest, unmindful of the blood and tears soaking his shirt.

"You have a home, Nora," he murmured against my hair, drawing his legs up on either side of me. Like a protective shield. "Your home is here."

I cried harder, fisting his shirt as I poured out the emotions I'd bottled up for far too long. He fell silent, offering me comfort without words. I continued to sob until my tears dried up. Until my body sagged against him, completely spent. He didn't move an inch the entire time, even when my cries faded and I simply laid in his arms. Letting him hold me. Letting his warmth lull me into sleep.

When I peeled my eyes open sometime later, I didn't know how much time had passed. I only knew that Kolton was still holding me, and he was fast asleep. I felt the steady rise and fall of his chest. Heard the slowed heartbeats and even breaths. When I stirred, his arms instinctively tightened around me.

Despite how numb and exhausted I was, I smiled. Just a little.

It felt good to be held. To be comforted and taken care of. I wasn't used to it. I'd learned at a young age how to self-soothe when things got bad. To not expect help from others. To only rely on myself.

But not needing to be self-dependent for once—not needing to hide my emotions from the world—felt amazing. And also terrifying. Because I was relying on *Kolton*. He knew practically everything about me now. He'd seen me at my absolute worst. He'd been to my home and witnessed how my pack treated me. If he decided that I wasn't the strong alpha female he'd been hoping for, he could easily kick me to the curb as well.

And all of this would be over.

I had thought I'd wanted that. To be freely independent. To make my own decisions. To be accountable to only one person. Me.

I'd wanted that for *years*. But that existence suddenly sounded . . . lonely.

Ah hell, what had he done to me?

He stirred at that moment, making my heart skip a beat. I shut my eyes again and waited for him to settle, only to hear him murmur, "You're awake."

Reluctantly, I nodded.

Before I could pull away, he added, "Want to talk?"

I hesitated, not sure if I had the energy to talk. Even if I did, unburdening my thoughts to Kolton probably wasn't a good idea. I already felt too comfortable around him. Too *close*. He didn't need to see me any more vulnerable. It would be like rolling over and exposing my underbelly to him.

When I didn't respond, he said, "I didn't mean for that to happen back there. I had every intention of keeping silent. But when I heard the way they were talking to you, I kind of just . . . lost it." His chest rose beneath my cheek, then fell as he heaved a sigh. "I'm sorry, Nora."

I smoothed the wrinkles on his shirt, belatedly realizing that I was stroking his chest. "It's not your fault," I quietly replied and fisted my hands. "All you did was expose the truth and defend me. Something I should have done a long time ago."

If only I'd had the courage.

"They were your family," Kolton said in return, as if that explained everything. I supposed it did.

"Yeah."

Silence settled between us again. But it wasn't awkward or uncomfortable. Neither was the position we were in. Instead, it felt . . . peaceful. Safe.

*Right.*

Holy hell, I was falling for his charm. *Hard.*

"It's late," I blurted, abruptly lifting my head off his chest. "We should go to bed." *Crap.* That didn't come out right. "In separate rooms, of course." That wasn't any better.

Time to go before I said anything else stupid.

I pushed off his chest, only for his arms to stop me. Surprised, I met his gaze. Then wished I hadn't. We were close. *So* close. And he was looking at me far too intensely. When I nervously bit my lip, his eyes dropped to my mouth. My exhaustion immediately fled as warmth filled me.

Oh, this wasn't good. He looked way too yummy right now and I was already under his spell. If he bridged the gap between us, I wouldn't put up a fight. Not even a little. I'd wholeheartedly melt against him and—

Kolton abruptly tore his gaze from my mouth and cursed under his breath. "Yeah," he roughly said, looking everywhere but at me. "It's late. We should get some sleep."

With that, he stood in one smooth motion, bringing me with. The second my feet were beneath me, he let go and stepped back. I immediately felt the loss of his warmth. Of his strength and touch. To hide my disappointment, I whirled and turned on the faucet to wash the blood off my hand.

"How's your injury?" Kolton said after a moment, still lingering behind me as if reluctant to leave.

Which was totally fine by me since I suddenly didn't *want* him to leave.

"Almost healed," I replied, barely glancing at my hand. I was too busy trying to sneak a peek at him in my peripheral.

"Good. Don't worry about the glass. I'll have someone clean it up tomorrow."

"Okay."

"Okay," he parroted. "I'll just be going then."

"Okay." I inwardly grimaced at how stupid I sounded.

When he hesitated, I held my breath, certain that this was it. That he was going to whirl me around and—

He strode from the bathroom, leaving before I could finish the fanciful thought. Okay, then. I'd definitely read that situation wrong. Which was a *good* thing. I was supposed to be keeping my distance from him. Letting him kiss me would only lead to other things. Like touching and exploring and hot, passionate *sex*.

Feeling faint, I leaned against the counter and dragged in air.

Why did I not want to have sex with him again? Oh, yeah. Because he didn't want love or a mate. Because this thing between us wasn't actually *real.*

Then how come he'd stood up for me in front of my pack? How come he'd comforted me in his arms? How come he'd made me feel *special?*

Confused and horny as hell, I finished cleaning up and headed for bed. What I needed was a solid night's sleep to clear my mind and straighten my priorities. Having sex with Kolton should *not* be at the forefront of my mind right now. Spotting my packed belongings next to the closed bedroom door, I walked over to it on autopilot and rummaged inside.

*Stop,* I scolded myself, but my hands continued searching. *You're only torturing yourself. He doesn't actually care about you. Not like that.*

My body ignored my protests, only stopping when it found what it was looking for. Pulling out Kolton's t-shirt that I'd briefly worn this morning, I buried my face in the soft material and inhaled. His smoke and woodsy musk with hints of bourbon invaded my senses, filling me with heat.

*Crap,* that smelled amazing. Like a calming drug, taking the edge off my frayed nerves.

I closed my eyes and walked backward to the bed, falling onto the mattress. After a moment more of breathing in his scent, I completely threw common sense out the window. Yanking off my shirt, I slipped on Kolton's. It wasn't the same as being held by him, but I felt closer, if only a little.

*You're insane. Insane!* I yelled at myself. But it was like shouting at a brick wall. Tugging off my shorts, I slid under the sheets with

Kolton's scent wrapped around me and prepared to sleep.

A minute later, I began to toss and turn, unable to quiet my mind. Thoughts of the past couple of days—more like past couple of *weeks*—plagued me. Namely, the many times Kolton had been there for me. He'd taken me in when I had nowhere else to go. Helped me free my wolf. Stood up for me when no one else would. Comforted me when my world fell apart.

And I couldn't remember. Couldn't remember if I'd ever once thanked him.

Finally, after what felt like hours, I reached for my phone to check the time. Midnight. *Ugh.* I didn't usually have problems sleeping, but thoughts of Kolton and everything he'd done for me wouldn't go away. Maybe it was time I did something for him in return.

An idea popped into my head. A terrible, *terrible* idea. But once an idea formed, it was hard for me to shake it. Especially bad ideas. Risky ideas. *Reckless* ideas. And this idea was all of those, plus more.

I ignored the idea for as long as I could, tossing and turning until the sheets were a twisted mess. And then I broke. Shoving the sheets aside, I hopped out of bed and tiptoed across the room. Listening at the door, I made sure all was quiet outside before turning the handle. I knew where everyone slept. Vi's room was next to mine. Melanie's beside hers. Griff and Jagger had rooms across from theirs, both on the third floor.

But Kolton . . . his room was on the second floor, directly below mine. I'd never been inside, but I knew exactly where it was. And that's where I went. Soundlessly slipping down the stairs, I beelined straight for his room. The others could wake up and find me at any moment, but that only fueled me onward.

My heart trilled in my chest, faster and faster with each step I took. Adrenaline gushed through me, giving me the courage to reach my destination. Once there, I barely paused. Without even knocking, I grabbed the handle to his bedroom door. My heart nearly gave out when it turned without resistance.

Before I could take back the decision I'd made, I pushed the door open and entered Kolton's room. It was dark, but my night vision allowed me to make out every detail. Including the man slowly rising from his bed.

My throat seized, cutting off my air, but my steps didn't falter. Quietly shutting the door behind me, I sealed myself inside.

Kolton stood from the bed and silently watched me. With a sweep of his gaze, he took in my apparel. I was still in his shirt but hadn't bothered to put on bottoms. He, on the other hand, wore sweatpants and nothing else.

"Nora," he finally said in hushed tones so as not to wake the others. "What are you doing here?"

Swallowing with difficulty, I whispered, "Can't sleep."

I watched as realization slowly dawned on his face. And something else too. Something that made his eyes flicker yellow. "And you want to sleep here?" he questioned, his voice deeper and huskier than moments before.

My body reacted viscerally to the sound. Warmth pooled between my legs and I quickly squeezed my thighs shut. Apparently, not fast enough. His nostrils flared as he scented the air. Scented *me*. His eyes glowed brighter.

"Yes," I replied, trembling from the effort of holding still. And then, "I want to sleep with my husband."

The words left me in a breathless rush, but I knew he heard them. Sharply inhaling, he stared at me like he'd heard wrong. But he hadn't. To prove that he hadn't, I crossed the room toward him. He went perfectly still as I approached. Only his eyes moved, tracking me as they burned brighter and brighter.

The sight stole my breath, but I didn't let that stop me. Reaching his position, I didn't hesitate to lift my hand and grasp the nape of his neck. Pushing up onto my toes, I pressed our lips together. He sucked in another breath and I swallowed the sound, kissing him passionately. There was no shyness to my actions. Only firm resolve as I wrapped both arms around his neck and opened my mouth to him. An invitation.

For a split second, he froze. Every line of his body went taut.

And then he moved, banding his arms behind my back to lift me clean off my feet. With our bodies pressed flush together, he swept his tongue out and caught mine. The air stuttered from my lungs. He did it again, thrusting his tongue fully inside my mouth. At the thrill it gave me, I gripped the hair at his nape and moaned.

He went wild at the sound.

His tongue tangled with mine, stroking and exploring at a frantic pace. I whimpered as heat shot to my core, drenching my panties within seconds. He turned and lowered me to his bed. When he settled on top of me, pressing me into the mattress, I fully surrendered to the moment.

Wrapping my legs around his waist, I kissed him with abandon, letting myself drown in sensation. His hands started to explore and I moaned again, reveling in his touch. They slid down my hips to grip my butt, pressing me against his hard erection. I trembled with excitement and drew him even closer with my legs.

He paused to release a harsh breath, then kissed me again. And again. As if he couldn't get enough. When I rolled my hips upward—another invitation—he tore his mouth from mine to quietly curse. I took the opportunity to yank his shirt over my head, leaving me in nothing but my bra and panties.

"Nora," he groaned, dropping his gaze to my chest. I threw my head back and thrust my chest upward. All the invitation he needed. His mouth fell to my breasts, greedily kissing and sucking at the exposed skin. I trembled harder as need whipped through me.

"Take me," I panted and fisted his hair. "I'm ready."

His cock swelled so big that I lost the ability to breathe.

"Nora," he said again, lifting his head from my breasts.

"No." I shook my head. "I'm ready for this. Take me now."

His hands on my waist stilled.

"Nora," he said for the third time, making me tense. Then, "You don't owe me anything."

My eyes snapped open. Still burning with need, it took me a moment to process his words. When I did, heat scorched my face. "I know that," I replied defensively, my voice sharper than I intended. "But I also know that you want this to happen. This is your chance. Take it. I'm giving myself to you."

He cursed again, digging his fingers into my waist. "You don't know what you're saying."

Frustration filled me. This wasn't going at *all* how I'd planned. "Yes, I do. We haven't consummated our marriage yet, so seduce me. I know you've been trying to, and now I'm ready for it."

He frowned. "Seduce you? Is that what you think I've been doing? Trying to get you in my bed?"

"Well, I'm here, aren't I?"

His expression suddenly hardened. "Have you ever stopped to consider that I might actually desire you, Nora? And not just your body, but *all* of you?"

My breath caught. This was going in a direction I had *not* intended. "Do you?"

"*Yes*, Nora, I desire you. I desire you *greatly*," he boldly confessed, his voice almost angry now. "If our deal ceased to exist, I would still desire you. And that's the problem."

It was my turn to frown. "What do you mean?"

"The problem, sweetness, is that I chose the wrong person to marry. I thought your tenacity was what drew me to pick you, but I was wrong."

When he started to lift off me, panic set in. "What are you saying, Kolton?" He didn't respond, removing my legs from his waist. I shot up in bed, trying not to shout as I said, "You can't just say that and leave. Why are you doing this?"

"Nora," he said, but I ignored the warning in his voice.

"Tell me!"

"Because I've grown *attached* to you," he roared, shocking me into silence. "This was supposed to be a business arrangement, nothing more. But you got under my skin. I tried to resist you, but now you're all I can think about. And the thought of us having sex, simply because you feel *obligated* to, sickens me. I can't. We can't do this, Nora."

When he reached out and grabbed my arm, I didn't react right away. But when he muttered a word under his breath that sounded a lot like "release," alarm flared through me.

"Wait. Kolton, what are you doing?" I gasped as a current of electricity jolted through me. Glancing down, I watched in horror as the snake tattoo began to shift. To *move*. It slithered off my skin and onto Kolton's. I tried to jerk my arm away but Kolton held fast. "Wait. *Please!*"

Seconds later, my skin was back to normal, as if the tattoo had never been there.

"I'm sorry," Kolton roughly said and let go of my arm.

With one final look at my unmarked skin, he turned and left the room.

# CHAPTER 21

"I don't care, Kolton. She's extremely vulnerable right now. You can't just leave her like this. You know what could happen."

From Kolton's study, Vi's voice had risen, confirming all too clearly what I'd feared. Kolton was gone. Judging by the sound of the one-sided conversation, Vi was on the phone with him. Before I could flee up the stairs again, the front door opened.

Jagger and Griff walked in, both wearing nothing but sweatpants. When they spotted me at the base of the stairs, they froze. At the looks on their faces, I grew all sorts of uncomfortable. Sure, they were half naked and sweaty as if they'd gone for a morning run, but their exposed skin wasn't the issue here. It was the way they were sizing me up, like they'd never seen me before.

"Um . . . hey?" I began, awkwardly shifting on my feet.

In reply, Jagger audibly inhaled, scenting the air. He glanced at Griff and muttered, "Yup. Definitely still a virgin."

My jaw dropped.

Griff groaned and shoved a hand through his spiky hair. "That fool bastard. What was he thinking?"

Embarrassed beyond belief, I sputtered, "Are you guys seriously *sniffing* me right now?"

The study door swung open and Vi emerged. Shooting death glares at Griff and Jagger, she barked, "Stop harassing Nora, you jerks. None of this is her fault."

"We know, Vi," Griff said, holding up his hands in surrender. He sheepishly glanced at me again. "Sorry, gorgeous. We're still in shock, is all."

I stared at them—at their *knowing* looks—and realized with growing horror what this meant. "Did you all . . . hear us last night?"

"Well, you weren't exactly quiet."

"Shut up, Griffin," Vi snapped, then threw me an apologetic look. "Yes, we heard. I'm sorry my brother left you in this position, Nora."

At the double confirmation, my chest started to ache. Blinking away the sudden moisture in my eyes, I nodded and said, "Guess I should pack my things then."

I jumped as a flurry of raised voices greeted my words.

"Hell, no. You're not going *anywhere*, gorgeous. Not like this."

"Pack your things?" Vi cried, looking stricken with panic. "Why would you do that?"

Jagger simply toed the front door shut and crossed his arms over his chest.

Startled, I replied, "You all heard Kolton last night. 'I chose the wrong person to marry,' he said. Since we haven't consummated the marriage, I assume he left to annul it."

Varying degrees of pity filled their eyes. Even Jagger's expression briefly softened. The sight made me want to burst into tears.

"Oh, Nora," Vi said, hurrying toward me. When she threw her arms around me, I almost lost it. "He didn't leave to annul the marriage. He might be a dickhead at times, but he's a man of honor. No matter what disagreements you two have, he would never go back on his word."

Try as I might, I couldn't stop a tear from falling. My knees weakened with relief, but Vi lended me her strength. Despite the way Kolton and I had ended things last night, I wasn't ready for this to be over. Something was brewing between us. Something intense. Something *terrifying*. I knew Kolton felt it too, even if he didn't want to.

Sniffing back more tears, I said, "Then why did he leave? And why did he remove the tattoo?"

Griff swore under his breath.

Vi pulled back to look me in the eye. "He needed space from you. I know that's not what you want to hear, but this is difficult for him."

"What is?"

"Being married to you. I know why he did it and respect his decision, but he's never allowed himself to get close to a female before. Not like this. Not when there are emotions involved. He has feelings for you and that terrifies him."

I frowned, trying to understand. "I'm terrified too. I mean, I pretty much gave up everything to marry a stranger." But I hadn't run away. Instead, *he* had. How was that for irony?

Vi sighed, a look of frustration crossing her face. "I'm going to kill him when he gets back. I don't care *how* scared he is. An alpha can't leave his virgin bride alone with unmated males."

Griff barked a laugh. "He knows she's safe here with us. If Jag and I even *look* at her wrong, he'll rip off our dicks."

Vi rolled her eyes. "Great visual. Thanks, Griff."

"No problem."

"Do I even want to know what that means?" I asked Vi.

"So innocent," Griff groaned, scrubbing both hands down his face. "I need to take a really cold shower."

Vi threw him an annoyed look over her shoulder. "Don't forget who Nora is before you start jerking off, pal."

What the hell?

Mortified, I nearly swallowed my tongue. Griff simply laughed and made for the opposite stairwell. Jagger stayed by the front door like a silent sentinel. I had no idea what he thought about this crazy conversation.

When we heard Griff close his bedroom door, Vi turned back to me and said, "So, you know how males get aggressive when a female goes into heat? Well, they also get this way around an unmated female favored by the pack alpha. The fact that you're married to the most powerful alpha in America and still a *virgin* makes you even more desirable. The only thing the males will think about is claiming you for themselves. It's pretty much their ultimate wet dream."

My face heated at her bold choice of words. "But wouldn't Kolton be mad if they touched me?"

"Oh, he would be more than mad," Vi said. "He would outright kill them."

Holy crap, this wasn't good.

"What should I do?"

"Lock yourself in your room and throw away the key," Jagger finally spoke up.

All the blood drained from my face.

"Not helping, Jag," Vi snapped. Sighing, she more gently said, "There's not much you can do until Kolton comes to his senses. But, if you want to go anywhere, make sure one of us goes with you to play referee. Because males *will* approach you. They won't be able to help it."

Great. Just great.

There went my freedom again.

Seeing my distress, Vi's expression softened. "Hey, this doesn't mean you're a prisoner here. In fact, with the tattoo removed, you can go out whenever you want."

"Vi," Jagger cautioned, narrowing his eyes on the back of her head.

She waved her hand dismissively. "Zip it. You might be Kolton's second in command, but he specifically asked *me* to take care of Nora. And making her stay in this house all the time isn't healthy."

"Yeah, but we don't want the pack to get suspicious—"

"Screw their suspicions and gossip. They've already spread so many rumors about her that it'll take *weeks* before everything gets sorted out. I'm sure Kolton will be back by then."

Weeks? I swallowed, suddenly realizing that Kolton might be gone longer than I'd thought. What was I supposed to do until then? I didn't even know what the duties of an alpha's wife were. Alpha Hendrix had never married, so I'd never actually been around an alpha female. My mom was an omega and had always taught me to be one too. I'd sucked at it though. And maybe for good reason.

I wasn't an omega.

But was I really an alpha female like Kolton had suggested? I didn't feel like one. I just felt . . . lost. Like I didn't even know who I was. Right now, I was technically packless. I might be married to a pack alpha, but that didn't mean his pack acknowledged me as their alpha female.

They were going to test me, I knew that much. It was the only way that wolves could establish pack hierarchy. They wouldn't respect or follow an unfit leader.

Why had I thought this marriage would be easy? Why had I made this deal just to free my wolf? A wolf that didn't seem to care about me or even *like* me?

She should have named herself *Ghost*. That's what she was. Barely even there.

Vi pulled me from my troubled thoughts, saying, "You know what? We should go on a run, just you and me."

I blinked. "A run?"

"Yeah. Your wolf and mine. I haven't seen yours yet, but Kolton said she's beautiful."

Several emotions slammed into me at once. Happiness that Kolton felt that way about my wolf. Excitement at the thought of shifting with Vi. Nervousness that my wolf wouldn't play nice with hers. But also sadness, the strongest emotion of all. Because, not only did I feel rejected by my hometown pack, but by Kolton and Storm as well.

They were both avoiding me for reasons I couldn't quite understand. And the rejection hurt. It hurt something fierce.

I thought I was used to rejection by now, but I was wrong. Being ignored by my wolf hurt worse than any mistreatment I'd ever endured. And being ignored by my husband—the man I was starting to rely on and care about—was a new kind of pain. One I'd never felt before. It robbed me of breath and left me feeling untethered. It pierced the very heart of me, making me wonder if I cared about him more than I knew.

So, instead of saying yes to Vi's request, I turned her down. I doubted my wolf was interested in a run anyway. Even if she was, I was still too upset, too *hurt* to let her have control.

She'd abandoned me when I'd needed her most. And now, so had Kolton.

I should have known better than to expect anything different. Relying on others was dangerous. It only ever hurt me.

Three weeks came and went.

Three weeks of living hell.

After the first week, I knew something was seriously wrong with me. I couldn't sleep. I could barely eat. And there was this hole. Right in the center of my chest. Gnawing at my insides, expanding in size with each and every passing day.

At first, I thought something had happened to my wolf. Maybe she was sick or even dying. But, after several hours of poking and prodding her, she finally admitted that something was wrong with *me*. Then promptly rolled over and fell silent.

Despite the stress my body was under, I'd spent the time slaving away in the estate gardens. Sunrise to sunset, I'd tend to the grounds without fail. So religiously that the groundskeeper had made a joke about me putting him out of a job. I couldn't seem to stop though. I'd become stuck in a purgatory of sorts. Always moving but going nowhere.

The story of my life, it would seem.

Another full moon came and went. From my bedroom window, I could hear the faint howl of wolves. Knew that members of Midnight Pack were on the prowl in the vast forest. For the first time ever, I hadn't felt the need to hide from them. A huge part of me yearned to *join* them. To shift and hunt and chase. To give in to my predatory instincts. To act like a normal werewolf for once.

But, for many reasons, I couldn't.

For one, I wasn't a normal werewolf. I also wasn't officially a member of the pack yet. Not to mention that I was still a virgin, and Kolton hadn't returned.

I knew he was safe though. Knew that Vi, Griff, Jagger, and even Melanie kept in touch with him. Although they were tight-lipped about where he was, as if he'd ordered them not to tell me, I could hear their whispered conversations. Knew they often spoke about me. About my latest . . . condition.

I hadn't left my bedroom in three days.

One minute, I'd been go-go-go, and the next, utterly burnt out. If I wasn't so downright miserable, I'd call myself weak and pathetic. Falling this deeply into a funk wasn't like me. No matter how bad things had gotten over the years, I'd always pulled through.

Something was different this time though.

The burnout went beyond exhaustion. Or sadness or even depression. It almost felt like a vital piece of myself had gone missing. Legit *missing*. And I couldn't function without it.

The bedroom door suddenly burst open. From my spot curled up on the bed, I didn't even flinch. Blinking slowly, I watched as Vi and Griff filed into the room.

"Okay, gorgeous, time to get up," Griff said, striding toward me. Before I could protest, he dragged me off the bed and into his arms.

"Griff," I complained, weakly pushing at his chest. "Put me down."

"Oh, I will. As soon as you agree to take a shower." He rounded the bed and headed straight for the bathroom.

"I don't want to."

"Well, you *need* to. For one, you stink. For—"

"Griff!" Vi barked as he carried me into the bathroom. "Just drop her off and get out of there like we planned. No commentary needed."

With a sigh, Griff walked right into the shower and set me down. When my legs wobbled, he looped an arm around me for support. "You're not making this easy, Nora. Kolton would flay me alive if he saw me in here with you."

"Sorry," I muttered, my heart weirdly fluttering at the sound of Kolton's name.

Griff only sighed again and gave me a comforting squeeze.

"Okay, *out* before I flay you myself," Vi said, barging into the shower with us. Griff let go of me and Vi took his place, shooing him away. When he lingered by the door, she snapped, "Out!"

As soon as he shut the door, Vi started removing my pajamas. I let her, knowing that resistance was futile. The girl was all alpha female and I didn't have the energy to stand up to her right now. When the last stitch of clothing was removed, she cranked on the shower.

I yelped as cold water hit me. Before I could jump out of the shower, she closed the glass door in my face.

"Get cleaned up, Nora," she said, her tone brooking no argument. "I'm not moving from this spot until you do."

I bared my teeth at her, only to receive a smirk in return. "Dictator."

"Why, thank you," she simpered, giving me a small curtsy. "Now wash yourself."

I stuck my tongue out at her but did as instructed, stepping under the now warm spray. For the first time in days, I cleaned my hair, struggling to hold my arms up as I thoroughly scrubbed the gnarled mass. Despite how weak and lethargic I was, it felt good to remove the layer of grime from my skin. I cleaned my body next, grimacing at how noticeable my ribs and hipbones were. I could only imagine how gaunt my face looked.

When I was cleaned to the best of my ability, Vi handed me a towel. As I wrapped it around me, she stepped aside and allowed me to exit. Only to shove clothing into my arms a second later.

"Vi," I protested, noting that they weren't pajamas. "It's late. I'm going back to bed after this."

"To hell you are," she said, stubbornly propping her hands on her hips. "I know the past month has been rough, but I've allowed this to continue for far too long. It ends now. We're going out."

I stiffened. "Out where?"

She shrugged. "Somewhere you can get your mind off things."

I gave her a droll look. "You can just say it, you know."

"Fine. *Kolton*. Somewhere you can get your mind off my annoying dickhead brother."

I snorted and dropped the towel. I still wasn't used to casual nudity, but at least Vi didn't make it weird. "Does he know you're taking me out?" I hedged, dreading and anticipating the answer.

"Nope. Not yet anyway."

At her cryptic reply, I narrowed my eyes suspiciously.

She waved off my look. "Don't worry. Griff and Jagger are going with us. They'll make sure any pack males keep their distance."

Still suspicious, I warily eyed her as I pulled on a white tank top and ripped jean shorts. They fit looser than they had a couple weeks ago. When I tried to exit the bathroom, she tsked in disapproval and pulled out the counter stool.

"No halfway attempt, sister. If you won't take care of yourself, then I'll do it for you."

Huffing, I plopped onto the stool and let her do my hair and makeup. Despite my outward protests, I secretly enjoyed it when she mothered me. It felt weird, albeit a nice weird. When I'd started to lose my appetite, I could barely walk two steps without her shoving food in my face. Her persistence hadn't paid off most of the time, but I appreciated the effort all the same.

The only other person who'd ever shown a genuine interest in my physical and mental health was Brielle, but she'd been extra busy lately with her new job. I hadn't even been able to tell her that I was married now. Or that my new husband was actively avoiding me. Or that my wolf had finally emerged. Or that my pack had cast me out.

Or that I felt emptier than I'd ever felt before.

A big part of me knew that I needed to snap out of whatever

this was. It wasn't healthy, for one. Obsessing over things I couldn't control only caused stress and heartache.

So, I allowed Vi to doll me up without further protest. If she wanted to take me out, then I would go without a fuss. Maybe a change of scenery was exactly what I needed to find my old self again.

Besides, what's the worst that could happen?

# CHAPTER 22

"Really, Vi? A *bar?*"

From her spot in the driver's seat, Vi answered Jagger with a firm, "Just trust me, okay? I know what I'm doing."

He settled against the backseat with a long-suffering sigh. "You'd better, or I'm the one who's going to pay for it."

"Chill, dude," Vi said, pulling into a parking spot. "We're here to have some innocent fun. No harm in that."

"Yeah, but Kolton—"

"Has already been informed of our whereabouts."

Jagger shot forward again, gripping the back of my seat. "What did he say?"

"Dunno," Vi sang, killing the engine. "I turned off my phone."

"*Violet,*" Jagger and Griff barked at the same time, but she'd already hopped out of the Jeep.

Rounding the front, she pulled open my door. When I hesitated, her free hand shot to her hip. "Don't make me carry you inside. I totally will."

Despite myself, I snorted at the mental image. "Are you sure this is a good idea?"

"No," she replied, leaning across me to unlatch my seatbelt. "It's a *great* idea. One I should have thought of weeks ago."

"Remember what happened the *last* time you meddled in Kolton's personal business?" Jagger persisted, slamming his door shut before joining us.

Vi deliberately flicked her ponytail in his face. "That was completely different. I was trying to *stop* him from seeing someone then."

I bristled all over, pretty certain I knew who she was talking about.

Jasmine.

"Well, I'm sure he won't be happy either way," Jagger replied, yet fell in line behind us as Vi grabbed my hand and beelined for the bar entrance.

"Too bad," she shot back over her shoulder. "This is his fault anyway."

"Yeah, but—"

"Oh, look!" she interrupted, pointing at a sign in the front window. "It's live music night."

I peered over my shoulder at Griff and Jagger, giving them a helpless look.

Griff offered me a small smile, but even *he* seemed on edge. "Don't worry, Nora. Just don't talk to any males in there. Or make eye contact with them. Or go anywhere near them. Or—"

"Great. Thanks," I said with an eye roll and turned back around. "But what if there are pack members inside?"

"Oh, I'm counting on it," Vi spoke again with a telltale smirk, reaching for the door handle.

"We're going to have words after this, Vi," Jagger lightly growled, but she swung the door open and music blasted our eardrums.

"What was that?" Vi mock-yelled. "Hey, I love this song!" She strode inside the building, leaving me with no choice but to follow.

Belatedly realizing that it was a Saturday night, I saw how packed the joint was. The city might be small, but it was smack in the middle of tourist season. Thankfully, I couldn't sense any werewolves yet. The crowd was predominantly human.

The first thing I noticed upon entering was their immediate reaction to our presence. It was purely instinct for humans to give the predators in their midst a wide berth, even if they didn't know it.

Up until now though, they'd never seen *me* as a predator. At first, I thought they were reacting solely to Vi, Griff, and Jagger. Wanting to know for certain, I slipped my hand free of Vi's grasp and put some space between us. The second I was on my own, the humans surrounding me noticeably leaned away.

I bit my lip, fighting back a smile.

Anyone else would feel insulted, but I'd been waiting my whole life for this moment. Humans no longer saw me as a normal, nonthreatening girl. They sensed something different about me. Something *dangerous*. For the first time ever, I was actually *happy* to be seen as different.

"Over there," Griff said from behind me, placing a hand on the small of my back to steer me toward the bar. Vi was already there, ordering . . .

I shook my head and placed my hands up. "No way. I don't do shots."

At my words, Vi whirled around. "Why not?"

"I'm a serious lightweight. Alcohol goes straight to my head."

"Oh, girl, that was *before*. You haven't tried it since *you know*," she said with a wink.

True. And maybe I didn't mind getting a little buzzed right now anyway. That would *definitely* help take my mind off things.

So when she handed me a glass, I accepted, raising it as she loudly toasted, "To fun and friends!"

"To fun and friends," we chorused back, clinking our glasses together. Vi and Griff tossed their drinks back, but I watched as Jagger lowered his untouched to the counter.

"Someone needs to keep a sharp mind," he explained and scowled at Griff.

"I've got a stomach of steel, my man," Griff replied with a laugh, nudging me when I hesitated.

"Screw this," I muttered and tossed the drink back.

Vi and Griff whooped in encouragement. I grimaced as the liquid burned down my throat, instantly warming my insides.

"Another!" Vi hollered, slamming her empty glass on the counter.

In no time, we'd each downed several shots. Except for Jagger. Despite my high metabolism, a heady buzz had taken over my senses. Probably because the only thing currently in my stomach was alcohol. I didn't mind though. The stress of the past few weeks had melted away, along with my constant plaguing thoughts. I could only focus on the here and now, not on the plethora of regrets I had.

When it became clear I was slipping into drunken territory, Jagger pulled us from the bar for a round of billiards. The corner of the building was darker and quieter. Even though I sucked at the game, I enjoyed listening to Vi and Griff's easy banter. The two were clearly into each other, despite their frequent spats. They just needed a little nudge.

"You two should totally be a couple," I piped up. They both stopped talking to give me surprised looks. I pointed my stick at them, adding, "Like all the time. Not just when Vi is in heat."

Griff's mouth fell open. He shot Vi an accusatory look. "You told her?"

Jagger groaned and scrubbed a hand down his face. "Now you've done it."

I blinked at him, confused. "What?"

"I had to," Vi responded to Griff defensively. "She was worried about Jasmine, so I explained the situation."

"By using *us* as an example?" Griff shot back incredulously. "Not cool, Vi. *Not* cool."

Her lips thinned. "I'm sorry, okay? I didn't think you'd mind."

Snorting, he dropped his stick on the pool table. "Then you don't know me very well, Violet."

When he turned and walked away, she blew out a sigh and watched him go.

I blinked again, suddenly realizing what I'd done. "I'm so sorry, Vi. I don't know why I said that. I really shouldn't have had that last shot. Alcohol makes me blabber like an idiot."

She shook her head. "You're fine, Nora. We should probably get you home though. It's past midnight."

Already? Wow. I'd managed to go *hours* without thinking about Kolton.

The second I had the thought, something pulsed inside me. Something sharp. And *hot*.

"Whoa," Jagger said, swaying forward to lean a hand against the billiard table. He took a moment to audibly inhale, then muttered, "That better not be what I think it is."

Vi's brow pinched. When she paused to sniff the air, her eyebrows jumped skyhigh. Cursing, she shot me an intense look. "Nora, is that you?"

Uh . . .

The pulse kicked inside of me again, nearly knocking the breath from my lungs.

"Oh, it's her," Jagger groaned and pushed away from the table. He made it two steps before the pool stick in his hands snapped in two.

"What's going on?" I said, noting how breathless I sounded.

Another pulse rocketed through me and I leaned heavily on my stick as my legs weakened.

Vi tossed her stick on the table and hurried toward me. "You're in *heat*," she hissed, grabbing my arm. "We need to get you out of here. *Now*."

Ah *hell*.

We only made it a few steps before the worst possible thing happened. A group of guys entered the bar. *Werewolves*. And I recognized the brown-haired one in the lead.

Rodney.

Vi swore and backpedaled, but it was too late. They spotted us and moved en masse in our direction. Unable to skirt around them, we desperately searched for another way out. "There's a rear exit," Vi said, whirling us around. "Come on."

"Hey, Vi. Wait up," Rodney called after us, but we ignored him.

We'd reached the billiard tables again, our focus set on a door just beyond, when a heatwave blasted through me. I stumbled, biting my tongue as a powerful mix of pain and arousal assaulted me.

"Crap, it's getting worse," I groaned, barely able to stand upright.

Swearing again, Vi shoved me toward the door and whirled to face Rodney and his friends. I caught myself against the wall as she said, "We're in a hurry, boys. So if you could back off, that would be great."

"Wow, no need to get testy, Vi. We just wanted to say hi," Rodney said, shuffling closer. Before I could fumble for the doorknob, he stopped dead in his tracks and sucked in a sharp breath. "Wait. Which one of you is in heat?"

I peeked over my shoulder, right as his gaze narrowed on me. Then widened as realization dawned.

Crap. *Crap*.

"Hey, guys," Jagger suddenly said, appearing out of nowhere to stand between us and them.

Griff joined him, his movements stiff as he slung an arm over Rodney's shoulders. "Looks like you could use a drink, man. Let me buy you one."

Rodney shrugged Griff's arm off. "She's still unmated," was all he said, but it was enough to make four more pairs of eyes focus on me.

"That's none of your concern," Jagger started, a clear warning in his voice. "I suggest you leave now. *All* of you."

Instead of listening to Jagger's order, Rodney straightened and puffed out his chest. "We're all pack members here. I say it *is* our concern. We want to know why the alpha's wife is still a virgin."

The other four guys murmured their agreement, shifting into more dominant stances.

Oh, this was bad. *Really* bad.

"Rodney, get out of here before I make you," Vi spoke up, grabbing her pool stick off the table and taking a menacing step toward him.

He stared at her for a moment, then slowly looked back at me with a feral gleam in his eyes. "I don't sense Kolton here. Which means that he's left his unmated wife to handle her heat alone. And I say that makes her fair game."

Everyone stilled at his words. No one even breathed.

Then Jagger quietly said, "Nora, run," and launched himself at Rodney. Horrified, I watched as the two collided in a tangle of limbs. With a roar, Vi charged next. Then Griff. Soon, the entire group was fighting like, well, a pack of wolves.

I only hesitated a moment, guilt freezing me in place.

Then I scrambled for the door.

They were fighting because of *me*, and the only way to make them stop was to run away. As fast as I could. When I wrenched the door open and Rodney howled his fury, I bolted outside. Clambering down a handful of rickety stairs, I hit the alley at a dead run. Only to double over in pain a few steps later.

The heat raged through my insides, nearly bringing me to my knees. I managed to stumble forward several yards, almost to the treeline behind the building, when my legs gave out. I crashed to the ground, falling to my hands and knees.

"Holy hell," I panted, shaking uncontrollably as a powerful need ripped through me. "This isn't happening. This isn't *happening*."

*Get up*, I inwardly screamed, but my body wouldn't obey. *You're still too close!*

Unable to stand, I resorted to crawling, wincing as each movement made the pleasure-pain worse.

*You're in heat*, a voice said in my head.

A crazed laugh burst from me. "No kidding. Anything else I don't already know?" I snarkily shot back at my wolf. She hadn't spoken to me in *weeks*, so I was more than a little peeved with her.

*You should let your mate help you.*

Startled, I froze. Then spluttered, "Just because he's my husband doesn't make him my mate. Besides, he's not here right now. I don't even *know* where he is."

No response.

Growling in frustration, I resumed my slow trek toward the woods. Seconds later, the bar's back door burst open. Expecting to see one of my friends, all the blood drained from my face when I spotted Rodney charging down the stairs. Even from here, I could see that wild gleam still in his eyes as he stalked toward me.

My body responded to it, but not in a way that I wanted. Heat engulfed me, making it impossible to run away. Biting back a groan, I pushed to my feet, just as he reached me.

"Rodney," I started, raising my hands to ward him off. "Don't do this."

He knocked my hands aside and slammed me up against the nearest tree. When his body pinned me in place, I gasped and struggled to shove him away.

"Claiming you is going to taste so sweet," he growled, grabbing my hair. When his grip painfully tightened, I stopped struggling. "Good. Now take me nicely and I'll make sure you enjoy this too."

As he reached between us to unzip his pants, fear rushed through me. Reacting on instinct, I dug my nails into his chest. Seconds later, my claws shot out, hooking into his flesh. With a pained roar, he grabbed my wrists and yanked. My claws ripped out chunks of his flesh. As blood gushed from the wounds, he roared again and shoved me. So hard that I stumbled and fell.

"You want to play dirty?" he bit out, towering over me. "Fine. Let's play dirty."

Before he could grab me again, a voice down the alley thundered, "Touch my wife and I'll tear your arms off, *beta*."

Rodney froze. So did I.

I knew that voice well. It had haunted my thoughts and dreams for weeks, never giving me a moment's rest. Hearing that voice now, angrier than I'd ever heard it before, I shivered. Not with fear, but with excitement. My instincts went haywire, flooding me with even more heat.

Above me, Rodney audibly inhaled, clearly scenting my increased arousal. With a growl, he turned and faced Kolton. "You've failed to claim her, Alpha," he bellowed back. "Now it's my turn."

From several yards away, I watched with a mixture of dread and anticipation as Kolton's eyes flashed a dangerous yellow. "Over my dead body."

At the quietly spoken words, Rodney hesitated, as if realizing how precarious his situation was. But only for a moment. We were suddenly joined by several others. Vi, Griff, Jagger, and Rodney's four cohorts filed into the alley. They were all bruised and bloodied, but nothing a little time wouldn't heal.

Spotting them, Rodney's confidence grew. Puffing out his chest, he took a step toward Kolton and shouted, "Then I challenge you. I challenge you for alpha."

Shock filtered through the group. No one moved or spoke, waiting to see how Kolton would react to the challenge.

They didn't have to wait long.

"Can't say I'm surprised. You've been sniffing at my door for months," Kolton said, slowly removing his shirt. Then, "Challenge accepted."

Holy hell.

Rodney yanked his shirt off as well, exposing the damage I'd just inflicted. Satisfaction filled me, along with another wave of heat. Despite how far away he was, Kolton went rigid, as if he could smell my heat.

"Vi, get Nora out of here," he said, never once taking his eyes off Rodney.

When Vi moved toward me, Rodney bared his teeth and snarled. Kolton answered it with a growl of his own, the deep sound raising the hair on my arms. I pushed away from Rodney and he didn't try to stop me, too intent on challenging Kolton. As Vi reached my side, I let her pull me upright. But when she attempted to lead me away, I resisted.

"You shouldn't be here for this," she frantically whispered, tugging on my arm. "If Kolton loses, we can't stop Rodney from claiming you. We need to get far away from here."

I shook my head. "I can't. I have to watch what happens." I *needed* to. Every molecule in my body screamed at me to stay. Even my wolf seemed to want me here.

"You'll only distract him," Vi persisted, laying the guilt trip on thick.

I grimaced but held my ground. "Sorry, but I'm not leaving. And if Rodney tries to claim me again, I'll use my claws on more than just his chest."

Despite her panic, Vi snorted. "I'd *definitely* like to see that."

When Rodney and Kolton moved toward each other, Vi dropped my arm. Instead of forcing me to leave, she let me lean on her for support.

"You know the rules?" Kolton said, stopping several feet away from Rodney to square off with him.

"Fight to the death," Rodney replied. "Winner takes all." He threw a leering smirk over his shoulder at me.

"Incorrect," Kolton rebutted, watching him sharply. "As my wife, Nora is next in line for alpha. Pack rules."

At the reminder, all the air left me in a rush.

"But she's not a member of the pack yet," Rodney said, turning back to him.

"Doesn't matter. She still has dibs on my position and everything it entails. Pack initiation will only be a formality."

Rodney's hands formed tight fists. "Fine. Challenging her won't be a problem anyway. With her in heat, she'll *want* me to dominate her. But I won't spare her. I'll take her hard and fast, making sure to come inside her several times before killing her. Maybe I'll call in more pack members to watch as I do it. Too bad you won't be alive for the show."

Without thinking, I lunged. My target: Rodney's throat. Vi

wrapped both arms around me and dug in her heels. I thrashed against her grip, screaming at Rodney, "Touch me again and I'll *kill* you!"

Kolton finally looked at me. *Really* looked at me. He took in my fury. Took in my fear and desperate need for vengeance. And his own anger fizzled out. The yellow in his eyes faded, and he quietly said, "He won't get that chance, sweetness."

Then he charged at Rodney.

# CHAPTER 23

Blood sprayed. Growls and grunts filled the air.

The fight was brutal. All carnal violence and no mercy.

They grappled for several minutes, each landing several blows. Their chests glistened with blood and sweat.

At one point, I feared that Rodney would best Kolton. He had Kolton in a tight headlock, one that looked impossible to break free from. And then, lightning quick, Kolton flipped Rodney over his shoulder. He landed on the ground with a hard thud.

Before he could recover, Kolton's knee came down on his sternum. Rodney's pained cry was cut short as Kolton grabbed him by the throat. "Beg for mercy," Kolton quietly growled in Rodney's face, causing me to shiver again.

"Never," Rodney spat, fruitlessly struggling to break free. "You're weak. You won't claim Jasmine or any other female in the pack. You won't even claim your own wife. You're not an alpha; you're a *mouse.* And if you spare me like the coward you are, I'll claim every single unmated female in this pack, including your—"

A sickening *crack* rent the air.

For the second time, I watched Kolton kill someone. Swiftly. Efficiently. Just like that, Rodney's eyes glazed over in death.

Oh, but Kolton wasn't finished. With a furious roar, he ripped Rodney's head clean off his body.

I was suddenly moving. Not toward Kolton, but away. Staggering into the woods. Desperate to put space between us. Lots and lots of it.

No one stopped me. Not even Vi. I would have put up a fight if they'd tried.

Fresh heat blasted through me, but it felt different this time. Sharper. All pain and no pleasure.

Storm was trying to emerge.

Wanting to disappear, I let her. After weeks of repression, she forced the change quickly. So quickly that I'd barely fallen to the ground before my bones began to shift and break. I didn't even have time to scream. Within seconds, she'd taken control, shaking out her fur as she adjusted. Then she bolted, taking off into the woods at breakneck speed.

For miles, we both stayed silent, our focus purely on running. It felt good. I hadn't tried to run away in so long, and I had missed it. Missed the thrill of leaving my troubles behind and forging my own path.

*He will come for you*, Storm said, finally breaking the silence.

*I know*, was my only response.

*But you don't want him to?*

I hesitated, a bit weirded out that I was having a heart-to-heart with my wolf—or celestial being familiar. It was so confusing. Sighing, I replied, *I don't know.*

A pause. Then, *He defended your honor today.*

*I know.*

*You should let him hunt and catch you. You are his to claim.*

At her words, my mind blanked. *Excuse me?*

*You are his mate. Show him your interest and he won't be able to resist you.*

*Okay, whoa there*, I loudly said to her. *I might have animal instincts, but I have human ones too. I'm not going to seduce him just because I'm in heat.*

*Why not? You were planning on having sexual intercourse with him right before he left, were you not?*

*Okay, la-la-la. This conversation needs to end. Besides, I thought you hated him.*

A pause. Then, *I don't hate him. Only the spirit that resides in his wolf.*

*But why? What did he ever do to you?*

*Oh, child, I will not burden you with these matters. You have enough on your plate.*

*Yeah, but—*

She abruptly slammed to a halt. Breathing lightly despite the ground she'd covered, she listened for a moment before whispering, *He comes.*

Already? But I wasn't ready. I hadn't been able to process all that had just happened. And I was still in *heat.* Just knowing that he was near made my body warm in all the wrong places.

Storm's hackles suddenly rose. A deep growl rumbled in her chest as she barked, *It's him.*

Alarmed, I quickly asked, *Who?*

*His wolf. Shadow.* She spat his name like a curse. *If I see him, I will attack.*

*No, Storm. Please don't do that.*

*I can't help it. It's my calling.*

*Calling? Look, we need to figure this thing out. I can't have you attacking every wolf you see.*

*Not every wolf. Just the bad ones.*

Shocked, I sputtered, *Are you saying Kolton's wolf is bad?*

*Yes. The absolute worst. I'm surprised he hasn't corrupted his host yet. If he does, I'll have no choice but to kill your mate.*

*WHAT?* I shrieked.

*Silence*, she whispered, flicking her ears back and forth. *I hear his approach.* After a moment more, the hackles on her back slowly flattened. *All is safe.*

Still bursting with questions, I was just about to press her for more answers when a tall figure stepped out from behind a tree.

Kolton.

Despite the darkness, I could clearly see him. At the sight of his stark naked form, heat flushed my insides. Blood still smeared his chest and torso, but I could tell the wounds were already healing.

Storm softly whined. *You want him.*

*What? No, I don't*, I was too quick to say. *I can't control how my body reacts when I'm in heat, is all.*

She didn't respond.

Still several yards away, Kolton crouched to my wolf's level. They silently watched each other for a long moment before he said to her, "Give Nora control, Storm. She needs my help."

*No, Storm. Don't give me control*, I commanded her. At the frantic tone of my voice, she cocked her head to the side.

Kolton waited for a beat. Then, "I know you're trying to protect her. She was attacked, and you have no idea how sorry I am for that. But she's safe with me. No harm will come to her."

*No, no, no. Don't listen to him, Storm. I won't be safe!*

She was silent a moment more. Then, *He would never hurt you, Nora. You are his mate.*

*Would you stop saying that?* I yelled at her. *I'm not his mate. He made it very clear that he doesn't want one. So clear that he left me. And—Hey, don't you dare shift back!*

But it was too late. There was nothing I could do as the transformation gripped me, forcing me back into human form.

When it was finished, I lay panting and trembling on the forest floor. Unlike my last shift though, I didn't feel pieced back together by tape. The pain was minimal . . . until warm fingers touched my shoulder.

Heat blasted through me and I yelped, scrambling to get away. A tree blocked my path and I whirled, facing Kolton with terrified eyes. "Stay where you are."

Without taking his eyes off mine, he slowly raised his hands. "I promise not to touch you. Not until you want me to."

"Well, I *don't* want you to," I viciously said, even as my core throbbed with need. He was so close. And *naked.* My body could barely handle it. Needing a distraction, I snapped, "You left. For *three weeks.*"

His eyes shuttered, but they stayed fixed on mine. "Yes. I'm sorry."

Not satisfied, I pressed, "Where did you go?"

A pause. Then, "I was visiting someone."

Another wave of heat smacked me, but it was different this time. Before I could stop myself, I demanded, "Who?"

A muscle jumped in Kolton's jaw. "Nora . . ."

"*Who*, Kolton?" I said through clenched teeth. "Was it *her?*"

His brow furrowed. "Her, who?"

"Don't play games with me," I bit out, feeling the heat rise to a boil. "Did you stay with *Jasmine?*"

He blinked several times, then scowled. "No, Nora, it wasn't like that. For the last time, I'm not a womanizer."

I stared at him. Hard. Trying to decide if he was lying or not. After a long moment, I said, "Then why did you leave?"

His gaze finally dropped to the ground in front of him. "I needed a reminder that I can't fall in love with you."

My heart clenched. At a loss for words, I simply said, "Then don't."

He huffed a humorless laugh. "It's not that simple."

"Why not? I'm not asking you to love me. I don't . . . I don't need that from you."

His gaze shot back up to mine. "You came to my room."

Now it was my turn to blink. I suddenly found it hard to breathe. "Because you *wanted* me to," I forced out, struggling to keep still as anger filled me. "Because you said we needed to consummate the marriage. I was just doing my duty."

Ouch. I knew the words were wrong the second I uttered them. I was upset, so I'd cruelly lashed out. Sure enough, hurt flashed in his amber eyes. Before I could apologize, he said, "That's the problem, Nora. I thought time away would dull my attachment to you. I thought distance would help me see you as my responsibility again. But all it did was confirm what I've been trying to ignore. I no longer want our marriage to be purely business."

My breath caught. "What do you mean?"

"I mean," he said, lowering to his knees before me, "that even though I shouldn't, I want more. I want more than your vow to me. I want more than your *obligation*. I want you to want me."

I violently shuddered from head to toe. Swallowing with difficulty, I whispered, "But you don't want love or a mate."

"You're right. I don't," he whispered back, easing into my personal space without touching me. "But I still want you. So badly that it hurts."

My stomach swooped with butterflies. *Drunken* ones. Holy hell, what was happening? What he said didn't make sense, and yet, it did. I completely understood, even if I didn't understand why love was off the table for him. What I did understand was that he no longer viewed me as a mere responsibility. He *wanted* me. *Me*.

When all I did was stare at him like a gaping fish, he continued to whisper. Continued to break down my defenses one damning word after the other. "Let me help you, Nora. Let me take care of you."

The apex of my thighs immediately grew wet. I squeezed my legs together, but it was no use. His nostrils flared as he scented my fresh wave of arousal. A growl rumbled in his chest, but he didn't touch me. Didn't do anything but wait. Wait for me to—

"I shouldn't," I said, the words embarrassingly weak.

His eyes started to glow again. Crap, he knew. He knew how weak my resolve was. "You're right. You shouldn't," he purred, leaning even more into my personal space until all I could smell was him. "Not unless you want me to."

A whimper burst from me. He trembled at the sound, but held perfectly still. I continued to breathe in his scent, a scent overlaid with blood and violence. It should have turned me off. Should have reminded me of the carnage and death I'd just witnessed. But the animal part of me, the primal part currently gaining more and more control, reveled in the smell.

He'd fought for me. Fought and *won*.

According to my instincts, that made him worthy of my body.

The last of my resistance suddenly crumbled to dust.

"I want," I whispered, beginning to shake.

"Want what, Nora? I need to hear the words."

"I want you to take care of me," I cried, suddenly desperate for his touch. "Please, Kolton. Please help me."

A long sigh shuddered from him and he breathed, "Finally."

Then, just like that, I was on my back. Before I could prepare myself, Kolton lowered his head to my breasts and began to kiss. And lick. And suck. And—

When he opened his mouth and bit down on my hardened nipple, pleasure shot through me. I arched my spine and gasped, staring up at the night sky in shock. He didn't give me a moment to adjust, kissing a hot trail to my other breast. As his mouth clamped down over that nipple, my eyes rolled back and I breathlessly moaned.

"God, Nora," he said against my skin, his voice heavy with need. "If you make that sound again, I won't be able to control myself."

Liking the sound of that, the junction between my thighs grew even wetter.

Kolton audibly inhaled and blew out a curse. The feel of his hot breath on my skin sent goosebumps skittering over my flesh. When I whimpered, he reached down and gripped my thighs. As he slowly opened them, I struggled to breathe. So close. I was *so close* to getting what I wanted.

"Please," I begged, unable to wait a moment longer. "I need you."

The words tipped his control over the edge.

Spreading my thighs wide, he settled himself between them and lowered his head again. And I wasn't prepared. I *couldn't* prepare. Not for this.

Already thoroughly aroused and ultra sensitive, my body responded viscerally to his warm tongue on my aching center. At the first sweep, I threw back my head and screamed. Wave after wave of pleasure pounded through me, stealing my breath and sanity. Just like that, I climaxed, coming hard and swift against his mouth. Digging my nails into the leaves and dirt on either side of me, I rode the blissful high, shaking uncontrollably. When I came down, he dove right back in.

"Kolton," I gasped, struggling against his grip on my thighs. "Too much."

He swirled his tongue around my clit before pulling back to growl, "This is not nearly enough, sweetness. I'm just getting started."

And I was suddenly turned on again, trembling as the heat built once more. He pleasured me mercilessly, doing things with his tongue that drove me wild with need. I begged and pleaded, wanting more, more, *more*. I was insatiable and he knew it. His tongue pushed me over the edge again and again and again. Giving me what I needed. Making me feel things I'd never felt before. Until I lay limp on the ground, a panting quivering mess. Completely satiated.

"More?" he said, lifting his head to watch me catch my breath.

I shook my head, too exhausted to speak.

In reply, he bent and kissed my inner thigh, then the other. The tender gesture warmed my insides. It was a soft warmth, unlike the raging inferno he'd finally snuffed out. I watched as he gently closed my thighs, then turned me onto my side. Moments later, I felt him settle behind me. As he placed a hand on my stomach and pulled me flush against him, my eyes flared wide. Holy hell, I'd almost forgotten how huge his dick was.

Before my mind could wander too far down the gutter, he said, "Get some rest, Nora."

I blinked. "Now? Like this?"

In the middle of the woods? While he spooned my naked body with his?

"Yes. Like this," he rumbled, pulling me more firmly against him. "We'll go again in the morning."

My mouth fell open. "Again?"

He chuckled softly. "Yes, again. Your heat won't fade for another day or two."

Oh. So he meant to keep me here in the woods, naked and alone with him, until my heat abated?

I could think of worse things.

My back vibrated as Kolton quietly growled, "Whatever you're thinking, stop. I need sleep and so do you."

I shut my eyes and bit my lip, fighting back a grin.

After a minute, he sighed and relaxed against me. Then whispered, "Sleep well, Nora."

# CHAPTER 24

The next morning, I woke up *starving*.

For the first time in weeks, my stomach rumbled with hunger. But even more persistent than my empty stomach was the powerful need for sex. My body yearned to be satiated, the feeling stronger than ever.

With the sun's rising, my heat had come back full force.

As if responding to it, Kolton tightened his hold on me and rubbed his stiff cock against my backside. My eyes popped open. Judging by his movements, I guessed he was still asleep. Certain parts of his body weren't though. They were *wide* awake.

He continued to rub against me, the delicious friction further tightening my core with need. I endured this torture for a solid minute, listening to his heart and breathing speed up. Then I snapped.

Shifting in his arms, I pushed him onto his back and straddled his hips. When his thick erection brushed my inner thigh, euphoria rushed through me.

"Kolton," I breathlessly whispered, willing his eyes to open. To see my need and give their consent.

Instead, his hands came up and grabbed my waist. Still fast asleep, he groaned my name and thrust his hips upward. The action pressed his swollen head against my slick entrance.

Holy hell.

I nearly came on the spot. My body went wild, flushing and

trembling with desperate need.

"Kolton," I repeated, weak with desire. Every inch of me wanted to press down on him—but not while he was asleep. Unable to hold still a moment longer, I whimpered and dug my nails into his chest.

He jerked awake. Our eyes met for a split second. Then he burst into action. I gasped as he flipped our positions and I landed on my back.

Towering over me, he pinned me with a stern look. "*No*, Nora."

Startled, I stared up at him with wide eyes. "But why? I want to."

My core still ached something fierce. I'd barely felt the swollen tip, but it had awakened a carnal need to have him inside me. *All* of him.

He bit out a curse before replying, "I can't have sex with you right now. Not like that. If I do, I won't be able to stop."

Confused, I said, "Why would you want to stop?"

He huffed a laugh. "That's just it. I wouldn't want to. But my body is primed to take you in a way you're not ready for yet. With you in heat, I wouldn't be able to control my instincts."

I noticed then how much he was trembling. If I pushed him a little bit, he probably *would* lose control. Despite how much I wanted him to, I forced myself to hold still and say, "And what way is that?"

His expression turned incredulous. "You've never heard of knotting?"

I wrinkled my nose. "Notting?"

"Knotting. Like a knot in a rope. Only an alpha has this ability. The base of the shaft swells during sex, making it impossible to pull out. It's our body's way of ensuring the female becomes impregnated. When she's in heat, the instinct to knot is uncontrollable."

My jaw dropped. Holy hell. Yet another important bit of information my pack failed to mention to me.

"Oh," was all I said, suddenly realizing how dumb I'd been. Yes, my body still wanted to have sex with him, but I did *not* want to get pregnant. At least, not right now.

Still horny as hell but unsure what to do about it, I savagely bit into my lips.

Kolton's attention dropped to them. Reaching a hand up, he gently freed my mouth from my teeth. "Do you need taking care of?" he quietly said, caressing my bottom lip with his thumb.

Resisting the urge to suck the digit into my mouth, I mutely nodded.

His gaze shot back up to mine. "Do you still want me inside you?"

Oh wow. He was going with full-blown transparency here. Feeling vulnerable, I looked away before nodding again.

He studied me for a moment in silence. Then said, "I can offer a compromise."

At that, way too much excitement zinged through me. I looked back up at him expectantly.

His lips twitched into the barest of smiles. When he slid an arm beneath me and lifted, I grabbed onto his shoulders. Instead of rising to his feet though, he sat down and placed me in his lap. The move spread my thighs wide, until I was straddling his waist. This close, my breasts nearly touched his chest. As for my throbbing core, it was inches away from brushing against his hard erection. I settled more firmly on top of him, needing to erase that distance.

Before they could meet, he placed a hand on my lower back and stilled my movements. "Let me make this perfectly clear, Nora," he gruffly said, drawing my gaze up to his. "My instincts are demanding that I take and knot you right now. The only way I can control that instinct is if you let me set the pace. Got it?"

Which basically meant that I needed to fully submit to him. A large part of me bristled at the thought. When I hesitated to respond, Kolton started to pull away from me. "Okay!" I growled, digging my nails into his shoulders to keep him in place.

His eyes narrowed dangerously. "Don't test me, wife. You'll lose."

I shivered. Losing to him might not be such a bad thing. Before I could picture what losing to him might look like, he pressed on my lower spine. The action pushed me down, aligning me flush with his erection. As our bare skin touched, I sucked in a gasp. With my eyes still locked on his, I watched his irises begin to glow a bright yellow.

"We'll do this nice and slow," he said, shifting both hands to my hips. When he gripped them firmly and slowly lifted me, my wet center slid up his shaft. The sensation stole my breath. A second later, he pushed me down again, rubbing my clit along his length. A tremor shook him and he softly groaned.

Enamored by the sound, I leaned forward and kissed him.

When I pulled back, his eyes were on fire.

"Oh, sweetness, you shouldn't have done that," he roughly said, before grabbing the back of my head and crushing our mouths together. Surprised by the abrupt move, I gasped. He took advantage and slid his tongue past my parted lips. As our tongues found each other, he took full control, setting a pace that was anything but slow. The thrusts of his tongue mirrored the thrusts of his pelvis, filling me with hot pleasure.

I gripped his neck and held on tight, moaning with each new sensation he wrung out of me. When I pressed my chest to his, he increased the pace, every thrust frantic with need. The air became saturated with our heady arousal and rough panting. I trembled as my core clenched. Instinctively, I tightened my thighs around him. He increased the pace even more.

It felt so good. *So good*. Wild and reckless and free. I gave myself wholly to the passionate moment, reveling in the pleasure my body was experiencing. A delicious tension built in my core. The tension grew and grew and grew until it abruptly *snapped.*

My world shattered.

As the orgasm barrelled through me, I broke our kiss to cry out Kolton's name. He crushed me to him and roared, stiffening as he climaxed against me. His cock swelled and swelled, becoming impossibly huge. *Knotting*, despite not being inside me.

The feeling made me come even harder, dulling all other senses. As I continued to orgasm, Kolton buried his face in my hair and held me tightly. The euphoria lasted so long that I nearly passed out, unable to breathe.

When I finally came down, I gasped for air and slumped against him. His cock remained engorged. Knotted. I waited for the shaft to soften, but it didn't. After a long moment, I weakly murmured, "Holy hell."

In reply, he swept my hair aside so he could nuzzle my neck. The tender gesture curled my toes. I tipped my head back to give him better access and he growled possessively, nipping at the vulnerable skin of my throat. I immediately stilled, realizing my error. I might not have known about knotting, but I *did* know about this.

Our werewolf instincts weren't all that different from regular wolves, and exposing one's throat like this was a sign of submission. Not only that, I was basically saying that I wholly trusted him.

He seemed *very* pleased with my unspoken message, continuing to nuzzle and nip at my sensitive skin. I hadn't meant to do it, but my instincts must have. They didn't care that it made me completely vulnerable to him. They didn't care that he could easily sink his teeth or fangs into my throat and rip it out. They didn't care . . . because my instincts trusted him implicitly.

The realization stole my breath. I'd never submitted like this before. Not to my parents. And certainly not to Alpha Hendrix. I hadn't felt safe doing it. But now, allowing myself to be vulnerable for Kolton felt right. Despite our rocky start and the past few miserable weeks, I truly felt safe with him. I even felt . . .

Like I belonged.

*Because he's your mate*, Storm abruptly said, as if she'd been listening to my thoughts.

My eyes flew wide. Not because she was a part of this intimate moment, but because her words suddenly held new meaning.

*When you say mate*, I haltingly began, *what exactly do you mean?*

*I mean that you're bonded. Soul-bonded. I felt the bond stretch thin while he was away. It's why you lost your appetite and struggled to sleep. But now that he's here, you slept peacefully and your appetite has returned. It's also why you want to have intercourse with him so badly. Doing so would merge your souls and complete the bond.*

"What the hell?" I shouted before I could stop myself.

Kolton froze, then pulled away to look at me. He slowly raised an eyebrow in question.

Ah *crap*. Nope. I was *not* ready for this conversation. Besides, Storm could be wrong. How was she the authority on *soulmates* anyway?

Soulmates were rare. So rare that I'd never even met a bonded couple. The chances of Kolton and me being soul-bonded was slim to none. Storm had to be mistaken.

"Sorry," I hurriedly said, trying not to blush at his perusal. "I'm just really hungry."

I mean, it was true. Still, his skepticism was clear.

Suddenly needing space—*lots* of it—I scrambled off his lap. My body inwardly whined at the move, already missing his warmth and touch. Too bad. This had just become *way* too complicated and confusing.

Soulmates? *Really?* What was I supposed to do with that information? Kolton didn't want a mate. That meant he *definitely* didn't want a soulmate.

When I scooted back several feet and pulled my knees to my chest, trying to hide my nakedness, Kolton searched my face. He was clearly confused by the abrupt move, but thankfully didn't press me for answers. After a moment more, he said, "I'll go get us some food. Will you be okay here alone for a little while?"

"Can't I come with you?"

"It's best you stay here," he replied, rising to his feet. "While you're in heat, I need you to remain isolated. Otherwise, I might kill any male you come across. Even ones I like."

My eyes widened at his words. Then accidentally dropped to his glistening penis, still stiff and engorged. My mouth dried as I realized that it was coated in *me*. The sight made the walls of my vagina spasm with fresh need.

Tearing my gaze away, I quickly said, "Okay, I'll stay here."

He was silent for a beat. Then, "Will you?"

The question dripped with doubt. I couldn't blame him. The itch to run was hitting me hard.

"I will. I promise," I said with more confidence than I felt, meeting his eyes for good measure.

"I'm serious, Nora. If I have to chase you, I'll make sure you're properly punished."

My throat seized with panic. Not because I was scared, but because the words elicited all sorts of naughty fantasies in my brain. I'd always been terrified of punishment in the past, but this time, I *wanted* to be punished. Badly.

When all I did was gawk at him, Kolton's lips slowly curled into a wicked grin. He knew. He *definitely* knew what his words had done to me. As if to throw fuel on the fire, he added in a soft purr, "And I won't be gentle."

With that, he turned and walked away, leaving me with my naughty naughty thoughts.

When an hour passed and Kolton hadn't returned, my restlessness got the better of me.

I didn't go far though, and I left an easy trail for him to follow. It should have felt weird walking through the forest naked, but I really was well and truly alone. The only life my heightened senses could detect was the occasional bird, squirrel, or rabbit.

My stomach loudly growled at the thought of catching one, but Storm had fallen silent again. Even the promise of food couldn't stir her awake. So much for our brief icebreaker moment. She was back to being her usual distant, moody self.

Giving up on the prospect of catching myself some breakfast, I went in search of the next pressing thing my body needed. I found a shallow creek about half a mile in and followed the winding path to its source. When the sound of splashing water greeted my ears, I grinned and broke into a run.

"Score!" I sang upon spotting the pool of water through the trees. A short waterfall on the far side fed it, creating a small and somewhat secluded oasis. I wasted no time slaking my thirst, kneeling at the edge to scoop up handful after handful of the cool water. Even in the middle of summer, mountain-fed pools like this were chilly. In the past, I wouldn't have dared swim in one. But that was before. My body was different now. Stronger in every way. Which meant . . .

Grinning once more, I hopped over the edge and plunged into the frigid water. Sure enough, instead of the coldness stealing my breath away, it barely touched me. With a laugh, I kicked off from the bank and completely submerged myself. The pool wasn't deep, but deep and wide enough that I could enjoy a short swim. Popping to the surface again, I flipped onto my back and floated for a spell, shutting my eyes when a ray of sunshine struck my face.

The unexpected reprieve from the past crazy day felt nice. *Really* nice. But after several minutes of quiet floating, something felt . . . missing. Or rather, *someone* felt missing. A tall, dark-haired, powerfully-built werewolf, to be exact. One who just happened to be my husband. And was also possibly my *soulmate.*

At the fresh reminder, a now familiar heat engulfed my body. Despite the cold water, it rushed through me, scorching my insides and leaving me aching with need. Groaning, I flipped over and made for the nearest edge. Once there, I leaned against a large rock to catch my breath. The fiery need continued to whip through me. So overpowering that I reached between my legs to ease some of the tension.

At the first touch, I closed my eyes and sighed with relief. Tightly gripping the rock, I continued to stroke myself, the water allowing my fingers to slide over my clit with ease. Just as my orgasm began to build, I heard a voice above me say, "I see you started without me."

Startled, I yelped and jerked away from the rock. Crouching in the water to hide my nakedness, I glanced up at the intruder. Kolton stared back at me, a devilish smirk on his face.

"You scared me," I snapped at him, trying to cover my embarrassment.

His smirk widened. "Only because you were *heavily* distracted. I could hear your moans a mile away."

My jaw dropped. "You did not," I sputtered, feeling heat flush my cheeks. Never in a million years did I think this would happen. The urge to duck beneath the water and never come back up hit me.

Kolton quietly chuckled, clearly enjoying my predicament. "I obviously interrupted something important, so I can come back later if you want. Or," he said, a wicked spark entering his eyes, "I could help you finish what you started."

Ah hell, he got me. He got me *good.* And he most definitely knew it.

Still, I stubbornly clamped my mouth shut and refused to play his little game. He waited for a beat. Then shrugged as if he didn't care and said, "Guess I'll be going then. Holler when you're done."

When he moved to leave, my stubborn resolve pathetically crumbled. "No," I blurted, hating myself a little for being so weak. "I mean, yes."

He turned back around and lifted an eyebrow. "Yes, what? Use your words, Nora."

*Bastard.*

"Yes," I said with false sweetness, laying it on thick. "I want you to help me finish."

That stupid smirk slowly reappeared. "Say please."

I was going to *kill* him.

"Please," I whispered, reaching between my legs again.

When I boldly stroked myself, his gaze shot to my hand below the water. Now it was my turn to smirk as every muscle in his body went rigid. A warning growl rumbled in his chest, but I didn't stop, stroking faster.

"Nora," he said, his voice guttural as he openly watched me. "Stop touching yourself."

I bit my lip seductively and crooned, "Say please."

His eyes burned bright yellow in one second flat. Oops. Maybe I'd gone a little too far. In a flurry of movement, he dropped the packages he'd been holding and removed the shirt and pants he'd worn yesterday. Naked once more, he jumped into the pool and bulldozed toward me. With a small shriek, I tried to evade him, but he easily caught up and grabbed me. In the next breath, I found myself pressed up against the nearest rock by a wall of naked male.

I sucked in a gasp as he wedged a thigh between mine and spread them apart. "Please," he rumbled in my ear, then wasted no time reaching down and finding my center. At the instant jolt of pleasure, a breathy moan escaped me. Spurred on by the sound, he pressed his thumb firmly to my clit and rubbed in tight circles.

"Kolton," I gasped out, jerking against the pleasurable assault. When he brushed his lips over the shell of my ear in reply, I wrapped my arms around his neck and drew him closer.

He continued to work my clit until I was a trembling, panting mess. But right before I could climax, he slid his index finger back and circled my entrance.

"I can't have my cock inside you," he purred in my ear, "but I can do other things."

Startled, I yanked my eyes open and stiffened all over.

"Shhh," he whispered, continuing to circle my entrance. "I've got you. Do you trust me?"

With my heart pounding in my throat, I wordlessly nodded.

"Good. Then hold onto me and relax. I won't hurt you."

My breath came in short spurts as he slowly, ever so slowly, slid his finger inside me. Overwhelmed by the foreign sensation, I whimpered and clenched my thighs. He paused as my walls tightened around his digit.

"I know, sweetness. I know," he continued to whisper, waiting until I started to relax again. Then slid his finger all the way in. Before I could fully adjust, he curled his finger, hitting a spot deep within that stole my breath. My body bucked as a wave of bliss shot through me. He did it again, expertly targeting that same spot. Unable to catch my breath, I silently shuddered against him. "You're doing so good, Nora. Breathe. Just breathe. That's it."

The moment I started to breathe, he began to stroke me from the inside, once again making me feel things I'd never felt before. I'd never pleasured myself this way. Not even with a vibrator. I didn't realize that a single finger could fill my body with such delicious euphoria. When I began to tremble, so close to coming, Kolton slid another finger inside me.

The fit was tight. Almost *too* tight. As pain chased some of my bliss away, his thumb pressed on my clit again. I moaned, relaxing enough to allow his second finger entrance. The combination of *two* fingers nearly blew apart my reality. Once I was sufficiently stretched, he pumped his fingers in and out, making me see stars.

I couldn't imagine anything feeling better than this. Not even having his dick inside me. Okay, maybe that. Definitely that.

Imagining it inside me instead of his fingers was enough to tip me over the edge. I climaxed on a scream, spasming so hard that my walls viciously squeezed his fingers. Yet, he somehow managed to keep pumping, prolonging my orgasm. When I could finally function again, all that left my lips was a breathless whimper.

Kolton softly chuckled before slowly pulling his fingers out. "That's just a taste of what I want to do to you, my sweet flower. You have no idea how good I can make you feel."

Holy. Hell.

I was so incredibly screwed.

# CHAPTER 25

He wasn't making this easy.

Not. At. All.

How was I supposed to keep my distance when Kolton kept pleasuring my body, whispering wicked promises in my ear, and offering me *food?*

I literally felt like I was in Heaven right now. He'd gone back to the bar and ordered several dishes to go. He'd also managed to find my phone, which thankfully still worked. My clothes were ruined, but Vi had dropped off a new outfit for me, which I now wore. It felt good to be covered again, allowing me to focus on other things besides nudity all the time.

After my latest orgasm, I was half feral with hunger and dug into the food like a rabid animal. Thinking Kolton would be repulsed by my poor manners, I tried to slow down. But when I flicked a glance at him, satisfaction lined his face. Like he was pleased that he'd contributed to my healthy appetite.

Butterflies erupted in my stomach and I quickly ducked my head again. Seriously though. If he kept looking at me like that, I was going to jump him, soulmate bond be damned. I was way too horny right now to think rationally, so he really needed to stop.

With the waterfall gently splashing nearby, we'd allowed a comfortable silence to settle between us. It felt natural and peaceful. Combined with the food, it almost felt like we were on a date. Which gave me *way* too many warm and fuzzy feelings.

*This is bad. Bad!* I tried to remind myself, thinking of Storm's earlier words. If we really were soulmates, then each time we got close would only strengthen the bond. And if we had sex, the bond would be complete. I was pretty sure we'd both know by then if we were soulmates or not.

I was half-tempted to get it over with so we could know for certain, but that wouldn't be fair. In fact, it would be the worst kind of betrayal. Kolton deserved better than that. He deserved to have a choice. And the thought of him being *stuck* with me against his wishes soured my stomach.

I knew all too well what it felt like to be stuck. I also knew what it felt like to be unwanted. Kolton might want me *now*, but only because he thought we were on the same page. I wasn't the love of his life or his mate. I was his wife with benefits, for lack of a better description. And I was okay with that . . .

Right?

But we couldn't go on like this forever. Eventually, we wouldn't be able to resist the urge to have sex. And if that happened, it could ruin everything. His trust in me. His commitment to be married to me. Even if we were soulmates, it didn't mean he *wanted* the bond. He could even try to break it. I didn't know what that entailed, only that it was painful. So painful that the separation often caused permanent emotional damage.

I didn't want that for either of us, but how could I bring up the subject without him freaking out? I could seriously be worrying for nothing. We might not actually be soulmates. Either way, if I brought up the possibility, he could well and truly abandon me for good. And the prospect of that happening hurt something fierce.

Kolton wasn't the only one who'd grown attached. A month ago,

I might have jumped at the idea of finding a loophole out of this marriage. But now, I ached at the thought of it.

"Hey," he said, startling me out of my thoughts. "Where'd you go?"

"Oh," I quickly replied, setting down my half-eaten chicken leg. "I just have a lot on my mind."

"Like?" he prodded, biting into his chicken at a much more controlled pace.

Panicking a little, I blurted, "Like, what happens next? Do we go back to your estate as if nothing happened? Do I have to worry about more incidents like yesterday because I'm still a virgin?"

He swallowed before saying, "*Our* estate."

I blinked. "Huh?"

"The estate is yours now too."

Those stupid butterflies started acting up again.

When I remained silent, he continued, "The next step will be to initiate you into the pack, regardless of your virginity. Rumors have already spread by now and there's not much we can do about it. Rodney's death will serve as a reminder of my authority, but many will still question my marriage to you. Only time will tell if they decide to do anything about it."

"Oh," was all I said, feeling that familiar pressure to please the pack, no matter the cost to my own happiness.

Kolton searched my face. "You're still not obligated to consummate our marriage, Nora. Despite the intimacy we've shared, you shouldn't have sex with me unless you want to."

But I *did* want to. Badly. That wasn't the problem though.

Before I could stop myself, I asked point blank, "Why don't you want a mate?"

Crap, I'd really done it this time. Sure enough, Kolton couldn't hide the shock on his face. Why, oh *why* had I asked him that?

Scrambling to fix my mistake, I continued, "I mean, is it just me?" Ah hell, that was *definitely* not better. "What I'm trying to say is, if you want love but not with me, I won't stand in your way. Everyone deserves to find that special someone to share their life with. We could stay married though, of course. She could be your mistress or whatever they're called these days."

"Nora . . ."

"Or, if you want to annul our marriage once you find that special someone, I'll understand. I'm sure you'd much rather be married to someone you're in love with anyway."

"Nora."

"But if you still need me as an insurance policy or whatever, you and your chosen mate could live at the estate and I could go somewhere else. I actually have a friend in Albany that I've been meaning to—"

"*Nora.*"

Startled, I jumped at the sharp tone of his voice. Snapping my idiotic mouth shut, I took in his rather angry expression. My heart sank. I'd really messed up this time.

"No, it's not just you," he spoke before I could flog myself some more. "I don't want to fall in love because I've seen what love does to people. I don't want a mate because a bond that strong only leads to pain and destruction. I won't do that to myself or anyone else. And I won't do that to my family. They've already endured enough."

My throat constricted. This was big. Bigger than I imagined. He wasn't just angry, he was *hurt*. He'd been through something, and I was dying to know what. "What have they endured?" I softly asked, praying I wasn't overstepping.

A muscle thrummed in his jaw. Seconds passed. He continued

to stare at me and I at him. After a moment that lasted an eternity, a resigned sigh fled his nose. "It's best if I show you."

With that, he stood and began to clean up our mess. I scrambled to help him, keeping perfectly silent in case he decided to change his mind. Something told me that I'd struck gold. For better or for worse, he was letting me in. Letting me see a part of himself that had been hidden up until now. I both dreaded and anticipated what he planned to show me.

It could change everything, or it could change nothing. Either way, we were doing this.

We walked back to the bar, the silence between us not so peaceful anymore. A part of me wished I'd kept my mouth shut, but this had to happen eventually. I was no longer content with keeping him at arm's length. I either needed to be all in or all out. Being stuck in limbo, not knowing where we stood with each other, was slowly driving me insane.

It was better to rip off the bandaid and see if this thing between us could go anywhere, or if I needed to back off. Like *really* back off. As in, move to a different part of the state where we never had to see each other again. Otherwise, I didn't think I'd survive being near him every day, knowing that he might be my soulmate and unable to do anything about it.

*Just tell him*, my wolf chose that moment to interrupt my thoughts. *He needs to know—if he doesn't know already.*

I nearly choked on my spit. *Crap*. I hadn't even thought of that. What if his wolf was telling him the exact same thing?

*I doubt his wolf is encouraging the bond*, Storm growled. *Unless he's trying to corrupt you too.*

*Stop listening to my thoughts*, I chastised, inwardly scowling at her.

*Can't help it. When they're really loud, I pick up on them.*

*Well, it's annoying.*

*Duly noted.*

When we reached Kolton's truck, she fell silent again. But only until I was settled in the passenger seat.

Then, *Tell him. Now is the perfect time.*

*Seriously?* I shot back, so frustrated that I almost spoke out loud. *You won't tell me why you were in hibernation all these years or what kind of celestial being you are, but you won't shut up about this? What's your deal?*

Ignoring my bitter words, she replied, *This has nothing to do with me and everything to do with you.*

I internally snorted, which wasn't easy. *You do realize that if this soulmate bond is real and we complete it, you'll get stuck with Shadow.*

She was silent for a long while, then said, *Yes. That is the price I'll have to pay. We cannot fight or change our fate.*

This time, I snorted out loud. From the driver's seat, Kolton threw me a questioning look. I pretended not to see.

*You can't really believe that*, I told her. *We have a choice in what we do.*

No response.

Sighing, I lapsed into silence too, *quietly* thinking about what she'd told me. Could Kolton already suspect that we were soulmates? Was that why he'd left for three weeks? The more I thought about it, the more certain I became that he must know. Why else would he be acting this way?

Before I could pluck up the nerve to ask him, he started speaking. "It's extremely important that what I'm about to show you remains a secret. Only Vi, Griff, Jagger, and I know about this. It's too dangerous for anyone else to know."

I blinked, uncertain how to respond. "Okay," was all I could think to say.

He tightened his grip on the steering wheel. "Promise me, Nora. Promise not to say anything."

Oh. Oh wow. He was really serious about this. And nervous. He practically had a deathgrip on the steering wheel.

"I promise," I said, making sure he could hear my sincerity. I had the sudden urge to take his hand and offer him a small amount of comfort. I resisted the feeling, knowing that it could cause more harm than good. He was super stressed, that much was clear. But that didn't give me a pass to touch him right now, even though I was still in heat and ached to be closer.

Instinctively, I knew he wanted space. Something was eating him up inside, and the closer we got to our destination, the more closed-off he became. I tried not to let it bother me. He was *showing* me something, after all, despite how conflicted he clearly was. I felt honored that he trusted me with whatever this was. That I was one of a select few who would know this secret of his.

That meant something. But what exactly that something meant, I would soon find out.

We arrived at our destination an hour later. The place was even more isolated than the estate, surrounded by miles and miles of forest and mountains. When an imposing stone wall cut off my view of the property, my nerves kicked in. What was this place? As we approached the front gates, a handful of guards with *guns* blocked our path.

My heart jackknifed inside my chest.

"They're human," Kolton explained, clearly having heard my racing pulse. "They don't know what's inside these walls. Only that they get paid handsomely to keep intruders out. There are several more stationed around the perimeter."

Holy crap.

He rolled down his window and they immediately lowered their weapons and stepped aside. At the gates, he pressed an intercom button. Moments later, a female voice said, "Back already, Alpha Rivers?"

I perked up at that.

"Yes, Darlene," he easily replied. "Something unexpected came up. I've brought a guest with me, so make the proper preparations, please."

"Of course, sir. Right away."

With a buzz and click, the gates slowly opened. Kolton drove the truck through without further comment, leaving me with more questions than ever. The drive was long and winding, leading us to a sprawling two-story house. Not as big or fancy as the Rivers' family estate, but at least double the size of my childhood home.

Still nervous about what awaited me inside, my legs shook when it came time to hop out of the truck. Kolton noticed but didn't comment, not until we were at the front door. "Don't be afraid," he murmured after ringing the doorbell.

I nodded, all too aware that he was deliberately keeping his distance. I squeezed my trembling hands into fists so I wouldn't reach for him. For his comfort. He obviously didn't want to touch me right now, even though my heat had begun to simmer again. He was either ignoring it or was too preoccupied to notice.

We didn't have to wait long until a blonde-haired woman in her mid forties answered the door. I stiffened as she broke into a pretty smile at the sight of Kolton. "What a treat to have you back so soon, sir," she cheerily said, flicking me a curious glance. "Come in. Both of you."

"Thank you, Darlene," Kolton replied. With the briefest of touches on my lower back, he urged me to enter before him. "We won't be staying long though."

"Oh?" she said, throwing me another curious look.

"Yes. Just a short visit to say hello."

Darlene's nose twitched. She blinked a few times, then cleared her throat. Crap. She could probably smell my heat, among other things. Which meant that she must be a werewolf.

"I'm Nora," I said, and stuck out my hand. Might as well get this awkward moment over with.

Darlene's hazel eyes widened. She grasped my hand with an exclamation of surprise. "You're the one then. Kolton's new bride. I've heard so much about you. I was hoping for the chance to meet you someday." I bristled at the familiar use of Kolton's name. But then she excitedly added, "It is *such* an honor, Nora. Truly. You're even more beautiful than Kolton described."

A blush rose to my cheeks at her open compliment. My jealousy started to fade.

"Darlene is one of our oldest family friends. She's the sole caretaker here," Kolton explained. "Unfortunately, she wasn't able to attend the wedding."

"He told me *all* about it though," she said, sighing wistfully. "Maybe we'll get an opportunity to chat sometime, Nora. I'd love a female's perspective on the happy event."

I gave her a small smile in reply, dropping my hand. She was no doubt bursting with questions but had the courtesy to turn the conversation back over to Kolton.

"Well, I'll let you two do what you came here for. Everything is prepared, sir."

My nerves immediately came rushing back full force. Darlene

had been so friendly and welcoming that I'd almost forgotten why we'd come here.

"How is she today?" Kolton said, and I instantly went on high alert.

"Quite restless, unfortunately," Darlene replied, turning to lead us up the stairs. "But I upped her dosage right before you arrived, so everything should be fine."

Dosage? I hung onto their every word, making sure to keep quiet.

"I honestly think your presence here these past few weeks calmed her," Darlene went on, and I nearly missed a step. "You have a way of soothing her inner turmoil, even without words."

A hard lump lodged in my throat. I didn't know who they were talking about, but I could testify that what Darlene said was true. Kolton definitely had a calming effect. Whoever this mystery person was, they must be important to him. *Very* important. Why else would he have come here when he left me?

As we reached the second floor landing and approached a closed bedroom door, everyone lapsed into silence. Tension filled the air, raising the hair on my arms. Not knowing what I was getting into, my heart started to thunder again. A large hand cupped mine. I shot Kolton a panicked look. His hold tightened in reply. He continued to hold my hand, long enough that some of my panic faded. The second I started to relax though, he let go.

Swallowing my disappointment, I focused on the door as Darlene pulled out a key and unlocked it. She stepped back and gave me an encouraging nod, whispering, "Move slowly and quietly and you'll be alright. I'll be just outside the door if you need me."

Trying not to panic again, I gave her a wobbly smile and followed Kolton to the door. I didn't fail to notice that he took the lead, slightly blocking me from what lay inside as he soundlessly opened the door.

But when he entered, he reached a hand back and felt for me. I stayed close on his heels, blindly letting him guide me forward.

Over his shoulder, I glimpsed something strange. In the room's center, what looked like a huge glass box rose to the ceiling. It was only when we reached the box that its purpose became clear.

A cage. It was a cage. And inside . . .

Kolton punched in a code on the wall's keypad. A door clicked open. I stopped breathing as he opened the door and slipped inside, approaching the sole occupant. A woman. She was lying on a bed with her arms strapped to her sides.

He stopped at the bed, pausing a moment before reaching down to grasp her thin hand. And then, he murmured two words. Two words that couldn't have shocked me more. "Hello, Mother."

# CHAPTER 26

Mother.

She was Kolton's mother.

I thought his mother was *dead.*

Apparently, I'd been wrong.

My head buzzed with questions as I watched him gently hold her hand. Now that a little of my shock had worn off, I took a closer look at the woman lying on the bed. Her long hair was dark like Kolton's, except for a premature white streak at her right temple. Her olive complexion was paler than it should be, her body wraith thin. Still, she was beautiful, in a haunted, faded sort of way. It was her eyes that captured and held my attention though. They were open but vacant, as if she couldn't see.

When Kolton spoke, she didn't react. Like she didn't even know he was there. He continued to hold her hand, appearing unfazed by her lack of response.

We stayed like that for a long moment. Suspended in time. Barely moving or even breathing. And then, Kolton bent to kiss her hand and let go. Still no reaction. Without a word, he turned and left the way he'd come, closing and locking the door behind him. I didn't move until he reached out and touched my arm. With a jolt, I snapped back to reality, tearing my gaze from his mother's face.

Kolton soundlessly guided me from the room, nodding at Darlene as we passed. Instead of joining us, she entered the bedroom and closed herself inside. Not a word was spoken until we were outside again and standing on the front porch. Once there, Kolton sat heavily on the top step. More like collapsed. Balancing both arms on his bent knees, he bowed his head and sighed. I felt the sigh in my bones. Felt its terrible weight. And sorrow.

My own legs gave way and I sat beside him, making sure to leave ample space between us. I let the silence stretch. Let him slowly regain his composure. Every line of his body looked . . . tired.

When several minutes passed, I finally said in hushed tones, "What happened to her?"

He slowly lifted his head and stared out across the lawn. His gaze was vacant. Unseeing. Just like his mom's. "She broke when my father died," he began, his voice tight with emotion. "I was nineteen at the time, halfway through my second year of college. We were celebrating Vi's sixteenth birthday when an alpha challenged my dad. He'd received so many challenges over the years that we barely batted an eye. But right in the middle of the challenge, my mom went into labor with Melanie."

He jerked a hand through his hair, blinking rapidly as he recalled the memory. "Everything happened so fast, I don't even know what went wrong. My father was winning, and then he wasn't, caught off guard when my mom screamed. The challenger took advantage of the distraction and killed him instantly. Just like that, he was gone before my mother could finish her contraction."

Horrified, I stared at him with wide eyes, my hand tightly pressed to my mouth. I hadn't known. I hadn't known any of this. I'd only known that Kolton had risen to alpha six years ago after his father's death. Needing to know the rest, I quietly asked, "What happened after that?"

"The challenger went after my mother," he continued, still not looking at me. "She was a strong alpha female at the time, but in her vulnerable state, I knew there could only be one outcome. Unable to bear the thought of losing her and Melanie, I made a challenge for alpha in her stead. I made sure he suffered before finally ending his life. It was my first kill."

"Oh, Kolton," I whispered, fighting back tears. "I'm so sorry."

"Yeah," he said, and lowered his gaze to his hands. They slowly curled into fists. "Me too."

Wrestling with what to say next, I finally settled on asking, "Does Melanie know about her?"

Kolton stared at his hands a moment longer, then released his grip. "No. After the challenge, only Vi and I were left to help deliver the baby. We thought to call for help, but Mother just . . . snapped. She was inconsolable. Violent. We had to hold her down. And when Melanie was born, she didn't even care. She just kept screaming. Crying my father's name again and again and again. Eventually, we had to make a decision. One we've wrestled with every day since."

Blowing out a breath, he confessed, "We faked our mother's death. We didn't see any other way. She was a danger to herself and everyone around her, lashing out like a feral animal. We feared for Melanie's safety, so we separated them. Mother didn't even notice. At the time, the only pack member we entrusted with the truth was Darlene, my mom's best friend. She suggested we keep Mother in seclusion and offered to be her permanent caretaker. If not for her, I don't know what we would have done. The pack would have certainly voted to put Mother down. Still would, if they knew of her existence."

"That's terrible," I said, wishing I could bridge the gap between us. Wishing I could *comfort* him.

"It is, but a feral werewolf is an incredibly dangerous creature. Not only to humans, but to *us*. They would expose our true nature to the public and put us all at risk. As the new alpha, my responsibility was to protect the pack. I had to think of their safety over my own feelings of guilt. At least she's still alive. She gets twenty-four-hour care, and either Vi, Griff, Jagger, or I come here every full moon to relieve Darlene while she shifts into her wolf."

"Is your mother like us? Does she harbor a spirit being too?"

"Thankfully, no. She shifts with the full moon. We keep her heavily sedated when that happens. Otherwise, she'd try to break free and kill anyone who crossed her path. It's awful seeing her this way, so empty and lifeless. But that's why I came here."

"To remind yourself not to fall in love," I quietly finished for him, sorrow tightening my chest. Even without his confirmation, I knew it was true. Knew that his parent's tragic love story had broken him too.

"Yes," he said, finally looking at me. His sorrow matched mine. "My parents had a powerful bond. They were inseparable. So in love that my mom couldn't fathom a life without her mate. The moment he died, she died too. I can't risk that happening to me, Nora. It would leave my family vulnerable again. Maybe even destroy them. And my job is to keep them safe. To keep *you* safe."

So overwhelmed with emotion, words failed me. I opened my mouth, but nothing came out.

"I'm sorry, Nora," he said, true remorse lining his face. "I care about you. More than I should. But, no matter how much I desire you, I won't let myself fall in love. I've already put myself at risk by marrying you. It's why you sensed my fear on our wedding day. I was afraid of *you*, not your wolf. Afraid of falling for your strength and beauty and generous heart. It took everything in me to say my vows, knowing that I could be dooming us both."

His words brought me no comfort. They only amplified my anguish. Barely able to breathe, I whispered, "You can still annul our marriage, you know. It's not too late."

Heaving a sigh, he shook his head and replied, "That's where you're wrong, Nora. It's far too late for that."

I didn't let him touch me again. As much as my body wanted him to, the pain in my heart won the battle.

I had wanted the truth. I'd known it could change everything. I just hadn't realized until now how strongly it would affect me.

Despite my heat, the last thing I wanted Kolton to do was help me again. When he offered and I rebuffed him, I knew he was hurt. Hurt and confused. He'd opened himself up to me and I'd thanked him by distancing myself. But what else was I supposed to do?

He would never fall in love with me.

He would never be my mate.

Even if we were soulmates, he would never want the bond.

And my heart was struggling to accept that. I'd thought I could be okay with this outcome, but apparently, I'd been lying to myself. I wasn't okay. Not even a little bit.

It was dark by the time we returned to the family estate. Although my heat hadn't completely faded, Kolton seemed to think that I could manage on my own now. Or maybe the sting of my rejection was making him rush the process. Either way, I jumped from the truck the second he pulled in front of the house, desperate to put space between us.

When I entered the house, I went straight up to my room and began to pack. Vi found me a few minutes later, gasping at the sight of the suitcase on my bed already half-packed with clothes.

"Oh, Nora, what happened?" she said, wringing her hands when

I barely paused in my task.

"Ask Kolton. I can't talk about this right now." As her expression fell, guilt threatened to crumble my resolve. "I'm sorry, Vi, but I really have to go."

She watched me for a moment before whispering, "I'm sorry too," then leaned out the door and yelled, "Kolton, get in here *now!*"

I stiffened and threw her an annoyed look, but didn't stop packing. Kolton arrived seconds later, quietly taking in the scene before saying to Vi, "Please leave. Nora and I need to talk."

"You sure do," Vi said, staring daggers at her brother as she backed out of the room. "And you better make things right, Kolton Anthony Rivers."

With that, she closed the door with a sharp click.

I continued to pack, preparing myself for whatever he had to say. I would not be swayed. My mind was made up. He—

"I thought you understood how this was going to work when you agreed to our deal."

Ouch. It almost felt like he'd dug his claws into my chest with those words. My steps nearly faltered on the way back to the bed. I knew he hadn't meant the statement to sound like an accusation, but that's the way I heard it.

"I did," I answered, dumping an armful of pajamas into the suitcase. "I still do."

"Then why are you running?"

I froze, but only for a moment. "I'm not running. I'll be back in a few days."

Or a few weeks. Maybe months. As long as it took to make this pain in my heart go away. But I wasn't going to tell *him* that. Better to leave and apologize later. The strategy had always worked for me in the past.

"Where are you going?" Kolton pressed, still watching me without moving a muscle.

"To visit my friend Brielle. She lives in Albany. I already texted her."

He didn't say anything for a long while. As I zipped up my suitcase, he finally said, "Please stay, Nora. Let's talk through this. I'm sure we can figure it out."

Pausing, I blankly stared at my suitcase. Then, with a quiet sigh, I picked up the suitcase and turned to face him. "I'm sorry, but I can't. I'll be fine though." Eventually. "Thank you for trusting me with your secret. You did the right thing by telling me. I just need a few days to process everything, okay?"

He stared at me, so hard that I was certain he could see through my flimsy words to the terrifying truth within. But all he ended up saying was, "Okay."

Overcome with relief, my legs nearly gave out. He was letting me go. At the same time, sadness filled me. He was letting me *go*. See, this was why I had to leave. I couldn't think straight anymore. Conflicting emotions were tearing me up inside, and I didn't know how to handle them. Especially when I was this close to him.

I understood how he felt now. Knew why he'd left. And now, it was my turn.

Straightening my spine, I approached the door with my suitcase in tow. Approached *him*. Every step was agony. *Stay*, my heart pleaded. *Leave*, my mind ordered. Round and round until I couldn't tell one from the other. When I was near enough to touch him, he finally stepped aside, allowing me to pass. The gesture nearly shattered my resolve.

I made a mistake then. I met his eyes. The pain in them stole my breath.

Unable to stop myself, I let go of my suitcase and erased the distance between us. He held still as I wrapped my arms around him and squeezed. Squeezed and squeezed with all of my strength. I memorized the feel of him. Memorized his scent. With a ragged exhale, he hugged me back. So tight that I could barely breathe. Tears burned my eyes.

I clung to him for a full minute. Allowing myself this one final moment. Then pulled away. For a split second, his arms tightened even more. Refusing to let go. Then, they fell to his sides.

Grabbing my suitcase again, I turned and opened the door. Right before exiting, I paused. Paused and whispered, "Goodbye, Kolton." Then left without a backward glance.

He didn't stop me. Neither did the others.

I walked out of the house and around the side toward the garage. The door stood open for me. I threw the suitcase into my truck and inserted the key into the ignition. The familiar roar of the engine didn't fill me with excitement like it usually did. Pulling into the circular drive, I glanced at the house and saw them all on the front porch. Vi, Griff, Jagger, Melanie, and . . . and Kolton.

Déjà vu struck me. We'd done this once before. The memory played through my head as I turned out of the loop and onto the road leading away from them. The decision to stay or leave had felt so simple then. To free my wolf, I'd been willing to sacrifice everything. But that was before I'd started to give away pieces of myself. Before I'd felt accepted, like I belonged. Before I'd invested my heart. And before . . .

Before I'd begun to fall.

When I glanced in the rearview mirror for one last glimpse of them, the tears I'd been holding back finally spilled over. Tightening my grip on the wheel, I focused on the road again. On the path I'd chosen. When I reached the gates, they were already open. Unlike last time, I didn't slam on the brakes. I didn't even hesitate. I kept my foot firmly on the gas and drove through the gates.

Half an hour into the trip, my phone rang. Thinking it was Kolton, hope rushed through me. Maybe he'd changed his mind. Maybe we could work this out after all. Maybe we were soulmates and that would be okay. *More* than okay. Maybe he'd want me. *All* of me. No matter the risk. No matter the pain. Maybe he'd . . .

I picked up the phone and answered. "Hello?"

"Nora? Oh, thank goodness."

My hope faded. "Mom?"

"Yes, honey, it's me. I know it's late and we haven't spoken to each other in a while, but something happened to your dad."

Despite our differences, worry filled me. They were still my parents, after all. I still cared about them, even if they hadn't protected me from Alpha Hendrix. "What happened? Is he okay?"

"I don't know," she said, her voice quavering. "He was fine and then he wasn't. You know we don't get sick like humans do, but he won't heal. I'm just scared that this is it, Nora. That—"

"Wait, hold on. Slow down, Mom. What are you saying?"

"I'm saying that I think your father might be dying."

Alarmed, I slammed on the brakes. Then wrenched the truck around in a sharp U-turn. "I'm on my way, Mom."

"Hurry, Nora. I don't know how much time he has left."

Trying to stay calm, I hung up and focused on driving safely. It wasn't long before I was speeding down the road though. Most werewolves had a long lifespan. We weren't susceptible to human illnesses and very few things could kill us. Maybe my dad had come into contact with silver. I didn't see how though. We didn't have any in the house and his farming equipment definitely didn't contain any.

I drove faster.

By the time I got there, I was so preoccupied with thinking the worst that I didn't notice the man standing in the driveway until it was almost too late. Swearing, I skidded the truck to a jarring halt just in time. Realizing it was Alpha Hendrix, my stomach dropped. Was I too late? Was my dad . . . was he already dead?

Pocketing my phone, I scrambled from the truck. "Is he in the house?" I called out to Alpha Hendrix, not even bothering to shut the door as I beelined for my childhood home.

"Nora, stop," he said.

"I know I shouldn't be here, but I have to see him," I hurriedly said, continuing toward the house.

"Nora, *stop!*" he bellowed, loud enough that I jerked to a halt. "They aren't here."

Startled, I whirled to face him. "Then where are—?" The words died on my tongue when I spotted movement behind him. Several figures emerged and my night vision kicked in, quickly scanning their faces. None of them looked familiar. None except . . .

My mind went blank. Only one word formed, one that I whispered out loud. "Keisha."

With a toss of her long braids, the witch paused next to Alpha Hendrix. "Hello, little wolf. Long time no see. But I promised that you would pay, and I never break a promise."

When she and Alpha Hendrix shared a look, ice filled my veins.

"You . . . you contacted them?" I asked, staring at my previous alpha in disbelief.

"They contacted *me*, actually," he said, victory darkening his expression. "When they explained the situation, I was more than willing to help them out."

Dread crept up my spine. "What did you do?"

"What I should have done a long time ago, young lady. Something's wrong with you, and the Blackstone Coven has agreed to fix you."

My heart thundered erratically. "And what do *you* get out of this?" Because I knew he didn't give me up simply out of spite. He was too pleased with himself. Too *excited*. The witches must have agreed to give him something in return.

He shrugged. "Just a little due justice. The witches were planning to kill Alpha Rivers and his family anyway for what they did to one of their own. But his death will benefit me all the same. I might even take over his pack after this."

Feeling faint, I forced air into my lungs, desperate to remain alert. I had to warn him. I had to warn them *all*.

Whirling, I bolted for my truck. The second I did, they attacked. Magic streaked past me, blasting right through the pickup's windshield. Another blast followed and the entire cab went up in flames. Fighting back a horrified scream, I veered away from the wreckage and took off across the front lawn.

Magic dogged my every step, biting into the ground inches from my feet. Yelping, I ducked and dodged, scrambling to get away.

*Give me control*, Storm suddenly barked inside my mind.

"No!" I shouted, whipping out my phone as I ran. "I have to warn Kolton that he's in danger!"

*But you need help*, she roared, with more emotion than I'd ever heard from her before.

Too busy avoiding the witches' magic attacks, I didn't respond. I was almost to the main road when a fireball struck me in the back. I screamed as the fiery blast knocked me off my feet. I tumbed and rolled several yards before coming to an agonized stop.

Groaning, I sacrificed precious seconds to catch my breath and dial Kolton's number. As I pushed to my feet again, another bolt of magic blasted me backward. Stunned, I lay on the ground, struggling to breathe.

"Nora?"

Through the ringing in my ears, I heard Kolton's voice and almost sobbed. Clawing at the ground to reach my phone, I managed to rasp, "Kolton."

The tone of his voice immediately changed. "Nora, what's wrong? Where are you?"

"The witches," I continued to rasp, inches away from grabbing the phone. "They're here. They're going to—" I cried out as a foot came down on my back, right where I'd been hit.

"Don't let me interrupt you," Keisha said above me, digging her boot in harder. "Tell him. Tell him what we plan to do."

Biting back a pained whimper, I said, "They're coming for you and your family. You need to—"

I was suddenly frozen. Unable to speak. Unable to move. Not even blink. The only thing I could do was stare at the strip of grass before me.

"Nora, where are you? Nora? *NORA!*" Kolton bellowed, with so much panic and fear that tears filled my frozen eyes.

"Your pretty wife is under a little *spell*, Alpha Rivers," Keisha said, removing her boot to leisurely stroll toward my phone. "If you ever want to see her alive again, then I suggest you pick up when we call you. We'll be in touch soon."

"If you hurt her," Kolton roared, "I will hunt you down and *kill* you. Do you hear me? I'll—"

Keisha raised her boot and slammed it down on my phone. "Werewolves. So violent and dramatic over every little thing," she muttered, crouching to my level so I was forced to meet her eyes. "Ready to go, little wolf? I'd tell you not to struggle, but I don't think that will be a problem."

With a smirk, she circled her hand in the air and a portal sprang into existence. The bright cerulean light burned my retinas, but I was unable to look away. Unable to do *anything* as she reached for me and the portal swallowed me whole.

Wind and flashes of light whipped around us, faster and faster until my stomach roiled with nausea. As quickly as it began, it abruptly stopped. Keisha let go of me, and I fell unceremoniously onto a concrete floor. Rolling me onto my back with a nudge of her boot, she crouched once again to smirk in my face and say, "Welcome to your new home, little wolf."

Then, without warning, she punched me out cold.

# CHAPTER 27

As a werewolf, I shouldn't have woken up with a splitting headache.

So when I did, I knew something was wrong.

The first thing I saw when I peeled my eyes open was metal bars. Thick ones. Covered in what looked like . . .

Silver.

My eyes flared wide and I scrambled upright. As I did, my bare arm brushed against something cold and—

Pain shot through my arm.

With a startled cry, I yanked my arm to my chest, peering down at what looked like a burn mark.

"Careful," a deep, unfamiliar voice said. "The cage is lined in silver."

*Cage?*

Breathing through the pain as my arm began to heal, I searched for the owner of the voice. Through the bars, I spotted a figure crouched not far away. He was also surrounded by bars. Even above his head. Trapping him. Trapping him inside . . .

A cage.

My breathing sped up. So did my heartbeats.

He turned to face me better, saying, "Stay calm. You don't want to shift in here. Your wolf is too big."

Panicking even more, I gasped out, "Why am I in a cage? What is this place? Where—?"

"Slow down, slow down," he said, raising his hands. "You really don't want to freak out in that cage. Believe me, I would know. Take a breath. That's it. Now another. Nice and slow."

I did as he instructed, focusing on his startling blue eyes. They were lighter than mine, crystal blue instead of aqua. The room we were in was barely lit, but I could clearly make out his features. He had long, white-blond hair to his jaw and a handsome angular face. I couldn't gauge his height, but his frame was muscular, albeit on the lean side. All-in-all, he looked like a woodland elf. I half expected to see pointy ears poking through his tangled hair.

Focusing on something other than the cage did the trick. My breathing steadied, as did my pulse.

"There you go," my fellow prisoner said and flashed me a lopsided grin. "What's your name?"

"Nora," I replied, not seeing a reason to distrust him. We were in the same predicament, after all.

"Arrow," he replied back, still grinning. He was awfully cheerful for being stuck in a deadly cage. Wait . . .

"You're a werewolf too," I said, recalling what he'd said to me.

"Yes. But not just that," he replied with a wink. "And neither are you, I'm guessing."

My eyes widened. "You're a hybrid?"

He wrinkled his nose. "Sure, if that's what you're calling it. I wouldn't say that too loudly though. They have ears everywhere."

A shiver crept up my spine. "How long have you been trapped here?"

"Hmm . . ." He glanced at the floor of his cage. What looked like a long tally of claw marks was etched into the metal. "Fifty-two days."

Dread soured my stomach. "That long? Why are you even here?"

"For the same reason you are, I suspect," he replied with another wink.

Not sure how much he knew or how safe it was to speak out loud, I whispered, "What are they going to do to us?"

He flicked a glance up at the corner to my right, and I followed his gaze. In the shadows, I made out the shape of a camera. They were spying on us. Looking back at me, he loudly said, "These witches seem to think we have *spirits* inside of us. Like we're *possessed* or something. And they've taken it upon themselves to torture us, simply because they're ignorant, superstitious *morons!*"

He was shouting now. Shouting at the camera. The tendons in his neck bulged from the effort.

I swallowed, disconcerted by the crazed look in his eyes. Then again, I'd be going insane too, trapped in a cage for that long. When he'd somewhat calmed down, I dared to ask, "What kind of torture do they perform?"

He stared at me for a long moment. Then burst out laughing. Okay, this dude had definitely lost it. I'd almost given up on receiving an answer when he replied, "They're *witches*. There's only one way they know how to deal with things they don't understand. A good old-fashioned exorcism."

He started laughing again, throwing his head back like an insane person. My skin crawled at the sound of his manic laughter. Even more so at his terrible words. They wanted to perform an exorcism . . . on Storm?

When panic flooded my body again, Arrow's laughter abruptly cut off. He lowered his head and fixed me with an unsettling look, then said something that chilled me to the bone.

"That's right, Nora. Be very afraid. You've just entered the gates of Hell."

# ALSO BY BECKY MOYNIHAN

A TOUCH OF VAMPIRE

Shadow Touched

Curse Touched

Fate Touched

Sun Touched (spin-off standalone)

THE ELITE TRIALS

Reactive

Adaptive

Immersive

GENESIS CRYSTAL SAGA

Dawn till Dusk

Fall of Night

Stars till Sun

# ACKNOWLEDGMENTS

I have a secret obsession with wolf shifters. It's been such a joy to write my own story about them and put my own spin on werewolf lore! I'm also so happy to be expanding the world that first brought you the A Touch of Vampire series. I'm hoping that my vampires will eventually make an appearance in this series too!

A huge thanks to Kate and Morgan for continuing to be my amazing beta readers. Your speedy reading and feedback are gold!!

All the hearts to my awesomely loyal ARC team who never fails to soothe my nerves and boost my confidence. Your reviews and comments mean more to me than you can ever know!

Lastly, I thank each and every reader who picked up my book(s) out of the millions of others out there. Your support is what keeps me writing!!

BECKY MOYNIHAN is a bestselling, award-winning author of paranormal romance and urban fantasy. Her books include the A Touch of Vampire series, Wolves of Midnight series, The Elite Trials series, and the co-written Genesis Crystal Saga.

When she's not writing, you can find Becky curled up on the couch in her North Carolina home, binge-watching shows and sipping Mountain Dew.

To stay up to date on new releases, sign up for her monthly newsletter: www.beckymoynihan.com/newsletter

Printed in Great Britain
by Amazon